The
GUARDIANS

GUARDIANS

A NOVEL

Ana Castillo

Random House New York

Copyright © 2007 by Ana Castillo

Published in the United States by Random House,
an imprint of The Random House Publishing Group,
a division of Random House, Inc., New York.

RANDOM HOUSE and colophon are trademarks
of Random House, Inc.

Lyrics from the song "Gabriel" by LAMB, written by
Andrew Barlow and Lou Rhodes, reproduced with the permission of
Warner Chappell Music Publishing, Ltd.

LIBRARY OF CONGRESS CATALOGING-IN-PUBLICATION DATA

Castillo, Ana.
The guardians: a novel / by Ana Castillo.
p.   cm.
ISBN 978-1-4000-6500-4
1. Mexican-Americans—Fiction. 2. Mexican-American Border Region—Fiction. I. Title.

PS3553.A8135G83 2007
813'.54—dc22   2006051128

Printed in the United States of America on acid-free paper

www.atrandom.com

2 4 6 8 9 7 5 3 1

Text design by Laurie Jewell

To all working for a world without borders
and to all who dare to cross them

I can fly

But I want his wings

I can shine even in the darkness

But I crave the light that he brings

. . .

I can love

But I need his heart

. . .

My Angel Gabriel

—"Gabriel," A. Barlow and L. Rhodes

chapter

ONE

REGINA

It was raining all night hard and heavy, making the land shiver—all the bare ocotillo and all the prickly pear. In the morning we found a tall yucca collapsed in the front yard. Everything is wet and gray so the day has not made itself known yet. It is something in between. As usual, I'm anxious. Behind the fog are los Franklins. Behind those mountains is my brother. Waiting. On this side we're waiting, too, my fifteen-year-old nephew, Gabo, and his dog, la Winnie.

Winnie has one eye now. She got it stuck by a staghorn cactus that pulled it right out. Blood everywhere that day. By the time Gabo got home from his after-school bagger's job at el Shur Sav, I was back from the vet's with Winnie, rocking her like a baby. You couldn't blame the dog for being upset, losing her eye and all.

I kept Gabo this time around because I want him to finish high school. I don't care what the authorities say about his legal status. We'll work it out, I say to Gabo, who, when he was barely walking I changed his diapers, which I also tell him. He's still embarrassed to be seen in his boxers. That's okay. I'm embarrassed to be seen in mine, too. Thirty years of being widowed, you better believe I dress for comfort.

"Stop all this mourning," my mamá used to say. "You were only married six months. The guy was a drug addict, por Dios!" She actually would say that and repeat it even though Junior died fighting for his country. That's why we got married. He was being shipped off to Vietnam. If the coroner suggested he had needle tracks, well, I don't know about that.

Mamá always had a way of turning things around for me, to see them in the worst light possible. It's probably not a nice thing to say you are glad your mother's dead. But I am glad she's not around. Can I say that and not worry about a stretch in purgatory? Then I'll say that.

We've been waiting a week, me and Gabo—for his dad to come back. He's been back and forth across that desert, dodging the Border Patrol so many times, you'd think he wouldn't even need a coyote no more. The problem is the coyotes and narcos own the desert now. You look out there, you see thorny cactus, tumbleweed, and sand soil forever and you think, No, there's nothing out there. But you know what? They're out there—los mero-mero cabrones. The drug traffickers and body traffickers. Which are worse? I can't say.

So the problem is Rafa, my brother, can't just come across without paying somebody. Eight days ago we got a call. It was a woman's voice. She said in Spanish that Rafa was all right and that he was coming in a few days so we had better have the balance of the money ready. Who did those people think they were, I asked myself. That woman on the phone acted so damn cocky. I swear, if I knew who she was, I'd report her to the authorities, lock her up for five years. How dare she treat people like that? Take advantage of their poverty and laws that force people to crawl on their bellies for a chance to make it.

Truth is Rafa should have just stayed here last time he came to work the pecans. That's when he finally let me keep his son. Someone in the family's got to finish high school, I said to him. Poor Rafa, all alone like that now, going back and forth, even though I think he has a new wife down in Chihuahua. He won't say nothing out of respect for Gabo's dead mother. Just the mention of Ximena and the boy falls apart. It's been almost seven years now but Gabo was just a child. His mind sort of got stuck in that time when his mother didn't make it. He was here with me that winter, too. When Rafa and Ximena were returning they got separated. The coyotes said no, the women had to go in another truck. Three days later the bodies of four women were found out there in that heat by the Border Patrol. All four had been mutilated for their organs. One of them was Ximena. It was in all the news.

I've been fighting to keep my sobrino since then but my brother gets terco about it and keeps insisting on taking him back to the other side. What for? I tell him. Because he's Mexican, Rafa says. As if I'm not, because I choose to live on this side. He's got to know his grandparents—meaning Ximena's folks. He's not gonna become a gringo and forget who he is, my brother says of his only son, as if getting an education would erase the picture the boy keeps in his head of how his mother died.

I stayed and worked here in Cabuche, first in the pecans and cotton. Because of marrying Junior, I got his army benefits. I could stay and not hide in the shadows no more. This meant no more picking, no more peeling chiles, and no more canning. Instead, I got up my courage one year and signed up for night classes at the community college. I did pretty good in my classes. I really liked being in a classroom. I liked the desks, the smell of the chalk and erasers, the bulletin boards with messages about holidays like Valentine's Day and Martin Luther King Day. So later I got more courage and applied for a job as a teacher's aide in the middle school. That's how I bought my casita, here on the mesa, where I can't see los Franklins this morning. But I know they are out there, playing with me. Like giants, they take the sun and play with people's eyes, changing colors. Like shape-shifters, they change the way they look, too. They let the devoted climb up along their spines to crown them with white crosses and flowers and mementos. They give themselves that way, those guardians between the two countries.

I do not know what Rafa is talking about his son becoming a gringo. These lands, this unmerciful desert—it belonged to us first, the Mexicans. Before that it belonged to los Apaches. Los Apaches were mean, too. They knew how to defend themselves. And they're still not too happy about losing everything, despite the casinos up by their land. "Keep right on going," they'll tell tourists when they try to pull over on the highway that cuts across it during dry season.

Ha. I wish I could say that out here whenever some stupid hunter wanders near my property. It's just me and the barbed-wire fence between the hunter and government land where he can do what he pleases, all dressed up like if he was in the National Guard.

One day we heard some shots. It wasn't even dawn yet, that Sunday. Winnie went nuts—the way heelers do at the sign of something amiss. Gabo got up—pulling up his jeans, tripping on the hems of them, barefoot. "What was that, Tía?" he said, all apurado and the dog, meanwhile, barking, barking. This was before the accident, when she could practically see in the dark. I let her go out, and la Winnie ran toward the fence that divides my property and BLM land. "HEY, HEY!" was all my poor nephew called out. He always freezes up. I think he remembers his mother.

Over in El Paso people have asked me if I'm not afraid of the coyotes and rattlers living right next to the wide-open spaces kept by the Bureau of Land Management. The worse snakes and coyotes, I always say, are the ones on two legs. People think that's funny.

"Hey-Hey," Gabo called out again in the dark of the new day out there, with a little less conviction the second time. But la Winnie kept right on barking-barking. I went in the house and got my rifle. When I came out I went up to the fence and pointed the rifle somewhere I couldn't see. What were they shooting anyway? We don't got any deer around here. "YOU ARE WAY TOO CLOSE TO MY LAND!" I yelled like I was Barbara Stanwyck or Doña Bárbara or somebody and I took a shot that rang out like a 30-30. It must've woken up la gente all the way in town. A little while after that I heard Jeeps taking off.

We couldn't go back to sleep after that so I made us some atole and put on the TV. I needed to fold up the laundry I'd left in the dryer anyway. Winnie didn't come in like she would have normally, ready to be fed. She stayed outside roaming the grounds.

"Your father will come back," I said to Gabo that morning at the table about my kid brother who you'd think was way older than me, his mind full of the beliefs of another time, another era, belonging to the Communist Party and all that. He's so proud of it, too.

Gabo's older sister ran off a long time ago with a guy over there in Chihuahua and no one's heard from her since then. So all Gabo has to count on is his father.

And me, of course, his tía Regina.

But he's lost way too much already in his short life to know that for sure. So that's what I'm doing right now, trying to do something good—for my brother and Gabo but for me, too—to see that my sobrinito gets a chance. One day I'm gonna take him to Washington, D.C.

"What the hell for?" Rafa asked me when I mentioned it.

"To see where the Devil makes his deals," I said.

One day I'm gonna take my nephew to New York, too, where I've never been but it's on my list—my very long list—of places to see in this life. I may even take him to Florence, Italy, to see the David. Well, actually I'm the one that wants to see the statue of David but it won't hurt for Gabo to know a little something about great art. What? Why not? All our lives we have to be stuck to the ground like desert centipedes? My nephew doesn't show any signs of interest in the arts. He don't talk about girls. He goes to Mass every Sunday down in Cabuche. If I don't drive him or let him take my truck, he walks. He observes all the holy days of obligation. My biggest fear is he's gonna become a priest. Wait 'til Rafa hears about it. He'll be so disappointed.

◦ ◦ ◦

The truth is when I fired that weapon I was trying to show my sobrino not to be afraid. I wanted to show him that if a middle-aged woman like me could confront things that went bump in the night, he could do it, too, that he could face anything.

Actually, I had used my .22-caliber rifle only once before in the ten years I owned it. It was when a coyote was getting at my chickens. For a while I had it in my mind that I was gonna get rich selling fresh eggs. Everyone started asking me for eggs, all the neighbors, the teachers at the school, but no one really wanted to pay for them. Then I started feeling for the poor familias I worked with at the school and I gave them free eggs. The coyote ate three of my hens before I caught up with it. After that, I said, What do I need all this for? And I sold the rooster and the hens I had left.

I've never been very good at get-rich-quick schemes anyway. But it don't stop me from trying. The only thing I will not do is gamble, go down to Sunland Park or up to Ruidoso and throw my money away in the casinos the way some of the ladies in town do. Oh sure, now and then they win a couple of hundred bucks. They get all excited. They forget how much they lost to begin with. They forget the dinner or the motel and gas money they put out to be there. And I surely will not play the lottery. Millions and millions in the pot some weeks. So I figure, what are the chances?

Instead I take that dollar and buy two avocados if they're on sale. Avocados, the food of the gods, are the only things I can't grow on my land— too arid; avocado trees don't grow in sand. Another thing I've done with one dollar is send a fax to the White House on that number they give out to people in case you got a complaint about how things are being run up there. I tried to send the fax out of the school office but Mrs. Martínez, the head secretary, said no, nothing doing. Plus, she voted for the president. So I took my letter of complaint to the place on the corner of Main Street and Washington in Cabuche where you can send out faxes, buy phone cards, or have your taxes done. It took five minutes and one dollar and I felt much better afterward. I know I am nobody; no one has to tell me that. But I still vote like everyone else. So if I feel like sending a fax and complaining about the president's latest pick for a Supreme Court judge, that's my prerogative.

That's a word I use with the students all the time: *prerogative,* as in, "It's a lady's prerogative to change her mind." The boys say they know all about that—about girls changing their minds. You cannot get a gallon of gas for a dollar these days. You might still get yourself something you don't need, like a thirty-two-ounce can of beer at the package liquors across the street from the "business" tienda where I send out my official faxes. Sometimes I have actually sat and thought out what you can and cannot buy with a dollar no more and it's very interesting—because you think you can't buy much, but in reality, if you think about it, it all depends on your priorities.

That's another good word I've given the students and my nephew. "What are your priorities in life, anyway? Go to jail or go to college? Get drunk with your friends or get a job and make a little money to get ahead?" Things like that. You would be very surprised at how little thought any of them have given those choices until I start telling them about priorities. Gabo's priorities are very clear and I am very proud of him for it.

He says he is going to college. That is, if the government lets him. If he can't get residency he won't be going nowhere but back to México. They don't give scholarships to migrant kids without papers.

We do the dollar game sometimes. I used to do it by myself, but now that my Gabo is with me we do it together. He's come home with a big bottle of shampoo for one dollar. Of course, you can get a whole lot of stuff at the Dollar General for a dollar or what shouldn't cost more than a dollar; it's so cheap and falls apart so quick. But this was the champú bueno that Gabo bought at el Shur Sav with his employee's discount. Shampoo is just a small example of how our dollar game works. We've gotten all kinds of things for a dollar.

What we won't get and what we'd never do with our dollars, we have agreed, because we got our priorities straight, I tell him, is nothing that would be harmful to our bodies or our souls. That's why I made him take back the pound of chorizo he bought for us one time. He felt so bad and I felt so bad because the truth was that we both love our chorizo with eggs for breakfast. But we know that spicy, greasy sausage is no good for your health, and what's bad for your arteries cannot be good for your mental well-being neither.

Gabo and I are figuring these things out—he, with his suspicious signs of priest potential and me, a woman who has been living alone so long I may as well become beatified. Santa Lucia, who cares for blind dogs. Santa Barbara, whose father locked her in a tower because he desired her so much. When I've thought of the martyrs and saints, I told Padre Juan Bosco down at the church one time when he reprimanded me for hardly going to Mass no more, it seems it would be very, very hard to become one these days. It isn't because we don't have diehard virgins, but because these days the pope is not about to proclaim every girl who fights a rapist a saint. As for the martyrs—you don't get thrown in the den of lions for refusing to renounce your faith as in early Christian times. I wonder why I always think of things like that—imagining myself tied to a stake, scalped, Roman soldiers demanding I give up on God. Mamá used to come and slap me on the head when she'd catch me daydreaming.

"Maybe you used to be a martyr or a saint in another life," Gabo said when I talked out loud about these ponderings.

"According to the Church, there is only one life and this is it," I told him.

My sobrino looked very disturbed by this reminder. The rest of that day he kept to himself, listening to his John Denver cassette in his room.

He got it for a dollar at the flea market.

                                      ¢ ¢ ¢

Gabo found a hawk. It was young, you could tell. It was the most beautiful thing you ever saw, brown and near-white with dashes of black on the wings. Nature is so geometrically precise. If you look real close at birds and fish, too, you see how everything—every feather, fin, wing, gill, is colored just so.

Somewhere I heard that baby hawks have a high mortality rate. This one didn't make it. It must've been trying to take flight when it got hit on the road. Its neck was broken but otherwise it looked like it was sleeping, as they say about people when they're in their coffins. (Except for Mamá. The mortician had painted on such bright orange lipstick and powder too light for her complexion she looked dead for sure.)

"What are you going to do with it?" I asked my nephew. He looked so sad. You'd think he had killed the hawk himself. He'd found it on the road. He was driving my truck back from work. I let him take the truck since he comes home after dark. When he saw it, he pulled over and put it on the passenger seat. "I'm going to bury it, Tía," Gabo replied solemnly, the way he speaks most of the time, "with your permission."

My nephew is so polite to the point of being antiquated. True, humble Mexican kids have better manners than American Mexican kids, but Gabo sounds like a page out of Lope de Vega. Lope de Vega, the prince of Spain's Golden Age. I haven't read anything of his; I heard the Spanish teacher at the school talking to the students about him. But Spain's Golden Age of literature is on my list of things to read—my very long list. I've done some reading on my own, García Márquez, for example. *One Hundred Years of Solitude* was assigned in one of the classes I took at the community college and then I looked for other books of his, like the story of Eréndira and her wicked grandmother, that, in some ways, reminded me of my own life with Mamá in the desert. I read the newspaper every day. But now with Gabo here I have become more conscious of the importance of broadening the mind through reading. The next book fair the school has I'm going to buy us everything we see that we think we'll like. We'll treat it like a candy store. I'll have to assure my considerate nephew, who behaves as if he may be overstaying his visit—the way he tiptoes around and hardly eats, although I'm not sure why; it's not because of anything I've said or done, I hope—that I have saved up for such a splurge. Otherwise, he'll hesitate to get anything, even if he sees something he really wants.

The hawk was on Gabo's dresser. He brought home a white veladora. He got it for a dollar with his discount at work. It took exactly seven days to burn through. When the candle was done, Gabo said he would bury the hawk. Every night he prayed over it. "You look like some kind of shaman," I told him when I peeked in to say good night and there he was, standing in the glow of the flame, head bowed, hands suspended just above the dead bird. It looked as if he were trying to resurrect it, although I'm sure that's not what he was trying to do.

When the candle had burned out I found it in the trash. Where was the bird, I asked Gabo. Had he buried it already? Where? When? I thought we were going to hold a funeral for it. I felt a little left out of his ceremonies.

"Yes," he said.

Later that day, I saw a hawk perched on the fence post by the gate. The front gate is about an eighth of a mile from the front door. It was brown with near-white feathers, black dashes on the wings. It looked a lot like our dead hawk. Maybe it was its mother or some other relation.

"Where did you say you buried that bird?" I asked Gabo when he came to the kitchen to make a sandwich for his school lunch. He refuses the money I offer so that he can eat in the cafeteria or go out with some of the kids. He saves his work money, spends only on what he needs. He offered his whole check to me at the beginning, but I looked at him as if he were crazy and told him to use it on himself. His sandwiches are very frugal, too—one slice of meat between two slices of ninety-nine-cent whole wheat bread.

"I didn't," Gabo replied.

"You didn't what?" I asked. "You didn't say or you didn't bury it?"

"No," was all he said.

"Maybe that bird was carrying that virus, Gabo," I said. "How much did you handle it anyway?"

"Do not worry yourself so much, Tía," he said.

As far as teenagers go, from what I hear at the school and from the students' parents, Gabo could get a lot worse on my nerves.

This is not why I am so anxious all the time—having a teenager to look out for now. It was not even part of the Change, like the doctor down in Juárez told me last year. The anxiety is just part of me. On any given day, a person can find several reasons to be anxious. If you don't find it in your own life at that moment, all you have to do is pick up a newspaper and read the headlines. Being a fifty-plus-year-old woman alone for so long, widowed thirty years, that could be cause enough. Every paycheck covers the bills to the penny—when I'm lucky.

Every three months or so I come up with another get-rich-quick idea that ends up not making me much money and sometimes ends up costing me some. I've delivered groceries for people out here in the boonies who can't or don't want to drive into town every week. I've taken orders for curtains and sewed quite a few up. Over the years, I've dog-sat, old people–sat, house-sat. I sold Amway, Avon, and Mary Kay products, even though I am allergic to most anything with a chemical scent. I had Tupperware parties. I sold red candy apples and pecan bread in the parking lot of el Shur Sav. For a time, I had a little business out of my troca selling pizzas. I'd buy them wholesale down the road at a place across from the police station. Then I'd drive them to an empty lot on Main Street and put out my sign. People didn't really want to bother ordering a pizza ahead of time. Just drive up and I hand them one into their car or troca or maybe they were on foot. On weekends I'd make a killing. Then a guy started doing it, right next to me, out of his car. He gave away free Cokes, so he ran me out of business. A long time ago I went door to door selling bibles, the King James version. Then my mother found out and told Padre Juan Bosco and he had one of his talks with me, so I felt morally inclined to quit. All these jobs I had in addition to whatever other full-time work I was putting in somewhere. And all of it caused me anxiety.

I keep almost nothing from my nephew now, except what I might look like in a swimsuit, but why he would care to see his fat old aunt half naked I wouldn't know, but nearly everything in my heart or that crosses my mind I share with him. He's been God-sent that way, I think. I had no idea how lonely I was until one day I found myself at my Singer stitching up his jeans, talking my head off, and he, so patiently, sitting nearby listening to it all. Or at least he looked like he was listening.

One thing I won't tell Gabo about is my money worries. He'd run off so as not to be another burden on me. The other topic I cannot bring myself to approach is the fact that we haven't heard from his papá yet. It isn't as if Gabo himself hasn't noticed. I heard him crying into his pillow one night. He probably envisions his father being killed by a coyote and left in the desert like what happened to his mother. It isn't like Rafa not to get word to me somehow, but then again, I wouldn't be terribly surprised if he changed his mind about coming. That coyote woman on the phone was horrid—he may not have wanted to pay them all that they wanted. The fact is, all Gabo and I can do is wait.

In the meantime I discovered where he buried the hawk. It was right near the fallen yucca. La one-eyed Winnie, or Tuerta, as I am calling her now, dug it up. My Mescalero Apache friend, Uriel, told me over the phone that Gabo's finding the hawk was very good luck for him. She said the hawk is good protection medicine. I wonder if finding where it was buried and digging it up was good luck for la Tuerta. Poor little hawk— with so many now trying to benefit from its death. I reburied it this time between two huge chollas, where I don't think the dog will go, seeing that she's cautious now about getting too near anything with thorns.

⸙ ⸙ ⸙

I'd rather be pricked by a thousand thorns than have to think about what my little brother may have endured. The fact is, however, that I don't know what exactly he had to endure. Sometimes I like to think he is back in Chihuahua with a pregnant wife and that we just never heard from him because he became too selfish and didn't care about Gabo no more or his past life with Ximena.

Another week went by when a foco went on in my head and I realized that the phone number of that nasty coyote woman that called me might be on the caller-ID box. We don't get many calls. All the numbers of anyone who has ever called since I put in the caller ID right around the time Rafa left my nephew here were still on there. We never erased them. Most of the time we didn't even pay attention to it. Without saying nothing to Gabo, I checked and, sure enough, there was a call from El Paso the very same day la coyota had called me.

"Bueno," she answered when I tried it. I knew it was her. It was a voice full of intriga and bad tidings.

I went on to tell her who I was and that we were still waiting for Rafa. "I don't know what you are talking about," she said and hung up on me, proving all the more that she very well did.

My heart started breaking with the sound of the dial tone on the other end and I knew that my brother had been done some awful wrong. Still, without mentioning my concern to my nephew, the next day I took someone into my confidence at the school. I consider most of the teachers much more intelligent than me, with their college education and all. One of them could give me some advice, I thought, but it would have to be someone I could trust, since my brother trying to cross without papers was obviously against the law. Most of the teachers at the school are Mexican or at least of Mexican heritage although half of them call themselves "Hispanic," which means they don't want to be considered Mexican. Or at least that is how Rafa and I feel about the word. It is one of the few political points we agree on.

Mr. Betancourt, the history teacher, calls himself "Chicano." He wears a long ponytail and while he obliges the system with a nice shirt and tie, he always has on jeans. All this about Betancourt told me I could trust him with my fears about Rafa, so I pulled him aside the very next day and told him what I thought.

"We might be able to find an address for that phone number," Betancourt told me. He said there was a phone number that you could call where, if the number you had was listed, you'd get a name and maybe an address. I thought I would try it when I got home, but he took out a cell phone from inside his jean jacket and, to my surprise, within ten minutes had obtained the woman's information for me.

"Will you go to her house?" he asked me.

Betancourt is about thirty-five but most of his hair has gone white. He looks old and young at the same time. I remember when I was in my thirties, I felt like that—old and young at the same time. Now I'm middle-aged and I feel old and really old at the same time. Yes, I told him that I would, that I would have gotten in my truck and gone right then and there but that my nephew would need it for work in an hour. Betancourt nodded. He looked at his watch and then he said, "Let me move some things around. I can meet you somewhere in an hour or I can go pick you up at your house. I'll take you. It's probably not wise for you to go there alone."

Miguel. That's his name. He told me to call him Miguel or Mike but to please not call him Mr. Betancourt no more. I never called him just plain Betancourt to his face but that's how the teachers called him in the lounge. Especially a couple of the young women teachers said it like they meant something more by it. Sometimes a single man is as likely to be the object of a lot of unprofessional interest as a single woman, in particular the attractive ones, of which, at the school, I can count only four. I look around, too. I may not say nothing, being a fifty-plus-year-old widow, but I still look.

Miguel was handsome in his own way but more important, for the purposes of our errand, tall and very strong-looking. When he showed up at my house he was still wearing his tie. He decided to keep it on, he said, because it made him look like he might be someone of authority. "I mean, I'm not gonna say I'm with La Migra or anything but it wouldn't hurt if they think we have some pull."

The woman's house was very close to the customs bridge going into Juárez. It was a little house like others on that block, nothing special about it, and if my brother was in there, if they were holding him for ransom, never in a million years would I have guessed it would have been in such an ordinary place and right there in the middle of everything. The woman herself opened the door. She looked us up and down, especially Miguel, who did start to look like some kind of agent all of a sudden, with his Serpico long hair and bigotes.

At first she denied knowing anything, even the fact that she was the one who had called. Then Miguel took me by surprise. He pushed her, and next thing I knew, we were all in the house, in a dark, tiny, crowded living room with a dirty beige couch and two little kids, one in Pampers, in a playpen. "Listen," he said right in her face, "you are going to tell us what happened to this woman's brother or you are going right to jail— today. Do you understand? Do you understand?" He pushed her again so that she went reeling back until she hit a wall. She started crying. She might've been around thirty or so, with a bulging midriff from babies, and her breasts already sagging. The house smelled of stale cigarette smoke. The TV was blaring a Spanish channel. I felt sorry for the babies who looked startled but hadn't started to cry. It was funny that they didn't cry when the mother was crying. Then she got hold of herself and looked me up and down. "What would I know about your brother?" she said to me with that same sneer I imagined that time she had called me. "Have you tried calling your family back in México? He's probably there."

Before I could even say nothing, Miguel took her by the shoulders and shook her so hard her head went back and forth like it was on a spring. "I'm only going to ask you one more time," he said. And before he asked again, she looked at me and with spittle coming out of the corners of her mouth and with more hate than I have ever felt from a human being, she seemed even glad to tell me, "Your brother must be dead, stupid. Why else do you think you never heard anything again? Do you think they come and tell *me* what goes on out there? I only know about the ones who make it. They come here until their people pay what they owe. Your brother? What do I know of him? They most likely left him to rot out in the desert because he was a tonto or maybe for being a pendejo he got himself killed. What do I know? Now get out of here before I tell my husband you were here and you'll both be sorry you came."

It was like a movie. In movies about drug traficantes they have women like that, in their nightgowns in daytime in gloomy rooms and living an obscure existence. And they have guys like the one who drove up just as we were leaving, wearing a big anchor on a chain around his neck and a diamond earring in one ear. They—everything, even their frightened little kids who wouldn't cry—looked like they were right out of a bad drug video.

El coyote looked at Miguel as we left as if he was memorizing him, taking a mental photograph in case he ever saw him again. But neither said a word to the other.

I turned around and took a last glance at the woman, who stayed inside in the shadows. She knew something about my brother's fate. I felt it in my heart. She could have given me some piece of information, however small, a gold nugget to take back to Gabo so that the poor boy would somehow, someday, find closure.

I wanted to go back in and shake her myself. Shake her until her stupid head fell off. Until her neck snapped and we'd carry her lifeless body to Gabo so that he could pray over it for seven days. Then he'd find a place to bury it even though his father had gotten no such consideration. And when la Tuerta Winnie sniffed up the corpse and started digging, fine; she could dig all she wanted. I'd let her dig up that estúpida's body so that all the coyotes that wanted to come on my little bit of land that I protected so well could feed off of her stupid flesh and lick her stupid bones clean. And then we'd all, me and Winnie and Gabo and Miguel, too, if he wanted, and even the coyotes with four feet, could go out to the BLM land and scatter the bones out there to dry in the sun, for sands and wind to wash over. And Rafa, wherever they had left him, would no longer be alone out there.

Then I felt Miguel take my hand. He had to pull me with him. "Come on," he muttered close to my ear. "We'd better get the hell out of here while we can."

GABO

Su Reverencia, el Santo Franciscano, Padre Pío:

Venerado Santo, gracias for permitting me this great honor to write to you in heaven. If there is one reason alone why your most humblest of servants is given the privilege of not being un analfabeto and not knowing how to read or write like my mamá or mis abuelos, I believe it was for this purpose. Because you are at God's feet perhaps He bothers Himself to converse with you about what is going on when you don't hear from me. If not, I will relate what has happened now, as best as I am able to express myself como siempre, Santito.

On that day walking up the dirt road after school, I saw my tía Regina coming down in a car with a man I did not know. I knew it had to do with mi papá. She smiled and gave that little wave that people give out here when they pass each other on the road. My tía Regina's wave is like that of the Queen of England. She waved and smiled that very sad smile of hers, her fading red hair flying in the wind of the hombre's old Mustang convertible. We did not know anyone like that, my tía and I. Most of the people on the mesa and out around these parts drive trucks. Old ones, mostly. One neighbor rides a Harley but only on weekends, with his bikers' club.

Tía Regina smiled with her little squinting eyes that make her look like a china poblana and then they passed me. I stayed on the side of the road watching them. As the Mustang turned the corner, a flock of blackbirds with long patas, feeding on a rich wet patch of worms, all together lifted their wings. For a moment all the birds hung in the air, shiny wings out. As soon as the car passed, all together they gently went back down to feed, not one losing sight of the feast below.

I watched until the car was no more than a small, fast-moving object surrounded by fields of green alfalfa, swaying right, then down, until it became a red speck and there was nothing left to think about anymore. I swung around and kept going up the sandy hill lined with cholla y sprawling nopales. Dogs barked aquí y allá, letting my Winnie know that I was coming.

At my tía Regina's I got ready to go to work. "El Estockboy" is what my manager calls me. I pack groceries and keep the shelves stocked with inventory. I know that God gives us drudgery to keep us from being idle, Padrecito. As I unpack cans of string beans y garbanzos to line the shelves, it is a meditation of our Lord. Sweeping is my favorite quehacer, Santito, because then I am free to contemplate God's eternal love. Sometimes the manager sends me out to wash the windows. He says I am the best estockboy he's ever had and whenever I want, I can work for him full-time.

The money I earn I put away. My tía has refused it. When mi papá comes, I will give it to him. He would never ask it of me. He will make good use of it to help my abuelos or toward building the house there. As for me, I have no need of dinero or material comforts. (But, on this subject, Your Reverence, I must ask you to help me, especially when my blanket feels so rico over my body, tan cansado. I find it difficult to get up in the mornings.)

When I return from work, after my shower, I do my homework in my cuarto, so my tía's sleep is not disturbed. I go to school. I go to work. I go to church. Meanwhile we wait for my father. He will decide if I stay or not but for now I want to stay.

My aunt had left the truck keys on the kitchen table. Truck keys and one aguacate. My aunt is good at rationing even while she knows we are not starving; although we have our share of arroz y papas all week. And of course, every day, beans, every which way you want to have them— first in the pot like soup; that's the best. You sprinkle a little diced onions and with a rolled-up corn tortilla—a man could not ask for much more in life. We can't add chorizo to them anymore because my tía says one day it will give her a heart attack.

Avocados are just about the only thing my tía doesn't grow in the garden that we can't live without. She has one of those green thumbs.

We get all kinds of chiles, tomatoes, yellow, red, and green for salsa, three varieties of squash, a patch of watermelon, and corn.

Mis padres thought my tía Regina had won the lottery with this property. All summer, from harvest to harvest, Mami kept badgering my father, "Why don't we settle down like your sister? Why can't you get us something like that? Por favor, Rafael—your sister did it by herself. Why can't we?" My poor mother; she was never happy. Who could have been, working in la pisca like we did, pulling up tomatoes, artichokes, cotton, grapes . . . pues, todo, pues, Santo querido.

That day in my tía Regina's kitchen, which is dark even in the daytime but from the window over the sink you can see the mountains, I decided to eat only the avocado. I picked out two corn tortillas, the hardest ones. Little sacrificios prepare me daily for the course I have chosen. I added a hot salsa of chile árbol that my tía makes so delicious, but that was all. (I tried not to enjoy it too much.) I ate the whole avocado because no matter what I try, once you cut one open, the leftover portion will turn black and go to waste. I've heard all kinds of trucos as to how to prevent that—cellophane, aluminum foil, cut the pit out, leave it in, Tupperware. My tío Osvaldo in California swore that the only sure way to keep an open avocado from spoiling was to place the open part flat down on a piece of cardboard. My mother's brother, he had picked avocados in California all his life so I accepted his word. Until I tried it. It did not work. But back then, when Tío Osvaldo was still alive, I was just a little boy. What did I know of life then?

One day my mother got word that Tío Osvaldo was dying of pneumonia. He had been working for a flower rancher near Fresno, allá in California. We were working the garlic pisca near Watsonville when the message came. Mami took me with her to see him. Tío Osvaldo was laying there in un jacalito. It was typical of the ones we migrantes were assigned in the labor camps. Since my earliest memory such a shack would be called home. There wasn't electricity in that one.

How does someone die of pneumonia picking flowers, Santo? You could die of heat exhaustion and overall fatigue. This everyone knew. My uncle was only twenty-nine years old. He was very strong and had never been sick. When we found him, he was trembling to death under a blanket another migrant had lent him. It was one of those soft colchas depicting whole scenes—an adobe house in front of a big yellow moon, a tiger looking at you, the Seven Dwarves dancing. This one had la Virgen de Guadalupe with a white face. The owner of the blanket did not want it anymore with the smell of death on it, so my mother let me keep it.

Before we left, a woman told my mother that my uncle died because the men were forced to stand all night in a shallow lake on the property. The rancher did not want them running away. The story sounded almost unbelievable but Mami said almost was not good enough. She wept real hard over her brother but she said she was also weeping over the things in life that we had to put up with.

That night of the red car y el hombre with the ponytail, after el Shur Sav closed and I went directly home, all the luces were off, even el portal light. La Winnie Tuerta, as my tía was now calling her, was lying quietly outside the door. The winds were blowing dust, knocking cans and chairs down and tools around. Inside, there were no potatoes and eggs on the stove kept warm for me. There was the owl I'd been hearing for the last week.

I knocked on my tía's bedroom door. She was in bed, covers to her chin, la eerie luz of the portable TV next to her bed illuminating her face and the volume turned down. She tried to smile. "I was thinking we might want to go to the city tonight and have dinner out," she said.

"Go out?" I couldn't imagine doing something like that without it being an occasion.

"Yes, like a celebration," she said.

"What are we celebrating?" I asked. (I do try to avoid such extravagances, Su Reverencia.)

"Your birthday, of course, mi'jo," my tía said. My birthday was not until March—a month and a half away.

It was the first time she called me "her son." It should not have been a big deal so that I noticed—even teachers at school called me "mi'jo"—but suddenly I felt hypersensitive. I looked around my tía's room. There was a draft. Algo. I reminded her that my birthday was a ways off. "Your good grades, then," she said next. Exams were not for another week.

"We could go to Applebee's or Chili's, if you like," she said, "or to the Taco Tote. You like that place, don't you, hijo? We're celebrating the trip we're going to take to the capital as soon as you graduate—how about that?"

My hands had turned cold and then my ears. If only she would have

gotten on with it, just said what she knew. I had never been all the way
in my tía Regina's bedroom before. It was smaller than my own. There
was the dresser that had belonged to my grandmother, back from her
days. It looked antique. The headboard matched. Over the headboard
was a small plaque of la Virgen de Guadalupe. There was a color picture
of a young soldier on the nightstand. The nightstand did not match; it
was modern, of unfinished pine. I was looking around, feeling my body
grow cold, first my arms, then down my legs, remembering again for
the second time that day how my tío Osvaldo had died. I fought the
hunger so familiar en mis entrañas and waited to hear what my tía had
to say whenever she got the courage to say it. I started staring at a
mancha in the corner on the ceiling. "Does the roof need repairing
there?" I asked. She did not answer.

My palms hurt. Sometimes I wake at night and they throb as if they
have been punctured. I look but there is nothing unusual about them.
(You know how long I have prayed for that grace.) I brought my right
palm up and scrutinized it. "What's wrong with your hand?" Tía
Regina asked. "Did you hurt it at work?" I shook my head and put the
hand behind my back. (I do not doubt, Padre Pío, that she knows
about my affinities with my Savior.) El Cura Juan Bosco said I had to
wait until I finished high school. The days do not pass fast enough. I
have already chosen los Hermanos Franciscanos.

My dad and my tía are a lot alike when it comes to not trusting the
Church. "Millions," they each say, like they had been saying it all their
lives, "millions of mexicanos among the faithful, living in poverty. And
the Church—so rich." "Religion is the opium of the masses." Mi papá
liked to quote Marx. At my age, he joined guerrilleros to fight the government.

My tía is a good woman, Su Reverencia. She does not know that I
know, but she was a virgin widow. I heard my mamá tell my father
about it when I was a child. They both laughed. Maybe they had no use
for aires of purity. But nothing about the room I found myself in that
night or the news we were both preparing for—one to pronounce and
the other to accept—was more than what it was. It was just our lives.
My father was gone forever. Like crumbs of bread, bits of his soul had
been leaving traces for days. A bit had landed on la Winnie la Tuerta's
eye and taken it. Another had hummed the young hawk to sleep on the
road. Still another piece was now in the owl's throat outside the door at
that very moment. And my father's soul was causing la Winnie to howl

like she had never howled before. The howling of a dog is an announcement of death. We could not possibly go to a restaurant pretending
cheerfulness to ease the ache that my father's soul had dispersed all
around us like motes in a ray of light.

Tía Regina, she is so simple. (Am I simple, too, Padre Pío?)

Slowly I made my way to her bed that night, crawling like a little cat
to one side and put my head on the pillow next to hers that smelled of
lilacs or jasmine. The scent of flowers in the desert, even from pot-
pourri, was always disorienting. I was dizzy and closed my eyes. I felt
Tía Regina breathing hard until her sobbing began. And while I cried
like that later, in my room, many times, that night I went to sleep to
the sound of her copious weeping.

Copious.

It is one of the many beautiful words I learned from reading your
most venerated teachings. Yes, I know what it means. *Copious* as in
"And yet there will be more."

As always, your devotee tan desmerecido

chapter

TWO

REGINA

Today I ate three tunas, one after the other, while I looked out at the snow covering the tops of los Franklins, gleaming like white frosting. I gave a little piece of the cactus fruit to la Tuerta, who was sitting there staring with her one eye. She ate it right up. Sometimes the dog forgets she's a carnivore by nature. Although it's midwinter and all the prickly pear cactus is dormant, I had a stash of peeled tunas in the freezer in a plastic zipper bag for a day like today, when my spirit needed a boost.

I came up with a new idea of how to earn a little extra money. I have a boy to send to college now and that's something to think about. The idea came to me when I started making use of the costal of pecans I collected from under my trees one weekend. First I baked two pies, then three, then the rest of the night I was baking pies. It gave me something to do when I couldn't sleep.

I wrapped a pie and took it to school as my way of thanks for Miguel Mike Mr. Betancourt. I'm not sure what to call him. Everything about my pie was homemade. It had a golden crisp crust y todo. All I know how to bake that always come out right are pies. I entered my pies one year in the county fair. I didn't even get honorable mention. Still, they're pretty good.

"Wow," the teachers in the lounge said, one after the next. I had to let them know it wasn't for them to share but for Betancourt. "Uh-huh," said Cindy López. She gave a look to Michelle Montoya. They're this year's student teachers. They think no one knows that Michelle dated Betancourt at the beginning of the year. The first week of school those two got together. Before September was over, so were they. What's this vieja fea think she's up to? they must've been saying to each other with their eyes.

I found Miguel out in the teachers' parking lot on his cell phone. He seemed real happy about the pecan pie and stuck a couple of fingers in to taste it right away. "I'm gonna leave it in my car," he said, smiling, meaning he didn't want to share it with no one. It's winter, which for us means not cold but not hot, so the pie would survive there. "I got more at home," I said. All the pies were lined up as if on display on kitchen windowsills and counters. No one was gonna eat them. I don't have the appetite with all my anxieties these days. That's when I got the idea to go into the pie-baking business.

When I had a break, instead of having lunch, I went home, got one of the pies, and took it to the school and set it out in the teachers' lounge. "Wow," the teachers said again. "Who's *this* pie for?" someone asked, trying with all his might not to help himself to a piece. "It's for auction," I said. "Bidding starts at two dollars, no tax. Hecho en casa y con aceo."

"That means one hundred percent homemade good. I'll bid two dollars," said Miguel, who had just come in the door so I hadn't seen him. "Regina's pies are to die for!"

That's how the whole enterprise got started. The pie ended up going for five bucks and, since that was set as its market value—as the math teacher explained it—the others would be that price. Pie-baking will keep me from getting too depressed.

◦ ◦ ◦

"Hey, Regina," Miguel Mike called out to me in the teachers' parking lot the next morning.

At least I don't call him Mr. Betancourt no more. Not when we're one-on-one. "One-on-one" is how the seminar leader talks who comes from the university in Las Cruces every few months to catch us up on how education is progressing in the world. "Why don't you go back and get your degree, Miss Regina?" she always says to me. "You'd make a great teacher." I hear things like that and I think, Who knows—maybe one day I will.

Miguel Mike came over to my truck and helped carry the pies without my asking. I noticed from the other day when we went to El Paso that he was a gentleman, with old-fashioned caballero manners. Except for the part about pushing that coyota around. But what can I say about that? I don't like the idea of any man laying a finger on a woman. There is a very high domestic-violence rate in this area, uf, not to mention Cabuche alone, from what I hear at the PTA, on the news, on the street, and on my shortwave ham radio. (That's what I used to do for entertainment before I got cable—listen to police calls.) How Miguel Mike handled the coyota, however, I don't think falls into that category. My opinion is when you buy into a life of crime you can only expect to get hurt, and that's what happened with her. That's as far as my moralizing went, because the truth was I was in a world of pain over my fears of losing Rafa.

"Call me just Miguel, okay?" he said. "Or Mike. Whichever one."

I decided on Miguel because it reminds me of my favorite archangel. I call upon el arcángel Miguel whenever I need serious help, with this side and the other side. By that I mean here and across the border in México and I mean this life and whatever's on the Other Side. I was telling him all this when I saw by the smile that he was trying to hide that maybe I was just amusing him, which was not my intention. There's no end to how people think that everything about old women is ridiculous. Of course, I know I am not that old, but to a guy with a fast red car, yeah, I'm pretty sure I'm old. Also, what I might be revealing and what made me shut up right away was how lonely I could get sometimes that made me just go on and on about things. Then Miguel said, "I was named after the archangel."

"No way," I said, figuring he was pulling my leg.

"No, really," he said. "My mom had a difficult pregnancy." Then he stopped and said, "What I wanted to talk to you about, Regina, is your nephew. I know how much you worry about him. But maybe now, you know, you could adopt him legally. This way he could get his papers in order and he could stay in the States and study later on. You said he's a good student, right? We could get him a scholarship . . ."

I was looking down at Miguel's white tenis and thinking how I'd like to be able to afford a pair of those for Gabo for his birthday because I know he likes to play basketball, while I listened to all that Miguel was saying, words that he meant to sound all happy, like that silver lining around a dark cloud but that just plain did not. I knew that as Gabo's guardian, I could probably try to adopt him and if I did, he wouldn't have to go back to México. But what Miguel was leaving out was the fact that we didn't know whether or not mi hermano was coming back for him. Who said my brother was dead? La Coyota? Like she was a reliable source.

"Gimme the pies," I said, suddenly upset with Miguel because he had already written off my last living known relative, besides Gabo. It wasn't his fault if my kid brother was dead. But why should I have to accept it with no proof yet?

Then in our struggle, we dropped one of the pies. "Ay!" I said.

"I'll pay you for it, Regina," Miguel said, looking like he genuinely felt bad.

The sky was full of rain clouds again. Though everywhere there were long slits between them where brilliant light came through.

Sometimes I dream that I live on the other side of the clouds. There I've seen my mamá again. I've seen my father. I've seen my grandfather Metatron. I can't believe he made it to heaven, but I'd know that bellowing voice anywhere. Even in heaven he's yelling at everybody. My mother and he, of course, did not get along.

Mamá went to my abuelo Metatron's rancho when she was only fifteen to work as a cook. That's who I learned to cook from and to know all about plants and everything about vegetables, my mother. My father fell in love with her. It's an old story, I know, the son of the patrón in love with the beautiful india servant. But it was their story for real. We lived on the rancho until I was twelve, when my father and my older brother, Gabriel, who was the most perfect brother and son anyone could have ever imagined, were killed together. A bull turned on them and gored them both in almost one motion. It was one of those bulls you could never trust. I know how funny that sounds. But this was truly a mean animal. It was not all that young, neither, but it was still fierce. It came out of nowhere, a ranch hand said, when they were branding the calves. Who let it out, no one knew or would ever admit.

Hell broke loose on my grandfather's rancho that day. He fired everyone. Then he threw us out—Mamá, Rafa, and me. Rafa was barely six. "I've had enough, enough of this life!" My abuelo said things like that in his grief over losing his beloved son and his perfect grandson. In heaven they're all having it out, I guess.

Mamá took us, with our few belongings, to live with one of her uncles for a few days. She came from very poor people. Then we started crossing over to the States to work the harvests. I had met my future husband not in la pisca but on my abuelo's rancho in Chihuahua. Junior used to come out there every summer with his familia to visit his own grandparents. His grandfather was my grandfather's rancho foreman. What did we know about who gave orders to who until my abuelo lost it that day and ran everybody off his land?

We used to play together out there in our carefree days as children. We took care of my pets. I bottle-fed a pet calf one summer. Throughout my childood I had a pet burrito, cabritos to watch, two pet box turtles for a long time, and I always got to take care of the baby bunnies we kept in cages. When I was about three or four, when my first pet rabbit was taken from me for an Easter dinner, I learned to let go once they were grown. Junior was a gentle boy, so he preferred my company to that of my brothers. One time, when I was twelve, Junior tried to kiss me. We were collecting eggs in the henhouse when he leaned over. I think he had been calculating for a long time how and when he would make his move. When I saw his puckered lips headed in my direction I stepped back so fast, I fell and dropped all the eggs we had been collecting. My mother gave it to me good that day. Junior didn't try to kiss me again until we grew up. But that's how I knew he was the one for me, that summer day when I was twelve.

My brothers and I had had a private teacher who stayed the whole week with us and went home on weekends. The school was too far away and my abuelo thought it was for common folks anyway. Rafa was showing himself to be one of those math-wizard kids. Our big brother was going to go to study medicine in México City and then my grandfather said he would send him to finish up in Paris. I'm not saying that I'm better than other people who crossed over to this side, risking their lives in the river or through the desert, just because I started learning Latin when I was a girl. But life would have been much different for us if it hadn't been for that bull.

That's where a lot of the "what-ifs" start for me.

"What if I had insisted that Ximena stay with me?" Rafa said one time when he got real down on himself about Ximena's tragic death.

"What if Junior had never gone off to war?" I said right back to him.

Well, then, you just have to keep taking those what-ifs to infinity. What if there had been no war and what if no money could be made on killing undocumented people for their organs? What if this country accepted outright that it needed the cheap labor from the south and opened up the border? And people didn't like drugs so that trying to sell them would be pointless? What if being a brown woman, even one with red hair, didn't set off the antennas of all the authorities around here, signaling that you were born poor and ignorant and would probably die poor and ignorant? That you were as ordinary as a rock, so who cared what you thought or what you felt?

I was huddled down staring at that splattered pie on the asphalt, just staring, and I could hear Miguel's voice far off, saying, "Leave it, Regina. The birds will eat it up." When I looked up at Miguel he looked so tall, like a poplar tree, so healthy and full of life and vigor and a future and, like some kind of fortune-teller, I felt it would be a glorious future at that, with babies and a house and his pretty wife smiling, so proud to see him when he came home from teaching at the school.

All these visions over a spilled pie and hopes for everyone but yourself. Then Miguel said, helping me up, on my stiff knee joints, "Okay, okay. I get it, Regina. We'll look for your brother."

Since then, I am wondering what Miguel's mother knew about the baby she had just had to give him such a suitable name.

MIGUEL

If I ever write a memoir I'll probably call it *The Too-Late Guy.*

It started when I was born—1969.

At least if I had been born in 1968—*the year that rocked the world*—I could have felt a part of it. Sometimes I lie and say it anyway. That's why I was a history major in college, to be part of something big.

But in 1968, it was rocking all over—from My Lai to Malcolm, from the Democratic convention in Chicago to Jim Morrison. The civil rights movement. Free Leonard Pelletier, qué viva Anna Mae Aquash and Pine Ridge. Trinidad Sánchez, Jr.—"Why Am I So Brown?" Los Flor y Cantos festivals, poetry and public art. The San Francisco Mime Troop at Dolores Park. I was only ten when my mom and I happened to see them when we were on vacation. They weren't mimes and I heard the message loud and clear. We sat on the grass of San Pancho's rolling hills watching the performance, me a squirt and yet thinking, "I know the CIA's lurking around here someplace."

That was back when the CIA was considered the people's enemy.

It was the age of hippies, yippies, and LSD. The Beatles were still together imagining an ashram utopia. Santana came down from the sky like Horus blasting "Black Magic Woman."

Communism was the government's number-one enemy and students, Black Panthers, the American Indian Movement, and anyone else who spoke up, close seconds.

That would've been me, man. Public Enemy Number One of Nixon's administration. I'd been on it, too, writing about this country's "incredible *whiteness* of being."

Still, I got plenty to rant about right here in the present.

My book's gonna be called *The Dirty Wars of Latin America: Building Drug Empires.* Or something like that. The research goes back to when I thought I'd get a Ph.D. My thesis was gonna be on the School of the Americas. It was a U.S. Army center located at Fort Benning in Columbus, Georgia, that trained more than sixty thousand soldiers and police, mostly from Latin America, in counterinsurgency and combat-related skills since 1946. Its graduates became experts in torture, murder, and political repression. Since the word got out on what the School of the Americas was really up to, in 2001 the school officially changed its name to the Western Hemisphere Institute for Security Cooperation. After 9/11 the government felt it could justifiably come out of its covert-training closet.

The School of the Americas and I go way back.

My father used to run the language program. Colonel John Mason III made the army his career. He did two tours of Vietnam. He learned Spanish, Russian, and Czech and taught all three. He was an astute investor and a shrewd spender. Colonel Mason was so proud of himself. "Not bad for a kid from Sunset Heights," he used to say.

When I was in my third year of high school, captain of the football team, and doing everything I could to get my father's attention (and not necessarily his approval, since I got thrown off the team for smoking pot), he died of a brain aneurysm.

We flew to Georgia and brought his body back to El Paso. He got a military burial at Fort Bliss. I cried no tears over Colonel Mason. "Maybe a KGB agent ejected some poison from a fake pen into his highball and that's what made his brain implode," I told my mother.

"Don't disrespect your father," my mom said, although she had not moved us down to Georgia when he took the post.

After high school I passed on UCLA, which would have been the colonel's choice, and decided to stay in El Paso to go to college. I took my mother's last name. My father left me a trust fund and my mother his pension. Maybe by then she figured her duties as wife and mother were done. She packed up and moved to San Antonio to start a new life. We always keep tabs on each other but she never mixes up in my business and I don't mix up in hers.

I never got to put my findings down on the dirty wars fueled by the School of the Americas alumni. Family life took over. Crucita and I were expecting our daughter, Xochitl, before we finished college. Soon after Xochi, our son, Little Michael, came along.

But I held on to my dream of getting into a doctoral program, so the research kept piling up. As time went by the thesis morphed into something different. Now it'll be a full-fledged book. I got notes, clippings, magazines, stacks of articles I've been collecting for years. My trailer looks like the forgotten archives of every record on Latin America disclosed under the Freedom of Information Act—from the Reagan administration's intervention in Central América to what some of the School of the Americas's graduates who found themselves unemployed were doing with the highly specialized skills that the narco cartels found so valuable.

Now that I'm divorced and all, maybe I'll be able to get it done.

Crucita and me split up last year—that's when I moved into the trailer. Our kids stay with her. But I'm right across the street from my old house, where they still live. No, I'm not stalking my ex-wife. She and I get along better now than when we were married. Besides that, she's found religion. Jesus is in her life. Jesus and the evangelical minister she got involved with when we were still together.

To be fair, Crucita and I still share some of the ideals around social injustice that we cared about in college. She doesn't only look for potential converts to her church, she volunteers to help women in crisis on both sides of the border. She kind of freelances on that count and goes from one grassroots organization to another, as time allows. Crucita came from a family where the father was one of those cabrón types so it irks her to no end to hear of women being abused in their homes. Lucky for me that I respect women. Otherwise, after my ex took a class in self-defense a few years back, I'd have ended up in the hospital.

Anyway, we—Crucita and I—still try to do things with our kids. "It's all about maintaining family values," she says.

"Whatever you say, hon," I'll respond, to avoid the obvious contradiction in statements like that. So keeping up appearances was behind our going up to Cabuche last August to the kermis at the church.

And that was when I was struck by the thunderbolt, blindsided, dumbstruck. I'm talking about Regina.

I took a teaching job a couple of years ago up there. It's a colonia that needs good teachers and if nothing else, I'm a good teacher. I dig that sleepy town, although rumors that an Indian-owned casino is being set up there prevail. Other changes are coming, too. What with Las Cruces,

New Mexico, expanding south and El Paso, Texas, growing north, the surrounding farmland is getting bought up by developers faster than you can say, "Poor people, get out."

Crucita was set on turning everyone she could into a born-again, so a bazaar sponsored by the Catholic Church seemed like an ideal place to find converts. At the kermis, which they held in the church parking lot on one of the hottest days that summer, my ex walked around with Little Michael. She's always favored our son, mostly because he's so sickly. Xochi had just turned thirteen and Crucita was her new archenemy. My daughter didn't even want to be there but, since I was the lesser of the two evils in her life, she deigned to walk around with me.

There weren't that many people about, being as hot as it was and all. "This is pitiful," Xochi said, typically bored. Everything was boring to her, except hanging out with her friends. But the bazaar actually was kind of pitiful. The booths were the usual church-fair variety—a cakewalk, darts, and shooting balloons with a popgun. The prizes, mostly kids' toys, were used donations. There was no cotton candy or funnel cake but there was a deep-fried-gorditas-and-beer stand. Yeah, the church was selling beer.

I went over and got a beer for myself and a snow cone for Xochi. I looked around for Crucita and my son. They were already busy trying to make converts, or at least she was. That's when I spied the redhead from the middle school. She had a chamba. She was managing the ring toss booth. Mi'ja and I went and bought a roll of tickets to try our luck. Or try my luck, since my daughter said she'd have no part of such embarrassing displays.

The teens had set up a stage and were dancing to music spun by a DJ. "I'm gonna check out the music, Dad," Xochi said and strolled over to watch. All kinds of old-school music came on—from "I'm Your Puppet" to "Achy Breaky Heart" and everything by Elvis. The most recent song I heard was "Macarena." When it played, all the kids and their moms jumped on the stage to do it. Even for an old guy like me, Cabuche was retro.

Back at the booth, the sun drilling down on my head, I had no competitors. The object of the game was to get at least two out of three knitting rings around the necks of any of the two-quart plastic soda bottles set up on the ground. The prize was the bottle you snagged—grape, orange, strawberry, root beer, cream soda, or cola—all generic brands. The roll of tickets I bought actually paid for the sodas I ended up winning. With scarcely a smile, the redhead would reach out and hand me the rings while staying in the shade in the corner of the booth. Every now and then Redhead would take out a hankie that was tucked inside the front of her white peasant blouse and pat her freckled chest and flushed cheeks. "This heat's insufferable," I said, trying to start up a conversation to no avail, while I won bottle after bottle. The game was really set up for kids—with short arms.

I scored ten bottles before I finally had the nerve to ask her if she remembered me from school. "I think so," was all she said. Then she looked away.

I'd never had much luck with gorgeous women. Cute ones—like my ex, sure. But not women who not only looked good but who probably rustled steer in their free time. You knew right away you'd better not mess with them.

Well, I had really remembered *her,* all right.

And that's why I made a fool of myself trying to get her attention.

"Come on, Dad," called Xochitl, who is her dad's flower princess and has already made me promise to give her the biggest quinceañera Sunland Park has ever seen. That wouldn't be hard, I figured, considering how small our town is. Still, Xochi and her mom are already making plans that could do a man's wallet a lot of damage. Mi'ja, up on the stage, wanted me to go and join the group doing the chicken dance. I knew the chicken dance. She and her brother had taught me at home. At home was one thing but in public was another. "Hey, Dad!" Michael called. He'd seen his sister up there and ran up, too.

I looked at Redhead. I thought I saw her smile. That was all the encouragement I needed. I ran over to the stage and jumped on. I was the tallest chicken shaking his butt up there. She was looking, all right. And she was laughing, covering her mouth with her hand. Shy *and* gorgeous, man, I thought. What a sexy combination. I kept shaking my butt, moving with the crowd and smiling over at her. And she just kept laughing. By then, I couldn't be stopped. Next, we started doing the electric slide. This time, I saw that Redhead wasn't laughing anymore. In fact, she looked a little disturbed. That's when I knew I wasn't exactly impressing her.

Afterward, to hold on to the little pride I had left, I didn't bother collecting my sodas.

But Redhead and I were destined, as they say. Five months later, something happened. Something terrible on the one hand. On the other, it turned out to be what changed the life of a guy whose heart needed some serious mending. She was wearing one of her homemade dresses, made of seersucker or something Mrs. Cleaver–ish. But she could make anything look good. Ms. Redhead came up to me just as I was leaving, to ask for help in a "highly urgent and personal matter."

She took me totally off guard. And before she even explained what it was all about, I blurted out, "Don't worry, camarada," like I was in the Partido Liberal Mexicano. The party had made its headquarters right in my hometown over a hundred years ago, just before La Revolución. Those guys were among my role models. "You can count on me," I blurted out and all but saluted my new generala.

Whenever I talked like that, all Chicanoed out, using old-school, *The Revolution Will Not Be Televised* jive, my ex used to say, "You want to be a revolutionary, Mike? Start with me. A social movement begins with one woman and one man at a time."

It was too late for that woman to be Crucita. Standing in front of Redhead so close I could almost count the freckles across her nose and those that splashed down her biceps, I thought, Maybe it isn't too late for the too-late guy.

GABO

Santo and friend of God, thank you for listening to me,

My saludos to you and to the Lord, my Father in Heaven. Please ask
Him to look down kindly on me—I am trying to be good.

Padre Pío, I know you do not measure faith by how much a person
dedicates himself to reading scriptures but I want you to know I read
not only the Bible but everything. It was no one's recommendation or
insistence. Reading just came to me. That was how I learned English. I
read it before I could pronounce it. When I first went to school en Los
Estados, my tía Regina made them put me in the right year for my age.
Because I was un chavito migrante they were ready to stick me in the
first grade. I was eight years old. I was so quiet they figured I did not
know anything. Two weeks later, they moved me up to the fourth.

By then I had read my papá's old copy of *The Communist Manifesto*.
He used to carry it everywhere with him. I was only six years old when
I first tried to read it. My father saw how hard I was struggling, so he
started helping me.

My tía Regina taught me a little Latin. My bisabuelo Metatron
believed in a classical education. Regina first learned to read with a
teacher who stayed on the hacienda. She always says, "rancho," but they
raised cattle, so I imagine it was more than that. Father Juan Bosco has
promised to teach me Latin but so far *nusquam*. I remember my papá
would stay up with me, no matter how tired we were, and my mother
calling, "Get to bed." He would light una velita if we did not have elec-

tricity and when the candle burned out, then it was time to sleep. By sunup we were all out there working in the fields.

My mother never learned to read and did not care about books. My older sister, Karla, was a lot like our mother. She was a hard worker, too, but unlike our mother, she never complained about anything. If my hermana had an extra piece of fruit or gum, she would share it with me. When I was little she was the one who would give me a bath, outside in a tina. Karla never had any toys, so I was her doll. Then she started getting a bosom. My sister was still a child, twelve or thirteen years old. She would get so embarrassed. She was upset all the time. She did not want to go to school anymore. The other labor-camp niños teased her. I have not seen my hermana in about four years, Santito. Please pray for her.

Mr. Vigil, my English teacher, said a serious young man like me who never smiles would probably appreciate the Russians. So he started me with Dostoyevsky's novels. I read *The Idiot* and el *Gambler. Crime and Punishment* was my favorite.

"Do you think that by Raskolnikov turning himself in, God forgave him?" I asked Mr. Vigil. My English teacher thought for a moment, then he said in that very slow way of talking that he has, like he is thinking of not just one book but all the books he has ever read, "I don't know, Gabriel." He is getting ready to retire soon. I hope our next teacher brings us up to the twentieth century. This is no reflection on the Russians, just on Mr. Vigil, who only likes very long books with a lot of details. I stopped in the middle of los *Brothers Karamazov* because of my papá's disappearance. It is hard for me to concentrate on anything anymore besides that.

In el Padre Juan Bosco's library in his casita all he has are religious books. He said I could help myself to read anything I found interesting. He has a collection of Bibles. One is so old if you try to turn the pages the paper almost disintegrates, like dead moths' wings between your fingers. He keeps it open to the Book of Psalms on a wooden book-stand on his desk. I had never been in a house where people owned their own books. I mean, so many. My tía Regina has a few. They are on the bookshelf next to the fireplace. I have read them all. I can stay up and read un libro entero in one night or at least by daybreak. If they are thick like Dostoyevsky's, then it takes me perhaps three nights. Afterward I must sleep. I sleep and sleep and then I start another book.

6   6   6

After *The Communist Manifesto* I went on to the teachings of Mao
Ze-dong. My father also had *Das Kapital* and some writings by Lenin
and Engels. Everywhere we went to work, following the harvest, the
books came with us. El Subcomandante Marcos was a hero of mi papá
for so bravely pointing out to the world that the NAFTA agreement was
not going to make things better for the Mayan people but worse. If it
were not for my mother who said, "No, señor," he would have gone
down to Chiapas to join los Zapatistas in their battle against the government. I was only about five years old, but I remember them arguing
about it. "My mother was an indígena," he'd say. "My own grandfather,
who thought he was the last of the great hacendados, threw us off his
land because he didn't want us to inherit it."

I remember tanto, San Pío; even if I am not sixteen years old yet,
sometimes I feel like I have lived many lifetimes, not just one. And not
just my own. I remember my papá's stories. I remember, too, when I
was left with my tía Regina when I was very little. I was so upset, being
left behind. I was too small to understand how mis padrecitos were
trying to spare me from working in los files. I did not think of it in
terms of them having so little food or not enough wood for the stove or
things like that once they got back to Chihuahua. I got into reading
even more because then I would not have to think about when they
were coming back for me. My tía Regina was always so good. It wasn't
that. I just missed my mamá. I missed my papá, too. Like I missed how
he would pick me up and carry me on his back, especially when I
would get tired of working out in the pisca. I would cry like el chavalito
that I was. My mother complained about everything. So she would say
to me, "This is why you have to go to school, mi'jito. So you don't end
up living the life of a burra, like your mamá." That made me cry. It
hurt to think of my mother as a mule. I cried a lot when my father told
me she was not coming back for me. I cannot remember a time when I
wasn't crying over something gone forever. But I am a man now almost,
and I know that tears are useless.

Mañana I promise, Santo apreciado, no reading, only meditating on
virtues of penance.

Your most undeserving discípulo

MIGUEL

We outgrew each other. That's what happened in my marriage. People talk about how a couple is supposed to grow to keep the relationship strong. Well, Crucita grew in her direction and I in mine. I got more involved in grassroots organizing and spent less time at home. She found comfort with a bubba preacher named Prescott from Silver City.

All I gotta say is I hope he does not move into my house.

"It's not your house anymore," my ex says. I may have moved out, but I still think I have something to say about it.

"That's always been your problem, Mike," she says. "You always got something to say about everything."

I shared the rather shameful news of my wife's infidelity with Regina, who somehow has managed to take over most of my life. Actually, she's not that kind of woman. I don't know what kind of woman she is but she's not the clinging type—that's clear. But that's how women do it. They sneak up on you. Before you know it, you're acting like a big tonto over them. Then, they got you hitched. Next thing you know, you're paying taxes on a house you don't even get to live in anymore. As for finding Redhead's brother, I said I'd help. He sounded like a righteous man, so I am sorry to even think it, but for my money, he's been long dead.

My therapist thinks I'm afflicted with a "narcissist personality disorder"—*possibly*. He didn't actually come out and say it. I snuck a glance at his notes one day during a session. He was getting over a bad cold and ran out of the room in the middle of a coughing fit. I kind of peeked into my file that he left on his chair. Great. So, that's the verdict, I thought, not as sure of myself at that point, as he thought I *might* be, and no longer having all that much confidence in my therapist, either.

It was Crucita's idea that I get counseling.

Maybe I *am* self-absorbed or maybe my affliction is paranoia but I felt I got no pity from Regina regarding my cheating wife. When a man comes out looking duped, women tend to feel sorry for him. They view him as a potentially good guy. Instead, she looked at me with those deep-set eyes of hers, which she seems to not even be conscious of what they could do to a man, and said, "Come on, Miguel, you know that everyone at the school thinks you're a Casanova. You've gone out with every single woman who's worked there."

Every single woman but her, that was.

Now that I'm a divorced man I feel free to date whomever I please. But a Casanova? Ouch. Every time I start going out with a nice girl, she gets serious on me right away. Crucita was a nice girl. A nice girl who sprung on me she was pregnant just as I was about to apply for grad school.

When I was in college I used to write poems about Zapata, Pancho Villa, Che Guevara—all my revolutionary heroes. "It is better to die on your feet than live on your knees." That's not a quote of mine but of Emiliano Zapata's. My own poetry stunk. Crucita followed me around everywhere. Girls love poets. You say, "I'm a poet," and they say right away, "Write a poem for me," or worse, "Write a poem about me."

Secretly, Crucita wanted me to give up all that "nonsense"—not just calling myself a poet but also my "radicalism." She said I should buy us a big house and join the country club—spend my time golfing, her doing charity work. When I refused to live like that, she settled with living in Sunland Park next door to her folks.

Her family convinced her that my teaching was a "noble profession" and even my involvement in community issues was nothing to snub her nose at. Maybe the kids gave her some satisfaction but I sure didn't. Then she became a born-again and gave her life meaning. That and her part-time crusade to end domestic violence everywhere.

My own activism keeps me going, especially on those days when you question every decision for yourself that you've ever made. I'm one of the few people around here who still calls himself Chicano. A lot of people don't like that word. They don't get it. They think it means gangbanging. It's like one of those outdated labels that most people never understood and now everybody hates and has no use for. Like *feminist*. Half the women I know don't like that word, either, but when you ask them what it means, they say they don't really know.

Things just keep closing in by the minute. One day the two-party system is gonna sound obsolete and even a bad idea. Mark my words.

GABO

Mi Más Querido Santo,

One of the greatest favors for which I feel so indebted to our Lord is that His Majesty permits me to unburden myself to his servant in heaven. But today, Padre Pío, allow me to tell you about un regalo that He has brought us around here. Father Juan Bosco told me that los Hermanos Franciscanos encourage friendship. For this reason, I am most grateful that we now have others to share our humble vidas with. By we, I mean mi tía and myself.

Sometimes I feel my aunt's loneliness like un león feroz slowly coming toward us from far away. One day I'll have to leave her and then who will she have? Everyone needs familia. And when your familia goes away or when they die on you, then a good friend around helps. She always mentions la Señora Uriel, but they never see each other. "Too busy with work and life," is what my tía has said about never seeing her only amiga. But my tía Regina has finally made herself a new friend in el Chongo Man. We know little about the schoolteacher but I sense in my heart he is well-meaning, even if he goes about it clumsily.

My best friend is Jesse Arellano.

(He is *not* well-meaning, Su Reverencia. Pero that is why I consider him such a great gift from Our Lord. He stands in need of God's consolation. Please keep him in your prayers, Santito.)

"Jesse Arellano as in *the* Arellanos, ese," he said to me when we first met on the basketball court at the Catholic high school in Santa Teresa. Being a private school, it has a very decent basketball court. Santa

Teresa is the town between Cabuche and El Paso. It also shares la frontera with México. The Santa Teresa border isn't used for a lot except the business of the narcotraficantes. The sheriff's deputies drive around and harass us sometimes because we are out there playing on what they say is private property. But usually they leave us alone when they see we are only trying to throw a few hoops.

I looked at Jesse like he was talking to me in Greek.

"What up?" he said. "You not from around here or somethin'? My older brother is El Toro Arellano. . . . You know, the guy who helped start los Palominos back in the day? He's doing time over there in La Tuna now. . . . Are you really that out of it, man, ¿o qué, ese?"

My new friend was not *exactly* claiming he was one of the notorious Arellanos from Nuevo Laredo. Everyone along the borderlands has heard about esos narcos. He just left it open so that you might come to that conclusion yourself. Obviously, los Palominos counted on people being stupid. But one thing seemed obvious, Padre Pío. The Palominos were penny-ante gangbangers compared to los carteles grandes that reign over the borderlands. (*Penny ante.* I read that in *The Jungle* by Upton Sinclair. It is one of the libros Mr. Vigil passed on to me. But penny ante does not mean the Palominos are not locos.) Jesse forgave my ignorance regarding his status, he said, because I was so good at basketball. (I almost always win.) We have started meeting there now and then when I have time between my job and school and Jesse has time between his penny-ante activities.

He has put aside the fact that I have plans on becoming un hermano of the Church. To him, that makes me a "nerd" or I have a lot of nerve. (He laughed after saying that because he thought it was funny that it rhymed.)

One day, maybe to test out which it was, Jesse slammed the ball right at my face. Blood gushed out of my nose. "It was an acci—" he started to say, sniggering like it was not. Next thing I knew, Santito, he was pleading for me to let go when I had his neck locked between my thighs. (I learned that movida at school, trying to get on the wrestling team.) After that, there were no more accidental slam balls from my new best friend.

Another time he said, "More than anything, I'm in awe of a guy who is voluntarily gonna be without a woman his whole life. Never. Not even once. Do you have to be a virgin before you go in?" he asked, tossing the ball from one of his boxy hands to the other. " 'Cause if you don't, you better get you some before you do." When my face went red Jesse really cracked up.

I am not sure what the big deal is about sex, Padre Pío. I know I might be saying that because I do not have experience, but that is not the point. When you give yourself to Our Lord, desires of the flesh must be sacrificed. (. . . *And be ye separate, saith the Lord, and touch not the unclean thing; and I will receive you.* Corinthians Two, Chapter Six, Verse Seventeen.) "Not just sex," I told mi amigo, "but you must keep away from alcohol, drugs, parties, all kinds of loud music, and cars with fancy hydraulics like yours and which you are so proud of. And while I am at it, you will not have use for sinful pride, either. You will have God to fulfill you." I tried to explain it like that to Jesse with all the conviction I carry in my heart, Santo.

Afterward, he just stared at me, like he does a lot. One of his eyes wanders, so it is not easy to tell if he is giving you a hard look or someone else. Then he spits out a big wad of phlegm and you move back anyway. "Man," he said finally, "you are really weird."

As long as he does not try to get me in the gang. All we do is shoot hoops. And talk or "chill," as he calls it. He tells me all about his "cool" world. "Sex and drugs, man. That's what counts, vato," he says; and then he spits.

Jesse himself knew a girl, in the biblical sense, when he was only eleven and was brought into los Palominos. He said his brother, El Toro, had been his sponsor. "You need someone to vouch for you," he said. Not just anyone could join the gang. "You gotta have what it takes," he says all the time. What it takes, from what he has told me, Padre Pío, is a wish for a life in prison or worse.

When a chava gets brought into the gang it is truly a tragic fate cast upon a female. Except in the Old Testament I had never heard of such barbarism, Su Reverencia. He did not say rape. But that is what it is. What he said was that a girl throws a pair of dice and whatever number comes up, that is the number of guys who will have sex with her that night. Some of the girls are barely thirteen years old when they join. They also have to get "jumped in," which meant that their future "sisters" all beat la chavita up together. I walked away from the ball court and leaned against the fence. I wanted to vomit.

What kind of mother and father are at home, I kept thinking all that night, who wouldn't ask what happened to their hija when she returned home half the chava she was when she left? Beaten up and raped by kids who told you that they were going to be your "familia" from now on. What kind of family does that?

In my English class there is una chava who is in los Palominos. She can hardly read. (They pass failing students at my school just to get rid of them, Padre Pío.) Everything comes hard to her, all the subjects, I mean. Tiny Tears already has a baby. I asked her one day if she was planning on getting married once she finished high school. She stared at me with almost a scowl, as if she resented my question. I wanted to ask if she even knew who the father was but I decided to leave her alone. Tiny Tears hardly ever speaks. But behind all the makeup I fear is a very scary girl.

Su Reverencia, at night, as usted already knows, I devote prayers to Jesse and his brother in prison and to all of los Palominos, for God's light to enter their demented souls. Even if they do not have mothers and fathers who care, I beseech God y todos los santos that they find a way to forgive themselves. Jesse likes to tell me he forgives me for being such a nerd. He says he hopes he never hears of me on the news that I only joined the Church to molest altarboys. Then he laughs that loud cackling laugh that reminds me of a hyena's.

I used to hear hyenas when we crossed over through el desierto toward California when I was un chavito. They frightened me for sure—laughing all together, somewhere in the dark, getting closer. They travel only in packs. That's how they can be so vicious—the fact that there are many of them, they can get hold of a man and just tear him to pieces. They could eat a man vivo and afterward, laugh, todos juntos.

San Pío, thank el Señor for me, por favor, for all His blessings and considerations of His imperfect servant, but most especially for sending me this boy who is a mirror to my own spiritual shortcomings.

Su servidor, undeserving as I am

REGINA

I was tilling the soil for this year's garden when Gabo showed up with someone I never saw before to lend us a hand.

His name is Jesse Arellano. He is a thin young man with a shaved head and growing a goatee like Gabo's, except that it looks drawn on with charcoal. His first facial hair, and apparently, it was also his first time working on a garden. When he started to rake I noticed on his right hand between the thumb and index finger a blue tattoo of a cross. It was crudely drawn with dots in between the lines of the cross. I've seen that cross around a long time. It means you belong to a gang. That also means I wish he wasn't the only friend my sobrino has ever brought home. But Jesse did his best to help rake up the dead leaves, pine needles, and dried mesquite that had blown in and collected in the garden during winter, so I kept silent.

Gabo was fixing the gate to our garden just like his father would have done. Just before spring we mend it and every following winter the winds yank it every which way. We needed to reinforce the fence with new chicken wire, too, to keep the cottontails out.

I've been preparing my own mulch since I first took over this place. I use compost from food scraps, coffee grounds, eggshells, and bring over cow or horse manure from nearby ranchos and mix it all up as top dressing. We loaded wheelbarrows and dumped it in the garden to fertilize the sand. That's all the soil we have here up in the mesa, where what grows normally is a whole lot of cactus and creosote with no help at all.

If you are serious about your garden you start getting ready about a month before spring. That's when it begins to look like winter's gone but

isn't yet, because on any night you might get a frost that will kill everything you just put into the ground with such loving care. Loving care is
what I try to bring to whatever I do—otherwise why bother? "This year
I'm planting three different types of tomatoes," I told Jesse, "because
Gabo loves his tomatoes. He eats them like fruit." Jesse stopped raking
and gave me a peculiar look as if up until then he had thought tomatoes
came from cans.

"Well, that is because they *are* fruta," said Gabo, who I have noticed is
becoming kind of a know-it-all as his sixteenth birthday approaches. I
gave him one of my looks and he went back to his nailing. Seeing him
hunched over I remembered exactly the time when Rafa taught him how
to hold a hammer. Gabo was about eight years old. "It's heavy," I said to
my brother. "He's too chiquito to hold up such a heavy tool. I'll do it." I
rushed to help. My brother put his palm up, while insisting that the child
draw back the hammer with two tiny hands. Concentrating, Gabo's bo-
quita was all puckered like an old man's. And then, *bam,* he got the nail
square on the head. "¡Eso!" Rafa shouted, lifting up his son in the air and
swinging him around. Gabo never let go of the hammer.

All summer crop dusters will fly low, spraying pesticides on the nearby
farmlands, not to mention on the workers. A neighbor here on the mesa
whose house is hidden by big pines sunbathes in the nude. The crop
dusters, she says, circle over her property when she's out there. I don't
care what they see as long as they don't accidentally spray any poison on
me, or my plants. This year I'm thinking of joining a farmers' market and
taking my pesticide-free vegetables to sell.

Miguel told me about a cooperative of indio coffee-bean growers in
Oaxaca that ended up making a prosperous international business just
because they couldn't afford pesticides and produced organic coffee. I
hadn't thought of myself as an organic farmer until Miguel put it that
way.

One day me and him drove down to El Paso again. We drove up and
down the street of los coyotes. We never saw nothing. What were we
going to see? The window blinds were down on the house. Doors shut.
No sign or nothing to give us any clues about what to do about mi hermano.

While we cruised around I did get to hear all of Miguel's life without
asking. He just went from one subject to another on his own. It didn't
even seem to matter that I was there. Miguel just likes to hear himself

talk. From organic farmers and his concerns about the environment to what he thinks about the immigration issue. He talked like he was in front of his classroom. Me, with my hands folded on my lap, I looked like the pupil. When people talk that much around me I tend to get inhibited. And irritated. It comes from living with Mamá all my life. Who put the nickel in the nickelodeon? I used to say to myself about her.

"What's wrong?" Miguel asked.

"That cat got my tongue."

"What cat?" He smiled. My friend was teasing me but I didn't know it. Not knowing when you're being teased also comes from being alone for inordinate amounts of time.

"You know? *The* cat," I said. "I'm not a teacher like you, with always something clever to say on the top of your tongue."

Miguel corrected me. "On the tip of your tongue."

"See what I mean?" I said and then I shut up for a long while.

So Miguel kept talking, telling me all about his comunidad and all that they do to clean up the environment. And maybe in an attempt to make no big deal out of it, he slipped in the fact that he was a divorced man. "Yeah, my ex-wife and kids live across the street from me," he said.

"Oh," I said. If I were the bold type I would have said, "Oh?" to get more information. He looked at me for a second as if he expected I might have a question. I didn't. I had a million. A million questions I didn't ask. Then he went back to talking about his community activism.

ɛ ɛ ɛ

That day, after we got the new garden ready, Jesse stayed to eat. Although he is on the skinny side, he devoured his meal, as my mamá used to say about such appetites, like he was going on a long trip. After gulping down two fat brisket burritos, he had half an apple pie. He got up from the table without picking up his plate. He was walking around the house, looking at my knickknacks on shelves and windowsills, when we both lost sight of him. I found the huerquillo in my bedroom.

"What are you looking for?" I asked. I was standing right behind him and startled him, I think.

"Nothing," he said, leaving right away, "just the bathroom."

I looked around. Nothing seemed out of place. At the school I've had money taken from my purse twice. I checked my purse. There were two dollars and change in my wallet. Just like I'd left it.

"We can shoot some hoops tomorrow, if you want," Gabo said, looking tall next to the shabby boy as he stood up to say good-bye to his friend with an extravagant handshake.

When Jesse took off in his old Impala, I asked Gabo about the handshake, the sprouting goatees he and his friend were growing, and the boy's hand tattoo. "Do not concern yourself with Jesse," was his only response. "He is just my friend." He started getting ready for work. "Tía, if Jesse keeps helping us with the garden, do you think it would be all right to share some of our vegetables with him to take home to his familia? I mean, we had a lot this past year and it's not good to let food go to waste, right?"

When had we let anything go to waste? I can all the surplus produce for winter. Anything that gets by me in the refrigerator or in the fruit bowl goes into the compost. But if it's halfway edible we throw it out to the cottontails, birds, stray cats, la Tuerta, and even the naked neighbor's dogs that she lets run all over the mesa.

I said, "Yeah, whatever," to Gabo, answering the way the students do when they think I'm just one more person in their lives who doesn't make sense. Then I decided to share my latest business plan. "I got an idea of how we could make a little extra money with our garden. We could take the vegetables to sell at a farmers' market."

"Ay, Tía," Gabo said, as if all my enterprises were just my idea of fun, "whatever happened with your new pie-baking business?"

Taking a good look at him then and there, I had to admit he was not the same boy he had been six months before, when my brother left him with me. You couldn't tell right away, especially if you didn't want to, but he'd gotten older, all right. His voice was deeper. The way he dropped his shoes at night when he came home from work and plopped down on the couch—he was Rafa, all over again—there, but always somewhere else in his head. It made me long for the child who said his prayers out loud every night. The last time I had seen him do that was before his papá had gone missing. All his innocence was oozing out of him a little every day and there was nothing I could do to stop it.

As for my business plans, after the splattered pie, I said, "Baking pies is risky business."

"Like growing vegetables out here is not?" Gabo asked, without waiting for an answer but heading toward the bathroom to shower.

At the window I could see it was pouring rain down in the valley. The sky behind los Franklins looked like a blackboard covered with chalk scratches. Soon, those heavy clouds would be heading our way.

The local forecasters had predicted clear skies.

ε   ε   ε

"A honey *and* an eco-activist. What more could you ask for?" is what Uriel said on the phone. I didn't know who to tell about my guardian angel in boot-cut Wranglers. Curled up on my TV chair, devouring a half-pound of sunflower seeds, I went on like a chiflada. My amiga got me all worked up, thinking of el Miguel as a honey. That's why Mamá didn't like me having girlfriends, who, in her opinion, were bad influences and boy-crazy. Chifladas, she called them. Chiflada now means I'm more flushed than usual. It was either my plant know-how or pollution that brought me and my "honey" together again. "Whatever it takes," Uriel said.

For years Miguel's greatest enemy has been a sleeping giant. The sleeping giant is Asarco, a smelter company, which was closed down in 1999 after more than a century of belching fumes into our skies. When I was a girl and came up to work in the fields, I'd see the humongous swirls of smoke coming up from the smelter. I'd feel like the way immigrants must've felt seeing the Statue of Liberty. Those puffing chimneys were a pair of lamps, calling the huddled masses. I didn't know no better. Now the American Smelting and Refining Company that had reigned over the region might open again. The company officials have been trying to renew their air-quality permit. That's where my "honey" comes in. Not just him, but all kinds of gente must do a whole lot of huffing and puffing to prevent the waking of the sleeping giant. The Texas Commission on Environmental Quality decided to postpone making any decision until further information was submitted to the state.

Miguel My Honey takes it personally. "The personal is political," he says all the time. Not only did the smelter take his great-grandfather's life, but Miguel believes pollution affected his own son. His hijo stays home from school half the time because of asthma. The ten-year-old also sees a speech therapist. "You tell me if all the tons of lead, zinc, cadmium, and arsenic the smelter emitted into the atmosphere for years doesn't have anything to do with people being sick around here," Miguel said to me one day. My eyes blinked in response like a flashing red light. Tests done by the New Mexico Department of Health and others had overlooked

Anapra, la colonia right next to Sunland Park where he lives. The residents became distrustful so they decided to do it on their own.

"We started getting these kids tested to see if they have lead contamination in their blood," Miguel said. They got some help from the local branch of the Sierra Club and others but hadn't gotten the results yet. Me and my honey decided to start a project in Anapra. We didn't forget that what brought us together in the first place was searching for my Gabo's papá. But I will be the first to say, being a teacher's aide and seeing what I see at the school every day, that me and my sobrino are not the only ones with problems. Anapra is located in a sink in a bend of the Río Grande at the foot of Mount Cristo Rey. Mount Cristo Rey is a holy place where people make pilgrimages to the top. A holy place desecrated by contamination. Impurities from the smelter settled there that either got blown or washed down los arroyos that drain the mountain into the community. A levee protects los Anaprans from the river but holds the pollution inside.

Container gardens seemed like a good idea if you were in doubt as to whether your soil was safe. We went loaded down with packets of seeds for planting basil, squash, lettuce, epazote, cilantro, and chiles, and a couple of twenty-pound bags of dirt he got at a nursery. I brought dozens of small plastic trays for seedlings from so many years of gardening and took them to start us off. We worked at the run-down house that his organization uses as a community center. They get it rent-free because the güera landlady who lives in El Paso believes in their cause. Their cause seems to be fighting every single problem that could afflict an American town at the same time. Pollution is only one. But with it, they figure, comes other complications. Children full of energy one day can't get out of bed when the air changes. They suffer everything from pulmonary infections and headaches to behavioral problems.

Five kids and two moms showed up for planting. All of them had been told that whatever they grew they could sell at a nearby farmers' market. The kids, ages seven to fourteen, seemed okay. "It's gonna take a lot of work, patience, and time," I warned our new gardeners, "and you can't be afraid of bugs." That got a little kid going. He started fussing so much and then screaming, the mother picked him up and they left. We hadn't even started. I wished Gabo wasn't working on Saturdays. Being young himself, he could set an example, I thought. He'd been growing food all his life. "Kids listen more to other kids," I whispered to Miguel My Honey when the fourteen-year-old wearing a tube top and low-riding pants quit next.

She didn't leave. She sat there contemplating her ombligo. It was a little more interesting than most belly buttons since there was a ring going through it. The girl looked about four months pregnant.

"Do you know that by piercing your ombligo you won't be able to give your child a blood transfusion if he ever needs it?" I asked the girl.

"Huh?" she replied.

"Whatever happened to '¿mande usted?'?" I said under my breath. I was ready to quit myself. "You're doing just fine," Miguel assured me. "Don't mind her," he added, pointing to his head and making circles with his index finger. Loca. A loca or living la vida loca. Whichever it was, she was a girl on the way out. Not just to herself and her familia but to everyone. "Come on, muchacha," I called to her. "I need your help here." I handed her an apron. She dragged herself over. "After we're done today, we're gonna go see a doctor, okay? Okay?" I kept saying okay until she said okay back. Now what? I said to myself. Then I decided that Miguel had to know a doctor who might volunteer her services. One project at a time, I thought. When we were done I told them all the dos and don'ts for the seedlings. Before taking the kids and one mom home, we assigned a rotating schedule for the new gardeners. I promised Miguel My Honey I'd go down to Anapra every Saturday morning to keep an eye on things. I'd better stop calling him that before I slip one day and say it to his face.

chapter

THREE

REGINA

As soon as Gabo announced that he was going to be an acolyte I figured I'd go check it out. Miguel came with me to Mass as my "backup," as he calls himself. Backup for what? We weren't sure. Instead of my archangel showing up, it was George Strait. George Strait is one of my favorite country stars, so that was okay by me. But Miguel's ostrich boots and Stetson did cause quite a stir in church. In Cabuche not too many people dress up for la misa. If they do, it's for a wedding, quinceañera, or a baptism and there's gonna be a pachanga afterward—the men in big hats and fist-size belt buckles, the women in silky rayon, and all the niños in their Christmas clothes.

My sobrino joined us afterward outside as the crowd came out. It was the first day without rain or clouds in a couple of weeks. Gabo gave me a kiss on the cheek. "Oye, Gabito," I said, feeling his forehead, "are you okay? You looked kind of sweaty up at the altar." He wasn't just sweating; I was positive he was about to faint.

Gabo nodded.

"Listen," I said. "If you want to be a priest when you finish college, okay. There could be worse things."

"Like what—joining the army?" he asked.

"For one, smarty-pants," I said, "although you have to have your residency to do that, anyway." Which choice for his son would enrage Rafa more—clergy or serving in the U.S. military? I couldn't guess. I know it's not fair to say, but Rafa had better show up soon if he is going to talk some sense into his son. Every evening I sit in front of my TV with a bowl of lentejas (which I eat a lot now during Lent), and with la Tuerta at my feet, we watch the news. They show the pictures of American soldiers who have died that day in Bush's war. At ten o'clock, the local news reports on the boys who have killed one another in local drug and gang battles. The president says, "No child will be left behind." Some of our kids at the middle school, chiquillos, eleven or thirteen years old, are not just left behind. They're plain abandoned.

Then Gabo asked, "What do you want me to do with my future, Tía Regina? Get married and have kids to carry on the family name . . . ¿o qué?" It wasn't like him to be hurtful. It infuriated me that my sobrino thought that all I would want from him would be to produce an heir. Why? To carry on the name of Metatron, who had disinherited us?

"O qué," I replied, forcing a smile. Placing my hands tight against his temples I brought his cabezahead down to plant a kiss on his pimply forehead. *Cabezahead* is one of our made-up words. Gabo's and mine. A hybrid vocabulary for a hybrid people.

After Gabo left for work Miguel suggested we go out to the coyotes' house again. "We might get lucky and spot something suspicious this time."

"More suspicious than crooked coyotes who disappear people?" I asked.

"Suspicious as in—what specifically are they doing that people who cross over with them 'disappear'?" he said.

All the gente who had been in Mass were slowly making their way to cars or trucks or walking down the street to El Sombrero, the one restaurant in town that made carnitas and barbacoa on the weekends.

"Hey, you hungry?" Miguel said next. "How about this?" He pushed his hat slightly off his forehead and then he made kind of a lunch invitation. I had not had a lunch invitation in a long time. This one was okay. "How would you like to come with me to my abuelo Milton's? He's near where los coyotes live. I take him menudo, fresh tortillas . . . all his antojos, on Sundays. My grandfather has no teeth left and a bunch of stomach problems but he still enjoys the aroma of comfort food." Miguel smiled, straightening his bolo tie. "Do you know the Chihuahuita barrio?"

Of course I did. It was next to the Puente. Before my mamá died we used to go right near that old barrio to buy used clothes. That was my mamá's get-rich-quick scheme, purchasing used clothes by the pound to sell to people in Cabuche and nearby colonias. We used to live in town and every weekend Mamá would have a yard sale where she'd sell used clothes. People came from all around, going through the tables of near-rags and the racks of the half-decent trapos we had washed and ironed.

Long before my mother died we stopped our venture as used-clothing retailers. Some people had made themselves millionaires hustling ropa, but it wasn't us. It was those who sold to us. They had bought tons of garras, which they stored in warehouses right by the Puente. Mexicans crossed over to purchase in bulk and sell them in México. Mamá and I didn't go south with our goods but up north to New Mexico. There were a lot of needy people here, too, but not enough came around. Mamá and I both eventually concluded that neither of us wanted to be washing and ironing all week and spending the whole weekend home just to make no more than twenty dollars in total.

Until her last year, my mother had been pretty active. She drove her own car. She got involved with the Church. She gave haircuts and permanents at home. Most of my life she forced her home perms on me. I looked like Harpo Marx, red hair and all. That wasn't too bad when the Afro was in style in the seventies and I could pretend I was going for that look. She thought my natural hair was too straight. Since she died I have not touched my hair once. Along with the canas coming out, it goes every which way. And I couldn't care less.

My Sundays are usually a solitary continuation of whatever chores around the house I didn't get to on Saturday so I had no problem saying yes to the outing for whatever reason. And obviously, we were not going to do something dumb like knock on the coyotes' door again, just check it out, like Miguel said.

So off we went speeding around the other side of los Franklins, which is where you'll find El Paso—the big city for us in las colonias, where you can count a few thousand, if you include the daily labor brought in from across the border to work on all the ranchos and in the vineyards and hatcheries.

El Paso is the last stop before México. Like Miguel said, as he talked about it on the way there, "Once upon a time Texas was México." Back in 1846 the United States invaded its neighbor. "People who are all astounded today at the idea that this country would go and invade another country minding its own business should talk to a Mexican," Miguel said. "It was all about Manifest Destiny—the WASP philosophy that the U.S. had a right to expand its territories." Since then, El Paso was delegated to the United States and the city of Juárez to foreign soil. "Two cities that coexist in an arranged and loveless marriage," Miguel said. I had always thought about la frontera as neglected, but a word like *loveless* would not have occurred to me. Miguel's got all kinds of hardly used words. My new friend is not only a history teacher, he's a writer. He talks like a book. A book with a quiz at the end of every chapter.

He even had a lesson about the Segundo Barrio, where the coyotes live. While we parked, right in front of the green house, Miguel kept making small talk. The coyotes' house didn't even look like anyone lived there—it was shut up, with basura piled up in the front yard. "In my class I assign *The Underdogs* by Mariano Azuela," Miguel said. "Dr. Azuela—he was a physician—was a Villista. He wrote the first novel about the Mexican Revolution while living right in this neighborhood."

"I bet Gabo read it," I said, trying to make myself feel less ignorant. Miguel had the convertible top down and the noonday sun was already upon us. There were flies dancing around our cabezaheads and there was no air. After about a half hour my stomach started growling like I had swallowed a live pit bull and it was trying to get out.

"You hungry?" he asked.

"I'm too nervous to think about food," I lied.

"Sometimes it helps just to eat," he said, smiling.

"In my case, it's cooking," I said. "Cooking relaxes me. Chopping, cutting, adding a little epazote or ajo, tasting—by the time the comida's done, I'm not even hungry no more. But I feel better."

"You're making my mouth water, honey," he said with a laugh and turning on the engine right quick. "Let's go get us some food."

Had he just called me "honey," I was asking myself when just then the coyotes' door started to open. My eyes alone must have said, "¡Mira!" because Miguel turned to look. First the door opened wide, then the dirty wrought-iron storm door was pushed out by a stroller. My heart started pounding at the first sign of life we had seen there since that time when we went and actually knocked on the door. My nails clutched Miguel's forearm right through his shirt. He turned to glance at me for a split second, then looked back at the door.

La coyota made her way out with her two hüerquitos. They were in one of those baby strollers that fit two little kids. It was brand new and the babies themselves were dressed in what looked like new outfits. La coyota, too, was in her Sunday best, a tight, white satin dress and spiky high heels. She came out with her babies like they were on their way to church. Right behind her was her coyote marido, more feo than I remembered him and more dressed up, too. He was wearing a shiny suit and brand-new-looking botas. I hated them chatting so happily together, like they didn't have a care in the world. La coyota was putting on a pair of designer sunglasses, her husband about to lock up the door, when he caught sight of us. How could they not? We weren't only parked right in front we were parked backward.

Me and Miguel both swallowed hard. I clutched his arm tighter but neither of us could stop staring. The coyote couple stared right back. They could plainly see us. It felt like an eternity passed with us four staring like that when el coyote said something to his wife and she went on her way, coming out through the front gate and pushing the double stroller down the street. As she passed us she gave us a nasty look. I gave her a nasty look right back. She didn't own the street. Meanwhile her husband leaned against the doorway, watching us. He wasn't going nowhere while we were out there. "So, it's gonna be a showdown, eh?" Miguel said under his breath. "Us or him."

"Well, we ain't going nowhere, Miguel," I said, gritting my teeth.

Can more than one eternity pass in the span of about five minutes? That's what it felt like while we three stayed like that watching each other before el coyote decided to go back into his house.

"Now what?" Miguel asked me. I stopped gripping his arm and he started rubbing it. "Now what?" he asked again. I covered my face. I couldn't bear to let him see me cry. Then I took a deep breath. "Let's go in and get him, Miguel," I said. "Let's just go in and beat on him until he tells us something." It was crazy. I realized how crazy later, but not then. At that moment it seemed right.

"What?" Miguel said, whispering like the coyote could hear us. "Do you think that jerk doesn't have a gun? Or that maybe someone else might even be there with him?"

"Yeah!" I said. My face felt so hot I knew I must look like my neck was being squeezed. "What do you want to bet Rafa is in there, Miguel?"

"I'm not arguing with you," he said. "I'm just questioning how safe barging in there would be. He knows we're out here. He's probably in there waiting for us. . . ." Miguel put his hand on mine as if to hold me back. If el coyote was waiting behind the door with a gun, I was prepared to take that risk. It was my only chance to find out something about my brother's whereabouts. Even if el coyote said he didn't know nothing, at least I'd have had the satisfaction of him knowing that I knew he was lying.

Without even thinking about it, I started to jump out of the car. I felt Miguel's fingers barely grab hold of some strands of hair when an SUV that had just whipped around the corner almost hit the car door I had swung open so fast. "Regina!" Miguel cried out. Without slowing down, the driver of the SUV started honking as he passed us, pressing down on the horn so hard that the three people on the street all turned and looked at the SUV and then at me. Now for sure the coyote had to be on the alert for us.

Then Miguel said, "He's right there." I closed the car door and settled back into the seat. You could hardly see him, but he was there, all right, standing behind the storm door, watching us.

GABO

Adorado Padre Pío, Surrounded by the Holy Angels, San Pablo, and All the Saints, and at the Feet of Dios,

At last, el Señor granted me a favor. Praise be to Him Who is truly magnificent and merciful. It came when I least expected it. It happened last domingo, Su Reverencia. My first time to read part of the liturgy during Mass. Little did I know that God had in mind to bestow on me such a great favor. (I have not told anyone yet, not even el cura, and he is my confessor.)

The church was very full for the noon Spanish Mass. (You know that I usually go to the 7 A.M. Mass before going to work but Padre Juan Bosco asked me to this one and I could not say no.) It looked like everyone from Cabuche was there. I was not surprised to see my night manager from work with his familia and my computer teacher with hers but who I was really surprised to see was my tía Regina. Next to her was el Chongo Man. The schoolteacher did not look like someone who ever went to la santa misa. But there they were. (May the grace of Christ enlighten the hearts of all so that we may love him.) They were obviously looking for me. When she caught my glance my tía Regina's eyes so fixed on me, they seemed to be trying to say something like, "What the hell are you doing up there?" (That is how she talks, Santito.)

My tía Regina, watching over me, as always, was dressed for a change, out of respect. Her hair was brushed down, long, way past her shoulders. Her shawl was made from an old curtain we found at la segunda. And she stood so straight, my tía looked like una reina. A queen who had come down from her castle to see how her people were doing.

Padre Pío, she hurts over my father, too. He was her hermanito, after all. Every time my father was at her place, he helped her—cleaning out the gutters, tarring the roof, whatever chore she needed done. She made big meals for him. "Aren't you going to sit down and eat with me?" he'd say. Mi papá did not like her to fuss over him. "You eat. Don't worry about me," she would say. My tía loves to see people eat her food.

As I sat up at the altar waiting, the top of my lip was moist with anticipation of my reading. My manos were almost shaking holding my missal. I'd never spoken in public before. I looked around the church at all the roasted pecan faces. A lot of the women around here are gordas. Some are bien flaquitas. I think it has to do with very bad eating habits, too much drinking. Y drugs, también. There were girls with squirming chiquillos who looked like big sisters forced to babysit, but it was usually the case that they were mothers. All the women, young and old, came to church to kneel before la Virgencita. All of them with frowns and tears seemed to whisper, "Someone in heaven, give me a break."

The older men's faces looked like they were made of the same leather covering as el Padre Juan Bosco's ancient-looking Bibles, fine cracks cutting into sunburned skin, from lifetimes of working in the sun. Half the rest of the men had caras de crudo, not crude faces but hung over. And as with every Mass, Santo, there were very few young or able men.

I always wonder—is it not considered manly to fear God?

It was then that it happened. I turned to face the altar, tan nervioso, as I said, and as I was looking high above, at the life-size crucifix that hangs there, the wisdom de Su Reverencia came to me: *"The One who is keeping you nailed to the Cross loves you and is breathing into you the strength to bear the unbearable martyrdom and the love to love divine Love in bitterness."*

That was when the grace of Our Lord was bestowed upon me. Even in church Satan could fool someone so desiring a sign as I had. But I saw it, Santo. At first, a single drop. Then a second and a third. Bright and red as the brightest, reddest rose in God's holy garden. Drops of blood slowly coming down the divine forehead of Jesus. I was not frightened at all. It was as if the thorns were piercing my own flesh.

I felt my head suddenly ache. I put my hands up to hold it. It could have been no longer than a minute of sheer agony. Then it vanished. And my body and soul were calm. Thank you, Diosito, I said.

When it was time to give my reading, I felt as if the querubines themselves carried me to the podium. God is all-merciful.

Su Servidor sin Mérito

REGINA

If the barrio of Chihuahuita is not the oldest in town, then it has to be the second oldest. It is small with little houses pressed together. Casitas of adobe, cinder blocks, or stucco and gated windows and with tiny yards and big, barking dogs. I had never actually visited anyone there before. Since we settled down on this side of the border, I have always lived up in Cabuche. Miguel opened el abuelo's rusted gate and drove the Mustang right over the curb and into the front yard to a small house, media caída. The stucco and paint were cracked and red shingles were missing from the roof. Pulling out a lock and chain from the trunk, he tied it around the gate. The hood of the car was nearly on the front steps. We both carried in brown, soppy bags we'd picked up on the way. I didn't feel I knew Miguel well enough yet to tell him how I had decided recently I thought the food we grew up with could kill you.

His abuelo was sitting in the kitchen by the window. El viejito was as old as Miguel had described him. Maybe older. But he was tall for a senior, his back not too curved and with a cared-for white beard. Although his shirt was yellowed at the cuffs and collar, it was starched and his pants were pressed. He was wearing a white straw hat—the kind my own grandfather might have worn to town. "My abuelo Milton has always sent his clothes out to be cleaned and ironed, even when my abuela was still alive," Miguel whispered. "He's real picky about his appearance."

"No doubt dapper runs in the family," I said, eyeing my archangel's Sunday duds.

"Ouch," he said. I would have liked the fact that I made a man blush except that I think I was blushing, too.

There was barely enough room in la cocinita with peeling, oil-based paint for the laminated table against one wall with three chairs. A trastero with gritty glass doors showed stacks of stored mismatched kitchenware and a yellow refrigerator practically took up one wall. Miguel smashed two cockroaches with his index finger before we put anything down. He had explained to me that his grandfather insisted on living there alone. Miguel's mother had tried to move him into her new house in San Antonio, and the old man had caught a bus back to El Paso.

"IT FINALLY STOPPED RAININ', EH?" el abuelo called out. The window faced a narrow alley and the backs of other deteriorated houses. He was holding a hand-rolled cigarette outside the window. In the other hand, he kept a fly swatter at the ready. "BUEN DÍA, SEÑORITA! ¿CÓMO ESTÁ USTED?"

I didn't answer him right away because he wasn't looking at me. He was shouting at a half-dead ficus in the corner next to him.

"PLEASE FORGIVE MY HUMBLE HOUSE AND ALL THE DISORDER. BUT SIT DOWN, POR FAVOR. YOU ARE IN YOUR HOME. MIKEY, HIJO, PULL A CHAIR OUT FOR THE YOUNG LADY," the old man shouted.

By then, I realized that he was blind or near-blind. And near-deaf, también. I got a chair out myself and sat down. Miguel hadn't mentioned that his grandfather couldn't see or hear so good but I guessed he had figured why talk about what would be immediately apparent.

Also for obvious reasons, Miguel got to washing out bowls, plates, and utensils, all the while making very loud small talk with his grandfather. They shouted back and forth about the weather and Miguel's job and then the old man asked Miguel about his family—as in "HOW ARE THE CHILDREN?"

"Fine, fine, Abuelo," he answered, glancing over at me.

"AND CRUCITA? TODO BIEN AT HOME?" the old man asked.

"Fine, fine, everybody's fine," Miguel said, killing the conversation like a cockroach, lickety-split. It sounded like he was still married. I was confused. And not all that happy to be there suddenly, neither. Even if it had been a halfhearted lunch invitation of carryout to his decrepit abuelo in the barrio, it had still been an invitation to spend Sunday together, hadn't it?

All my life my mother had warned me about married men. They were everywhere—the butchers who flirted with us at the market, the postal carrier, managers, and neighbors. Todos big liars. "You know the good ones are already taken," she'd say as I got older. "At least the ones your age." And she was right, like always. That was the problem with my mamá. She thought she was always right and she was.

Now one of the good ones was eating up everything we'd brought for his grandfather. He fixed tacos that spilled over with fried pork and heaps of pico de gallo, guacamole, and sour cream. His abuelo only pretended to eat, for the sake of having company, I figured. I pretended, too, and nibbled on a rolled-up tortilla. But I did gladly accept a cold can of Fanta out of the refrigerator and drank it down in almost one gulp. All that kept playing in my head was, Funny, no matter how old you get, you always think someone could find you a little interesting.

EL ABUELO MILTON

"I was born right here in this house." I started my story that morning for the sake of my visita, who had never heard it before and not so much for my favorite grandson, who had many times. Let el Mikey stop me whenever he was ready to go and had had enough of his old abuelo Milton's long-winded cuentos.

El Mikey, like we started to call him when he was playing football in high school and could eat you outta house and home, hombre. El Mikey will eat anything we used to say, kind of like in that commercial on TV. That kid hated everything. Our Mikey ate anything. What a comilón that kid was. But he needed to eat a lot—playing football like he was doing then. I went to every one of his games, too. His father was so busy with his military career and all. Who else was there for him, if not me, his grandpa?

Now, there I was that Sunday, like every Sunday, expecting my nieto, all grown up, a teacher y todo, and the only relative I've got left who gives a damn about me, when this time, without warning, he comes walking in with a goddess—una mera diosa. La Helen of Troy. Helen of Troy was not a goddess. I think she was a queen. It don't matter. This one here, like her name, smelled like una reina.

Mi nieto told me that he and his new lady friend were out looking for her missing hermano. "Ayayayay," I said. What more could I say? But then, so they wouldn't take off so fast, I decided to tell my story. At my age, that could take a while. I geared myself up. "I know it ain't no comfort to you at this time, miss," I said, "pero back when I was young, I don't want to tell you how bad it was around here. You might not know this, but el Chihuahuita is one of our oldest barrios. Some years back now the neighbors got together and went to City Hall to make this one of those historic districts. They did it, too. Yes, ma'am. But plaque or no plaque, it hasn't stopped being our barrio. There's still a lot of criminal element. Pero hell, there's criminal element everywhere, from here to the state capital."

Thinking of the corruption that politicians had always been famous for gave me a lil laugh. I think my company agreed with me because I thought I heard them laughing some, también.

"You know," I went on, clearing my throat. Damn cigarettes are gonna kill me some day. But how I figure it, there are so few pleasures left an old blind and nearly deaf widower, it would be just as well. I'd been cheating death all my life. "When I was a chamaco, I nearly died of smallpox," I said. "Children were always sick of all kinds of diseases around here—smallpox," I said, "scarlet fever, diphtheria. El Río Grande was a breeding ground for mosquitoes, flies, and who knows what all. There was waste seepage . . . it was terrible. And those were terrible days, when I look back on them. The whole country was in despair but we here, los mejicanos, were really desperate. Too poor to afford doctors. Too poor to afford medicine. And if los americanos were going through hard times, you best believe so were all the people escaping the ravages of La Revolución, escaping battles with the Indians, suffering the results of Porfirio Díaz's days of everything for the rich. Pa' el chicharrón todos los demás. To hell with everyone else, in other words."

I paused because it sounded like Mikey was going to the refrigerator again. The door on my icebox rechina un poco. Then I heard him sit back down—because the chair squeaks, too. In fact, everything around here needs oiling, including me.

"Did you know I fought in the Second World War?" I asked la reina. Of course my grandson knew. "I was married by then," I said. "After I came back, we moved in with my jefitos. Later, when my wife and I were able to afford the materials, we set out to build a nice lil house for ourselves, right next door. That's how we were in those days, señorita, always staying close to our people. Nowadays, kids grow up y poof. They're living in Australia or some such place on the other side of the world, like they don't owe nobody nothing.

"Anyway, I know this house is falling apart and don't look like much now. But in its time it had its chiste. And I know it's pretty small but we all fit. In those days we didn't complain. We were glad to have our own casita. If I had not been kicked out of el army maybe we could have done better. Pero . . . bueno, one can't sit around all the time regretting everything. ¿Pa'qué? Ain't that right, Mikey?"

"That's right, Abuelo," my grandson said, chewing on something, like always.

"This is my home, where I was born and where I will die. Hopefully no one will be foolish enough to take me to a hospital, where they'll kill me before my hour." I paused as if I needed a moment to contemplate my ever-so-nearing death, but the fact of the matter was that I heard what I took to be la reina's petticoats rustle. Most likely women weren't wearing petticoats nowadays. It was something else, rustly moving against what had to be a pair of fine and shapely legs, as she made herself comfortable on the rickety chair.

Híjole, hombre.

A man could die happy just hearing sounds like that in the same room. Maybe I had already died and gone to heaven.

"Go on," Mikey said, interrupting my bliss.

I drew in a deep breath. He didn't have to worry none. I had all the time in the world. Thinking about Regina's missing carnal, I got to recalling how long the United States had been giving Raza—los mejicanos—a hard time. I said to the woman, "You know, back when I was a kid, just a mocoso, besides the poverty of the people it was even more harsh during the Depression. I got pretty sharp at making ends meet. For example, this city used to have a few, how would you say, houses of ill repute. Bueno, when I was a boy I was the one who used to run errands for the women. They'd give me coins, sometimes silver, sometimes gold. And now and then they'd even give me food. Sometimes they'd give me a peek. But as a bonus. I'd always say no, I want my pay first. Because I would hand it all over to mi jefita to help out."

I stopped to roll me up un cigarrito. I been smoking since I was about twelve, believe it or not. After a good puff, I started up again. "I didn't go to school. I never liked it. Segregation of los Mexican kids ended about that time but there was still a lot of racist attitudes. From the teachers, too. Calling us 'dumbbells,' 'niggers,' and 'dirty Meskins.' Sending us to shower. 'Don't be speaking Spanish'; 'You got lice . . .' This. That. I got in too many fights. You see me old, all shriveled up, today, but once I was a big strong guy. At least I saw myself as big and strong. Ha-ha. Until someone bigger and stronger came along and gave it to me good, because I wasn't afraid of nobody. No, ma'am."

And it used to feel real good, not to be afraid of nothing.

"The Border Patrol got started up in 1924, the year I was born. That's when Mexicans got to be fugitives on our own land. Whether you lived on this side or that side, all Mexicans got harassed. Sometimes the police would come knocking on your door and pull you out. It didn't matter if you were born over here or not. When I went to fight in Germany I'd tell people, Here los Anglos are fighting the Nazis. Over there, where I live, they treat us Mexicans as if they were the Nazis. One of my superior officers heard me one time. 'How dare you say that?' he told me. 'How dare you compare the great Americans to our enemies? We don't put people in camps.'

" 'The hell you don't,' I said, putting my chin up against his, remembering how los chinos y los japoneses had been treated, how los indios americanos had been treated and how los mexicanos were being treated.

" 'Everyone in the United States has the same opportunity,' he said. He was a gringo, much bigger than me. Muy grande.

"I didn't care. I didn't shut up. I said, 'Bull . . .' I won't say what I said but you get my drift. 'Right this very minute while I am here fighting for you to go back and have a good life, the United States is importing braceros to do the dirty work for me until I return.'

"We started fighting right then and there. Who knows who threw the first punch, but I was the one thrown into the stockade. After a while, they sent me home. What did I care? I came back. We won the war. Nothing changed for us around here."

I stopped to put out my cigarrito when Miguel interrupted again. "Tell Regina about your negocio, Abuelo," getting ahead of me, as usual. "Regina's got a dream to get her own business going someday."

"Well, it's true I've tried a lot of things," la reina said timidly, "but not with too much success. . . ."

I shook my head out of sympathy. There was still so much to tell in between, but I obliged my nieto. "When I got back from the war with a dishonorable-mention discharge—not that I was proud of it, pero what could I do about it?—work was hard to find. There were millions of braceros, maybe not millions but maybe thousands, working over here thinning sugar beets and weeding cotton. Haciendo de todo. Many of them knew how to farm because they came from ranchitos in México. That wasn't the first guest worker program they set up here to get cheaper labor. Los obreros signed away all their rights. They didn't even know what they were signing since everything was in English. And who was going to explain nothing to them, anyway? Desgraciada gente. They couldn't even go back if they wanted to unless it was an emergency and only with permission from the growers who hired them. They were promised all kinds of things, too. They thought they'd get pensions. They got nothing, señorita, just a big kick in the trasero back to México when they weren't needed no more.

"Where would this país be without the labor of the obrero, especially in agriculture, but in the railroads, factorías, and canneries, too, I ask you, señorita? Up in el Norte, 'onde hace tanto frío, in the steel mills and stockyards, too. That was before your time, I'm sure."

"Yes . . ." la reina started to say.

I was all wound up and couldn't stop myself from cutting her off. "Anyway, I came back, and since I was never good at taking orders and needed to be my own boss, I opened up my own business. Right here in downtown El Paso. It was just a cantinita, un lil hole in the wall, you could even say. But I'll tell you what, it made me a good lil profit most of my life—between los braceros, las cantineras, and the gringos looking for a good time, my lil bar stayed open every day except Christmas. I even opened on Easter Sunday. My old lady never liked that, pero ni modo. She liked that our hijos always had shoes on their feet. She liked that we never went hungry, I'd tell her. In any case, I myself never drank. I always saw how tonto people got in my establishment and I'd laugh . . . all the way to the bank, as they say."

I stopped to catch my breath. All you could hear was a steady tick tock, tick tock. I brought that old cuckoo clock back from Germany. It still runs like new.

"Okay, so you want me to say that I made my living working in a cement factory or in the mines blackening my lungs? So I wasn't a cobbler making boots for the gringo military like ese Tony Lama or with a lil barbershop, where half the time you'd have caught me sitting on my own barber chair waiting for someone to come in. Maybe my business wasn't what you could call the most respectable, especially for a family man, but I'll tell you what—I never stood around waiting for a customer. People like to drink and it ain't my fault if they do. At least it's nothing like what makes money today. Now all you hear about are these mafiosos who don't care about nobody or nothing. All they care about is making a lot of money selling drugs. It's blood money. That's all. What kind of life is that, I ask myself. Always looking over your shoulder, afraid that una rata bigger than you will eat you up if you don't watch out."

Híjole, I thought to myself as I said that, if my visita only knew what went on around my barrio these days, they'd go running. The things I could hear with my half-deaf oídos—coming from the alleys, entrando por las walls, coming just in the night air . . . pero, bueno. What could anybody do?

"I wasn't a greedy man and never did nothing illegal," I said, reaching the end of my story, "but I was never no santo. I did have an eye for the pretty ladies."

Who was I kidding? Even blind, I had an eye for them.

"My poor wife. She knew it, too. But back then, it was expected of a man to have, well, you know, a life outside his home. And the kind of business I ran I can't tell you how many muchachas used to go in there. Mostly, they were looking for un jale. Working gals, we'd call them. Anyway, that was all a long time ago. Everyone I ever knew is dead now. Except for my children, gracias a Dios. Even though they never come to visit. Only this boy, el Mikey." I reached over and he let me scruff up his greñas. "When you going to cut off that girlie ponytail, anyway?" I asked. Then I said to la reina, "El Mikey's mother was my favorite." I said it because it was true. Too bad mi'ja married into the military—a colonel, at that. "You know, señorita, you should never force your personal beliefs on your children. The first chance they get, they go off and do just the opposite of what you wished for them."

chapter

FOUR

REGINA

What was going to be a quiet celebration with only me and my sobrino turned into a barbecue party one Saturday, thanks to Miguel, who had started out by inviting himself to celebrate with us and then took over. Taking over might be just his nature but it's not hard to see why a woman divorced him.

Gabo hadn't wanted a party. I wouldn't have known how to organize one, anyway. And with no word from Rafa so far, neither of us was in a mood for a fiesta. But Miguel said, "Sixteen is a big deal, guys," and before we knew it, we had a barbecue planned. The invitation list was mostly left to my nephew since he was the one having a birthday, but like other cambios about him that I am noticing, you just couldn't predict who that might be. So there were a couple of people I anticipated being there and a few others I most definitely had not.

To top it off, Miguel invited people of his own, too.

El Abuelo Milton, for one. He was already there when we arrived at Miguel's traila. That's where he stays since his divorce. He's in a traila and across the street is his family in a nice big house. The old man was sitting outside in the yardita, if you could call a fenced-in empty lot that, at a patio table under the shade of its big umbrella. The patio furniture really stood out in contrast to its surroundings, where there was no grass, just weeds and dirt. But across the street, at his family's house and all down that side of the street, the yarditas had flower gardens and neat lawns.

"VEN. COME SIT BY ME, MI'JA"—the old man acted like we were long-time amigos—"SO I CAN HEAR YOU BETTER." I used to take care of ancianos, not to mention my mother, so I understand how desperate for company they get. But the second time el abuelo let his veiny hand plop down on my lap like the frisky paw of a wolf pup, I jumped up and made myself busy.

We had a taste that day of the hot spring ahead by two in the afternoon, when, like they say, you could have fried an egg on the pavement. We weren't frying eggs but grilling chicken and steaks on Miguel's brand-new gas grill and drinking down pitchers of limonada as fast as we could make it. Meanwhile, Miguel was directing the whole event. His need to take charge was getting to me—I can't lie. I'm a woman who's been on her own a long time. Then I said to myself: He might have control issues but I got problems of my own. My problems started way back. "Oye, muchacha," my mother used to say. "Now what are you up to? Why don't you do something? Like stitching your calzones or cleaning out los frijoles." That woman never left me alone.

Sometimes, when Gabo's not home, I grab a hairbrush and pretend I am at a karaoke bar lip-synching to Isabel Pantoja. I shake my hair loose and everything about me feels all loosened up. I always idolized Isabel Pantoja. She was a beauty, so talented and a long time ago was even married to a famous bullfighter. That was until he was killed in the arena. Besides both having loved ones killed by mean bulls, Isabel and I had something else in common. We were both widows. In the living room, pretending that I am doing Isabel Pantoja in karaoke, I also imagine I have the entire nightclub mesmerized. It's pathetic, I know—pretending about pretending. That's why I keep it to myself. But what harm does it do? Still, I look over my shoulder now and then like my mother is going to come out of nowhere and start on me.

That's why I say I've got my own issues.

The funny thing is, when I realized Miguel was reminding me of my bossy mother, something inside clicked—not quietly, neither. It started happening since turning fifty. "The Big Five-oh," Mrs. Martínez at work called it. She and a few of the staff surprised me after school on that birthday. They all pitched in and gave me a walker as a gag gift. What this click was trying to tell me was: *Everything is going to be okay.* It came in handy, like when Miguel's ex showed up.

Crucita had come to check me out. She checked me out. But I checked her out, too. What I concluded about Miguel's ex-wife was that she was perfect. Perfect manicure, perfect hair, flat stomach, and spotless white shorts. Not everybody can get away with shorts like that. Crucita could. She looked like a tennis pro. She held her glass with a pinky in the air and with a lip-gloss smile, she'd say things to Miguel like, "Don't burn the meat, Mike. I know you've never barbecued before." After a little while she said she had to go pick up their kids from swim class. What a relief, I thought, since I had been holding in my panza the whole time.

It might have been Gabo's schoolmate Tiny Tears who made Miguel's ex skedaddle as fast as she did. "Tiny Tears, like the doll that could cry," I said, when my nephew introduced her. She only laughed and sat down next to Crucita. "Are those real gold?" she asked Miguel's ex about the chains around her neck. She tried to touch them but Crucita pulled away. Five minutes later she was out of there.

Although I knew that Gabo's friend Jesse would come, I was very surprised to see Gabo's new shoes on him. Not just surprised but thinking my sobrino had some explaining to do. I knew that kid could not have gotten the shoes from my nephew honorably. My nephew may have a corazón that overflows with generosity but I'd seen Gabo's face when he opened his present. It was the finest gift he'd ever received. Mi sobrino said it himself.

Then I got a look at Jesse's older brother, El Toro. "Válgame Dios," I said under my breath when I first saw him.

"The Bull?" Miguel leaned over and whispered to me. "He looks like a giant amoeba."

It was true. There seemed to be no form to the man. "Do amoebas smell?" I asked Miguel.

"Bacteria does," he said with a wink.

The Giant Germ had just been released from the nearby prison. "Yeah, La Tuna ain't all that tough," he bragged, as if he were talking about Harvard. "I'd been there before, anyways." Nobody asked El Toro Arellano what he had done time for—more than once. Just by looks alone, you could imagine him capable of anything.

And the party was not over yet.

Padre Juan Bosco showed up. I figured Gabo would invite him. But the priest brought along his mistress. He didn't even bother to make excuses for her. I'd known Herlinda Mora from Cabuche for years. Not as anybody's girlfriend, neither. All her brothers and sisters got married and she was left to dress up los santos in the church. Now she and the priest were there making goo-goo eyes at each other. "What the hell do they think they are," I said to Miguel, "Episcopalians?"

"Be nice," he kept saying. "It's Gabo's day."

When the sun started to set I was glad that me and my sobrino could soon head back home. Then El Toro managed to get up from the bench he had been plunked down on all afternoon and gave a "vámonos" gesture of his big cabezahead to the kids. Not just his Palomino sidekicks, Jesse and la Tiny Tears, got up, but Gabo, too, followed them to Jesse's car. He didn't thank us for the party, say good-bye, or even look at nobody. He just hurried off and got in Jesse's car with the others. It wasn't like my nephew not to mind his manners.

GABO

Apreciado Santo y Amigo de Dios:

Holiest, dulce Santito mío, I beg you to intercede for me. I am not
worthy to ask God to forgive me. The last thing that I wanted to do
was to offend Him. Again, I succumbed to temptation. Again, I lost the
test to cleanse myself for Him. But as a weak excuse I only say on my
behalf, in the name of Jesus Christ crucified and of sweet María, how
much I have missed my papá and cannot bear to think I will never see
him again. And my tía—her eyes get so sad when we speak of my
father. If it were not for You, how would I bear this darkness? The truth
is, Su Reverencia, I made a pact with the Devil.

"My brother, El Toro, just got out, man," el Jesse said the night
before my fiesta at el Chongo Man's. "If anybody can find out what
happened to your old man it would be him. He got his ways and he got
his people. Me among them." We were shooting hoops with Jesse in my
new cross-trainers that my tía Regina had given me for my birthday.

I did not doubt Jesse's claims. The Palominos are everywhere. "What
would I have to give in return?" I asked right off. I hoped he knew all of
myself was pledged to the Lord and nothing would change that. Father
Juan Bosco has told me: God is the ultimate word on everything.
Besides that, a concept el padre wasn't sure I would grasp, God is not a
man and the Devil does not wield a pitchfork or smell of sulfur. God is
everything. We were all part of God. Christ died for the Palominos,
too. That night, Padre Pío, like tiny dandruff specks from God's head,
the Palominos had fallen on me.

"Well, first off," Jesse said, pulling up his baggy jeans that just dropped right back down past his hips again, "your calcos, ése." Then he added, "That's just for me. I can't speak for the rest, much less my brother. But that's all up to you, man. I mean, it all depends on how much you wanna find your old man."

Jesse and I traded shoes before parting ways. I hoped my tía wasn't by the door when I got in without my new pair. She had been so excited about her gift. Yes, I felt guilty for it. I know she had been up nights doing a lot of sewing in order to afford my present. Yes, I was filled with anguish about my deal with Jesse. Yes, I feared the embers of Inferno. But most of all, San Pío, I was ashamed, because I knew that God was watching. I would have gone to Father Juan Bosco, as I had done in the past during such torments, but knowing what I did about him, I could not bring myself to visit him. Father Juan Bosco told me in confidence that he was leaving the priesthood to marry Herlinda Mora.

"You're very young," el padre said. "You don't understand yet about love." What greater love could I ever have than my love for God? It would have been disrespectful to say out loud what I really felt. As if he were anticipating what I wanted to say, el cura explained, "This is a different kind of love, hijo. My love for God will always be there, but I'll have to devote myself to Him in a different way."

Su Reverencia, I am sixteen years old and already having a spiritual crisis. But I am not like other teenagers. I know that. My father is missing. My mother has been taken from me. My hermana, too. (Where is Karlita, Santo? Is she there with you y mi mamá? I have prayed that whoever she went with did not treat her badly.) I turned to my spiritual adviser and what was he now telling me? God was not enough for him.

According to Jesse, los Palominos were going to do whatever it took to find my father. Even la Tiny Tears, who had pledged her loyalty to the gang, had come to do whatever was necessary. Those tattooed tears of hers, one under each eye, is part of the Palominos' code. Each tattoo tear represents a life taken. Tiny Tears has already killed, Padre Pío. That is what el Jesse said. And not out of self-defense. She killed enemies de los Palominos. All El Toro had to say was, "Do it," and Tiny Tears did it without hesitation. Even from behind bars he had that kind of reach. Jesse told me, You had better not question the orders given by the jefe.

"So what?" Tiny Tears herself said when I asked. "My homies would do it for me."

Jesse talked it over with his brother and a plan was made. Somehow, some way, we were going to get those coyotes down in El Paso who had called my tía asking for money to tell us what they ended up doing with my papá. "Do not doubt for a second that they know what happened to your old man, homes," Jesse said, all too happy to take my new shoes as payment for his help. "But even if you let yourself doubt that, do not doubt that los Palominos will take care of business."

Ayúdame, Holy Saint. The darkness falls like a shroud now all around me,

Your Servant in God's Love

Amado Santo,

Our Lord may have bothered Himself to tell you, but here is my side of it.

At my party, when el jefe of the Palominos gave the sign, we all got in Jesse's car, El Toro, Jesse, Tiny Tears, and me. I did not dare turn around to look at my tía or any of the other adults. If I gave her the chance, my tía Regina would have twisted my head off like I had seen her do with a chicken when I was little. We drove straight to el Segundo barrio in El Paso, where the coyotes live. It had not been difficult to find out la coyota's address. My tía had told me how she found it.

On our way to El Paso, the fate of my papá looming over my own, I could not help but try to tell the gangeros what I believed about death. "It says it right there in Hebrews," I said. "Your earthly self dies but if your choice was to go with the good then you will have eternal union with Our Lord."

"Hey, man," El Toro half snorted from the backseat, "La Muerte is always good. Lookehere." I turned around. He pulled out the charm of La Muerte that he was wearing on a chain around his neck. It looked like the Grim Reaper. "La Muerte is the Palominos' patron saint," he said. (How that could be, I was not sure, Santo, since death was never a person to begin with.) "I call her La Niña Blanca," Tiny Tears said, pulling out a similar pendant hanging on a chain around her neck. "Before I go out, I pray to her."

"You pray to her?" I asked.

Tiny Tears nodded. "Hell yeah. I light candles to her and everything." She kissed the pewter pendant and stuck it back inside her polo.

"What do you ask her for?" I asked.

"I dunno," Tiny said, suddenly hesitant. Maybe, I thought, it was because she was being asked to speak from her heart. Then she said, "Like, if we're gonna go hit a convenience store or something and I go in with my kid to cause a distraction. I say, 'Por favor, Niña Blanca, protect my baby from getting hit by a stray bullet.' " Then she smiled.

"That's right," El Toro said from the backseat. "You just gotta ask La Muerte to watch out for you and you'll be all right."

El Toro told us, "Tonight, all we're gonna do is scope out the place." He was so big he took up all of the backseat. Tiny Tears sat between Jesse and me in the front. "Whatever you mensitos do," El Toro said, "do not let anybody there see you."

How we were going to manage not being seen hanging around by the coyotes' I had my doubts immediately, since, as soon as we found the house, El Toro told the three of us to get out. "Find a hiding place to stake out the pad," he ordered, wiggling out and jumping into the front seat to squeeze in behind the wheel. "See if you spot anyone coming in or going out. We need to know who we're dealing with. Jesse, you know some of the coyotes around here. See if you recognize anybody." Jesse nodded and scurried off so fast I did not even see which way he went.

El Toro drove off without saying another word. I hoped he was coming right back. I had to be at Mass at seven in the morning. After la misa I had to go to work. "I guess you ain't exactly cut out for a life of crime, huh, dude?" Tiny Tears said when I told her I was worried that El Toro would leave us out there all night. Before I could answer, she took off, también. Esa Tiny Tears was fast for being so chiquita. She could not have been even five feet tall but she acted as tough as a man.

Left alone and needing to hide, too, I looked up at the trees, mostly elms, to see if there was one I could actually climb. There was not. If I crouched behind a parked vehicle someone would find me suspicious soon enough. Then I spotted a big garbage bin that looked empty. It was directly across the street from the casa of los coyotes. How to get in without anyone noticing was the challenge.

I let a few people go by, a lady walking her dog, taking their sweet time, a couple of chavalos on skateboards, then un hombre yelling in Spanish at someone on his cellular came. He actually stopped right next to me as if I was not even there, he was so busy shouting swear words. I became anxious, knowing El Toro could come right back. He would find me still out in the open. I just went for the garbage bin with the cellular man standing nearby. Either he was used to seeing things like that in his barrio or his phone call was taking up all his attention, but even in the bin I could hear him yelling.

My heart was pounding and even though the bin was totally empty, it smelled like dead rats. Somehow, I made myself get used to it by focusing on the crack I left by leaving the lid slightly open. I had a full view of the house. The modest casita was un verde all faded with a small front yard that looked neglected, with all kinds of trash thrown around. Big plastic bags of garbage. There was an empty kids' wading pool and every now and then a flaco Rottweiler came around from the back. There were iron bars on the windows but that was not unusual on that block.

Was my father in there? I wondered.

When no one was around I pushed the lid up and I gave out the whistle my papá taught me. We used it when we crossed the desert. "In case you lose your mamá or me, hijito," he said, "give out this whistle as loud as you can. We'll hear you."

I whistled again.

"Papá!" I called out next. My eyes searched for any sign of movement coming from that house—all boarded up as if it were abandoned. Pero no one came out. I crouched back down, out of sight.

A long while passed.

How many times had mi tía Regina begged my father not to return to México, to take his chances and stay, Santo querido? But México had a pull on my papá. It was his country. "No soy un gringo," he'd say. He came up to el Norte only for the sake of supporting his familia.

Tears came to my eyes from the stench, the pain in my back and knees, and so much unsureness de todo.

Eli, Eli, lema sabachthani? Jesus had cried out on the cross. All I ever have to do is remind myself what Our Savior suffered for us to know what I am capable of enduring, Padre Pío. I did not dare move, just like I used to have to do when we were crossing el desierto and helicopters were hovering over us. "Stay put," my dad would say, pushing my head down between my knees, hoping I would blend in with a nopal. "Shhh."

Su Servidor

Praise Jesus Christ in His Angels and in His Saints, Santo Pío:

Perdón that I take so much of your time as I continue with my poor excuse for offending God. That long night that I watched out for los coyotes and never saw anyone, finally there was some whispering outside my garbage bin and then *zas, zas, zas,* on the lid. I jumped up like un jack-in-the-box. It was El Toro and Jesse. "Come on, man," Jesse said. I climbed out and followed them down the street to Jesse's car.

"Where's la Tiny?" I asked, looking around and seeing no sign of her. Once Jesse and I were in the backseat and El Toro behind the wheel, Jesse said, "She made it back home a while ago. Ésa's got a kid, now. It's all good. She can't be out in the street all night like before."

"Anyway, la cholita did all right," El Toro said. "She got in the house—"

"What?" I said. "But how—"

"Don't worry about it," El Toro said. "She got in. She got out. She got some information for us."

While we stayed parked and I waited to hear whatever information they had found out, El Toro lit up a marijuana cigarette and offered it to me. I shook my head and he passed it to his brother.

It was not the first time I had been around people smoking marijuana, Su Reverencia. Not only en los baños at school did I see muchachos smoking but even as a child, working in the fields. Sometimes the men would be outside los jacales we stayed in; they would smoke cigarettes and sometimes marijuana. They drank beer and played guitar if anyone had one, anything to forget the day they'd just had and the next one coming up just like it. But smoking in a car at two in the morning, with Border Patrol and police cars cruising for people like us, made me duck down.

"Hey, pendejo, whatchu afraid of?" El Toro barely breathed out, holding in marijuana smoke.

To begin with, I did not even have a green card.

I stayed down while El Toro kept talking. "Man, you got yourself some real sh-- to deal with." (Forgive me, O Holy One, as I repeat more or less accurately only to show you how the Devil made himself manifest before me with so many temptations.) He took the marijuana cigarette back from Jesse and kept it for himself from then on. "Those coyotes that got hold of your old man are with los Villanueva—a small but very powerful family. Ambitious. They're into pushing meth, kids, females, all kinds of sh--. That's who we're talking about, none other."

"Aw, man," Jesse said under his breath. He looked out of the window into the quiet of the street at that hour and I waited to hear more of how exactly I was going to descend into hell forever. I knew there was no turning back from the threshold of eternal damnation. Padre Pío, even if I had good intentions at the hour of my death I was not sure I would be able to avoid God's anger.

I had no idea who were the narco familias or carteles, Santito. All I could think of was how had my father gotten involved with them? Usually he and my mother would find a coyote in Juárez who would set a price, maybe a couple of hundred dollars for each of us, and he would cross us all over. It was harder for first-timers and people coming from farther away. It was a lot more money, too, as much as fifteen hundred a head. They would be brought over through the desert, like herded goats that needed no consideration, sometimes not even water.

One time, back when we were crossing into California, mi hermana became so dehydrated we were sure she was going to die. My papá had to carry her. The coyote had just left us out there, having no use for us once he had his money. All I could see was white. My mamá started to carry me, too. After a time, I became too heavy for her. Then my father and my mother both dropped to their knees. It got so bad, we had no choice but to drink our own urine. It is disgusting to admit, but it saved us.

"They came from Tornillo," El Toro said. "These newcomers have got to fight it out for control like a buncha muthaf-----s. And when I say *fight*," the Palomino jefe said, "I mean AK-47 wars with the police in Juárez, man. In la pinta I heard these people threw a hand grenade into the police station."

El Toro stopped to admire the marijuana cigarette he held up in his hand. "They must grow this sh - - in Acapulco, man," he said, taking in a long puff before continuing. "Not only that, the Villanueva family's got some meth labs set up. That house right there? That's one of them.

Tiny checked it out. Move out the way, Scarface, the Mexicans are here to stay. Coke, horse, weed, ice . . . snot—they're all coming to a school ground near you. Little brother," he said to Jesse, "if we can get in on that, you and me are gonna be rolling in some major feria."

Not just what he was saying but even his tone was ominous, San Pío. El Toro's hair was all messed up, thick and black like a hairy dog's. In silhouette, so huge, greñudo, sweating and breathing down on me like Cyclops—I could not imagine anything ever terrifying me more.

That was until a light flashed on us.

The sheriff's car pulled up right behind Jesse's. Two deputies got out and started walking toward us with their hands on their holsters. One of them was an older lady.

"F--- me," El Toro muttered, as he turned around to face the front and he banged the steering wheel with one of his manotas. I did not know what he did with the marijuana cigarette. As if it was all we had to worry about, Padre Santo. When the authorities pulled the three of us out, they not only found marijuana in El Toro's back pocket, but he was carrying a knife inside his bota.

"And you, boys?" El chavo deputy asked Jesse and me, while we were made to lie facedown on the sidewalk. "What will we find out about you?" (I call him un chavo because he looked almost my age.)

La señora deputy was radioing in to see who we were. All I had in my pocket were a few dollars and my student I.D. that said I was in high school.

"How old are you, son?" I felt a slight kick on the back of my shoe. "Yeah, you. How old are you?"

"Sixteen," I answered. "Today was my birthday," I added, like they were going to drop everything and start singing "Las Mañanitas" to me.

"Well, happy birthday," the woman deputy said, coming back from the squad car. "Let's take them in," she told her partner. It turned out she was a chief deputy and his superior.

"Nice company you're keeping with this guy," said el chavo deputy, who yanked me up off the ground. We were already handcuffed. He meant El Toro, since the next thing he said was directed at him: "Well, I hope you enjoyed your vacation since it didn't take long for you to violate your parole."

First they drove us to the jail downtown, where they took los hermanos Arellano. The chavo deputy went with them. The woman chief deputy took me across the street to what she called the "holding tank" and stuck me in a cage. She left me there with no explanation. Of course she did not owe one to me. Then she went about her business as if I was not there. My wrists were still cuffed. I just stood watching like an animal passes the time watching the people at the zoo, Padre Pío. All kinds of gente went back and forth, police officers, state police, their prisoners, and victims. Y las familias coming to find out what to do about it all, in their bedtime clothes and faces. After about an hour, la chief deputy came back and let me out. She said she was going to process me. I was not sure what that would entail but the sound of it made me feel like a slice of cheese.

She took me to her desk to fill out forms, which I figured would end with me being deported. But she never bothered to ask if I was legal or not. At the time I figured it was because of my perfect English or the nuevos jeans I was wearing that my tía got me. "You look like a dorky white boy," Jesse always told me. "Who'd suspect you of anything?" Maybe that was it, I thought. But later, I found out from el Chongo Man that they would not have reported me to Immigration because it was not their job.

I did not realize I was shaking until la chief deputy said, "I'm going to take the handcuffs off." Then she asked me where I lived, and for some reason, Su Reverencia, everything that came out of my mouth was a lie. I would open my mouth and a lie would spill out. She would ask something else and out would come another lie. San Pío, by then I knew I was condemned already, maybe not in the eyes of the law, or even with los Palominos, but in my soul. "I live with my grandfather here in El Paso," I said, thinking about el viejito at my barbecue party.

"CALL ME ABUELO MILTON—EVERYBODY DOES," el señor had told me. We had talked for a while about school and what I wanted to do with my life and then Miguel's grandfather gave me his address and phone number. "COME BY AND VISIT ME WHENEVER YOU LIKE, CARNALITO," he told me.

He had probably seen me as a good boy, not like my "pachuco" friends, as he called them. I think that was the way they called bandilleros in the old days. But el Abuelo Milton had not seen how dangerously close I was already to becoming one of them. Steadily, they were absorbing me, like through osmosis. (I am excusing myself again, I know, Padre Pío. Perdóname.)

"Your school I.D. says you go to school up in Cabuche. What's up with that?" la chief deputy asked, sitting on the corner of her desk and acting like she was my friend. "Call me Diputada Sofia," she said. She reminded me of the painting of the beautiful lady holding the Mexican flag that they showed in history books in school in México, proud and so resilient.

There was no way I was going to call my tía Regina and give her a heart attack, like she always said she was going to have one day. "I go with my uncle, Miguel Betancourt, who teaches at the middle school there." The lies kept coming. I lied like I was Dostoyevsky making my tale longer and longer. (And worse, Santito, deriving pleasure from my cleverness.) "He thinks the school is better for me up there than down here, where my abuelo lives."

La Diputada Sofia nodded with her kind eyes and her equally kind smile, lips painted dark pink and her mouth going, "Tsk, tsk." "Your parents?" she asked next.

"Dead," I said, which was only half a lie, I hoped. I also hoped God would not punish me for that lie and take my papá away, too. My father had to still be here on earth—somewhere. That is what I really wanted to tell la Diputada Sofia, Padre Pío. I took a deep breath, hoping that when I opened my mouth next I'd have the courage to say the truth. *You want to catch real criminals?* I wanted to ask. *Go check out that house where los coyotes live. They are not just coyotes, they are really mala gente. Find my father. Leave kids like me alone who only want to study in peace.*

She was staring right into my eyes and I wondered if she was reading my mind. My thoughts kept going loudly, *I belong to the Lord, not to your laws.* "My kingdom is not of this world," I muttered. She did not hear me, I was sure. And I did not repeat the blasphemy. I was shivering like I had a fever, like my tío Osvaldo trembled, lips quivering, just before he died. Maybe I was going to die, I thought, and not just wished I would from shame. Maybe I had contracted something in that garbage can, tetanus, malaria, or maybe the West Nile virus. My arms and ankles itched painfully from the mosquito and fly bites I got in the garbage bin.

La Diputada Sofia sighed. "You kids," was all she said, while shaking her head. I could not tell if she was feeling sorry for me or was just repulsed. I kept my head down. I wanted to look up but I could not.

She did not ask any more questions. Instead, she got up and let the clipboard fall hard on the desk. It knocked down a pencil holder. Another officer nearby looked up for a second. "You okay?" he asked her. She nodded and crossed her arms. Here it comes, I thought, the scolding, the verdict. They are going to take me off to jail with the Arellano brothers. Who knows what will become of me. I should have told her the truth. At least about my tía Regina. Now my aunt would never know what happened to me. She would die of a broken heart for sure. Then la Diputada Sofia said, with those kind eyes and kind smile and most of all a kind voice, "You know what, Gabriel?"

I dared to raise my eyes to meet hers.

"I think we're going to give you a break this time. You may be heading down the wrong path hanging around with the likes of those two we found you with tonight, but I got a feeling it's not too late for you. I'm going to call your grandfather to come down and pick you up."

With my gratitude y mi devoción
Your most unworthy servant

EL ABUELO MILTON

Whew, hombre, I sure do hope the summer don't turn out like that one back in el ninety-four, when it was up past los one hundreds for two months straight.

That was when I lost my Lola. Fifty years we were together. Her heart gave out with the heat. La pobre. I was in the process of trying to put in an air conditioner when I heard a glass fall. I had left her in bed resting y drinking una Fanta. Orange Fanta was her favorite. "¿Qué te pasa?" I yelled from la sala, where I was struggling with the heavy unit by the window. I couldn't just let it go to run and see what happened. There was no answer. Nada. I only heard the hum of all the lil fans we had set up around the house, like always. We never needed no air-conditioning before. We'd grown up with the heat.

But that summer was a bad one. And my Lola was not doing too good by then. Our daughter, el Mikey's mamá, came over from San Antonio to arrange the funeral. I couldn't do it. I was too broken up. Mi'ja was so mad at me. She acted like I had killed her mother. "I'd been telling you two to come live with me, hadn't I?" she kept saying. It wasn't me who had not wanted to leave our home. It was my jefita.

Anyway, this is going to be one of those summers—I can already tell.

Besides everything else that can go wrong when the weather gets this hot it seems that people's tempers blow up faster. La other night I thought it was firecrackers going off in the alley that woke me up. No, hombre. Firecrackers, ni que firecrackers. It was bullets. I got up and came over to the back window like I always do at night when I can't sleep.

I rolled myself un cigarrito. And what did I see? Even though I can hardly see in the day, the funny thing is I can see almost perfect at night. No, the doctors can't explain it. But I ain't surprised. There's a whole lot of doctors can't explain.

That night there was a dead man lying on the ground right there in front of my window. Oh, I knew he was dead, all right. Blood spilled out all around him, especially around his head. He didn't move. I didn't move, neither. Caramba. I was afraid if I did, someone out there might see me by the window. The lights in the kitchen were off so I didn't think I could be seen. But I can never be too sure about nothing around here. Before I finished my cigarrito, keeping it low so the light wasn't showing out the window, I heard footsteps running back. Two pachucos came and dragged off the corpse. In the morning I asked the neighbors. No one saw nothing, heard nothing. That was just last month. It ain't the first time I witnessed something like that in the back of my casita, where my chamacos used to play a long time ago and where now it ain't even safe for your dog to go out.

Yes, sir. Things can get pretty bad during these times, so I wasn't all that surprised when I got the call from the police station about Regina's boy. At the little barbecue party that Mikey had for him, I gave el muchacho my phone number and address because with the likes of those hijos de la mala vida hanging around him, I just figured he'd need someone to call sooner or later. I didn't figure on that very night.

But then again, I suppose I wasn't surprised.

That big vaca that called himself "El Toro"—I recognized him right away. I can't see how my grandson didn't. A couple of years back that was the pachuco they arrested for train robbery in Sunland Park. Imagine robbing trains in this day and age. He was the ringleader. Nothing but kids, punks from Anapra, México—the other side. There's an Anapra on this side, too. And this big castrated bull, hijo de su . . . leadin' them all to perdition. The train stopped right where the U.S. and México meet unnoticed. The punks would run over in the middle of the night, jump on the stopped train, break into the cars, and throw off all it was transporting—TVs, stereos, whatever there was, you name it.

One night, the FBI got a tip, planned a sting. They caught the gang in action. But then a couple of the FBI got beat up so bad they ended up in comas. One eventually died. As far as I see it, the revenge of the officials that followed was near merciless—allá, on the Mexican side. Whether la chota or el FBI, I don't know who exactly, but right after all that went down they went around in the middle of the night like King Herod's soldiers, banging on doors, arresting everyone and his mamá.

I remember that ugly old cow from the TV news. He was the very same vaca who now calls himself "El Toro." His ganga ain't nothin' but a bunch of kids. He uses los cabroncitos to do his dirty work. Usually since they're minors or don't have records the chota can't prosecute to the full extent of the law.

And that El Toro Arellano—ol' heifer—likes young boys in more ways than one. The news said he had been arrested before as a sex offender. I'm glad he got thrown back in el bote, where he belonged.

Ay, no. I saw Regina's boy and I said, No way, hombre. That cow ain't going to ruin this one. Even with that crazy pelirrojo like a scalp on fire, you can tell ese muchacho is with God. Maybe a man like me, who made his livelihood with a saloon, has no right to say who is with God and who ain't. Then again, a man like me might know better than most. That boy, without a doubt, has un halo. I kid you not. I don't know if I'm the only one who can see it but it's plainly there. A gold ring y todo just like in all the paintings.

So when Sofia, la chief deputy ésa who told me later she's from up around Albuquerque, quesque some lil village nearby there, called me about picking up my grandson, I said, "Yes, ma'am, right away." It was four in the morning, just about the time I usually get up anyways. I got on my clothes, made un cafecito, and smoked the first cigarrito of the day.

Then I went outside and got the tarp off my troca. I cover my pickup to protect it from the elements. (And by elements I don't just mean the sun and windstorms, I mean those elements who come around to see what they can steal or vandalize.) My troquita is a 1953 International, in mint condition, just like the day I bought it. You can't even find parts for it no more. I got in my white truck and went straight down to the police station, hoping to beat the daylight, when afterward the lights in my ojos would go out on me. That is, until dark came around again. And night would become day.

chapter

FIVE

REGINA

My Gabo has been gone for four days. I know where he is.

He is a boy trying to figure things out. Even if you are a hundred, how do you make sense of your parents being killed or disappearing trying to make their way to the Land of Gold? Muchos dólares en Los Estados. That's what a lot of people hear in their villages. Rafa and Ximena knew better. The reality is that it don't make sense. People have to make peace with it—otherwise they might start a revolution. That's Miguel talk, but sometimes I have to agree.

At sixteen, my Gabo's got the bad luck that follows each member of our familia. So my nephew grabs on to God for the answers.

He is at the priest's house next to the church.

I went to see el Padre Juan Bosco when my nephew didn't come home from work. I already suspected something. The boy hadn't come home to pick up the truck. I pounded on the church first, using the huge door-knocker. *Zas! Zas! Zas!* Dogs started barking. I woke up the neighbor-hood. "Open!" I yelled, wanting to make a mitote. I never got along with Padre Juan Bosco. I kept banging until someone going by in a car stopped and said, "The church is closed, señora! Why don't you go around to the house?" I knew all that. I just wanted an opportunity to make trouble for el cura for being such a hypocrite. Who in Cabuche doesn't know that Herlinda Mora is his mistress and not there just to look after him? You'd only have to have a glance inside the house to know she was no housekeeper. I don't want to be mean but it's the truth.

Herlinda is the youngest of thirteen kids. Thirteen. Count them. She's been staying with el padre since her parents died. Mr. Mora the boot maker was ninety-seven. His wife was eighty-nine. They went one day apart. Herlinda found each one in the morning in bed, cold. She had always looked after her folks. Suddenly, no one. Then she went to take care of Father Juan Bosco. Right. She was taking real good care of him at the barbecue party, from what I saw. I went around the church to the house. Her dog started yapping from behind the door. Of course it was her dog. What priest owns a Shih Tzu?

I rang the bell. It was el padre who answered. "Yes, he's here," he said as soon as he opened the door. He didn't invite me in but I tried to peek around him. I could see from where I was standing what a mess the house was. The coffee table was covered with evidence of past meals in front of the television set, big empty soda bottles, plates and forks, even a pizza carton. Clothes thrown on the couch and chairs. Like I said, a mess.

For a second I caught sight of Gabo's red hair. It's indio hair, like my mother's but red, like mine and my papá's. Gabo's stands up like a maguey plant, all over the place. It was his cabezahead poking over the couch.

"I've given him sanctuary here," the priest said.

Sanctuary? I wasn't the secret police. With hands on my hips, I started tapping my foot. I couldn't look him in the eye, knowing what I did about him and Herlinda. She wasn't showing herself, neither.

Over twenty years of Father Juan Bosco as my confessor and he never once let up on me about my not knowing a man. "How could you not, Regina?" His silhouette would lean against the screen, all ears. "You were married."

Sure, for one day. Junior was shipped out the morning after we had gone to the courthouse in Las Cruces. We planned on waiting until we could have a church wedding. In those days people waited. Father Juan Bosco never believed that we did not spend even our "wedding night" in the same bed. We weren't ready for that. We only married because Junior had a feeling he wasn't coming back. "I want to make sure you're taken care of just in case," he said.

"Is my nephew all right?" I asked.

"Yes," Padre said. Still, he didn't invite me in. "He'll be safe here. We'll . . . I'll take good care of him—don't worry," he said, looking ready to close the door on my nose. He was acting like I was one of los Palominos. "Are those hoodlums harassing him?" I asked. The priest didn't say yes or no, but made a face that said, "You can never tell."

"Make sure he goes to school," I said.

Padre Juan Bosco nodded. "Yes, of course, Regina. *I* wasn't the one who let him hang around with that gang. Remember that. Just don't worry so much. He doesn't miss work, either. He's a good boy." Buen muchacho, he called him. That's why I wanted to fetch him home. I didn't want my boy corrupted by Church hypocrisies any more than I had ever wanted him hanging around with hoodlums.

"When he's of age he is going into the seminary," Father Juan Bosco said, treating me like an unfit parent. "Go on now." That did it. I tried to get around him, but he succeeded in blocking my way.

I sized him up. I could've taken him, I thought. Stepping away from the door and on tiptoes, I tried to look past the priest again. Red spiked hair jutted out from behind the couch.

"Go on now," el padre said, shooing me with his hands like I was a bug. "When your nephew's ready, he'll go home on his own." The door slammed on my face. Maybe in big, enlightened cities you could call the authorities on a priest for holding a minor. Pero in Cabuche I doubted very much that the sheriff would force Gabo to go home when the priest was looking out for him. Everybody liked Padre Juan Bosco. Except me. More than ever now. "I'll be back!" I shouted, all Schwarzenegger-like after the priest shut the door with a *pom*. It sounded as if he might have slammed it on purpose to be rude. But I wasn't sure. It was a heavy door, so there was no telling.

Los curas had always been like that, in my experience, back in México and in Cabuche, New Mexico—hard to decipher. *Decipher* sounded like they were encoded beings. But that's the word that came to me, hurrying back to my truck in the cold. A big word for a big pain in the butt. When he wore his collar (which Father Juan Bosco was not doing that night at home), a priest would look like trustworthiness incarnated. You could surrender yourself entirely to him, your penas, and all your woes. He would understand you. He would help you. He would look up to the heavens and intervene for you if you had lost your way from God. But not Father Juan Bosco and not the ones I knew growing up. They were men. Just men. And a couple of them had been good and a few had been bad. El cura was not always a good man but not always a bad one, neither. That's why I say he was hard to figure out. Slowly walking off, I hoped in the case of my Gabo he was planning on being good. If he called La Migra on Gabo, I swear I didn't know what I'd do to that hombre.

"He's at the top of his class," I shouted from the corner. I knew the priest was watching me from the window through a crack in the Venetian blinds. "I want him to graduate!" I said.

Then the door opened and Gabo came out. Just for a second. "Don't worry, Tía," he called.

I wanted to ask him if he was eating all right (I knew Herlinda Mora was no kind of cook) and let him know that if he still needed help with calculus I had found a tutor for him. Before I could make a move toward the house, he went back in again.

El Padre Juan Bosco said he was giving him sanctuary but it feels more like he's being held prisoner. All I do every night is plan Gabo's breakout. I know my nephew is there of his own free will. But maybe he needs deprogramming. I learned all about this years ago on a TV special. Kids like my Gabo, suffering, could get brainwashed by cults and political zealots. Their parents had to hire someone to find them and deprogram them. Rafa would have agreed with me. He would have thought his son was being brainwashed by the Church. Just like Mamá used to think that my brother was brainwashed by communism.

While I waited up, hoping Gabo would just come home on his own, all kinds of fears crossed my mind. I'd heard somewhere that there was a shortage of priests lately. Maybe they were resorting to drastic measures now to keep the numbers up. Sequestering undocumented orphan boys like my Gabo with promises of being taken care of here for now and by God for eternity. I'm not trying to be a smart-ass. All we want is our buen muchacho to come home—me and la Winnie Tuerta. One night she was whimpering outside Gabo's bedroom door. We both slept on the couch, like we expected him any second.

GABO

Most Holy Padre en Jesús Cristo:

Primero, thank you for delivering me from the possibility of going to prison. Santo mío, I am sinking. Pray for me.

"Turn these stones into bread," Satanás told Our Lord while He fasted in el desierto. Use God to help you, is what he meant. Jesus refused. Not I, Señor Santo. I fell into temptation as easily as a rabbit falls into a trap.

The dawn when el Abuelo Milton came for me, he let me drive his truck from the police station to his house. All the way el Abuelo Milton would not stop casting aspersions on El Toro. "CABRONES LIKE HIM WOULD STEAL FROM THEIR OWN GRANDMOTHER," el señor abuelo said, riding next to me. (He looks like Don Quixote, Padre Pío. One day I will finish reading that book. But, as you know, my mind is consumed lately.) El abuelito was right about the greed of the Palominos. Jesse had gotten my new sports shoes but El Toro had taken the medalla my father left me. It was of Saint Christopher, the santo of travelers. My mamá gave it to him. It was all I had that El Toro said was worth anything. It did not even fit around El Toro's fat neck but he took it anyway.

As soon as we were in the house of el abuelo I ran to the bathroom, sick, mostly from self-disgust. When I came out he was fumbling around at the stove scrambling up eggs. "MAN DOES NOT LIVE BY BREAD ALONE," he said out of nowhere.

I stopped in my tracks, "Sí, Abuelo. Man shall not live by bread alone. . . ."

"BUT BY HUEVOS AND SOME CAFECITO, TOO," el Abuelo Milton said, pulling up a chair at the mesita for me, "SO COME AND EAT. ÁNDALE, CARNALITO."

The toast was burned y los eggs dry. He served us both café from a little pot on the stove that looked like it came from the cowboy campfire days. It was so tarnished you could not see its original color. The coffee tasted like high-octane. I never eat breakfast but I ate like I had just come back from forty days in the desert, wiping my plate with a piece of crust. I was so grateful for my freedom. After I washed the dishes, I called in to work.

But it was el abuelo who telephoned my tía. "LET ME START BREAKIN' THE NEWS TO HER," he said. He told my aunt I had spent the night at his place. An explanation to come later—or maybe not—he added. It would be up to me, he said afterward, letting me know I could take him into my confidence. I imagined mi tía Regina at home yelling after they hung up. She would yell until she scared away la Winnie, all the birds and creatures around and she became hoarse. By the time I got home, so tired of being angry, she would not even speak to me. That was when I decided to go to see Father Juan Bosco. He offered to take me in; at least until my tía calmed down.

Mientras, with el viejito, he seemed determined that we should bond. "WHY DON'T YOU TELL ME SOMETHING ABOUT YOUR PEOPLE DURING LA REVOLUCIÓN? FOR EXAMPLE, MY JEFITO FOUGHT WITH PANCHO VILLA. . . ." (Sí, Su Reverencia, he shouts to the point of hurting uno's eardrums so that I must put my fingers in my ears. He cannot see me, anyway.) Old people liked to talk about el bandido Pancho Villa turned revolucionario. I tried to recall the cuentos I had heard about my great-grandfather Metatron's hacienda. Pancho Villa's men had ransacked his home when he was a little boy. They pulled down los chandeliers and even carried off the ornate roperos and brass beds from Spain. Later, the new government gave most of the land to the peons who worked on it. "All this made my papi's grandfather grow up to be a bitter man," I said.

"YOU SEE HOW THAT WORKS, MUCHACHO?" El abuelo was all smiles, as if the fact that my ancestors and his father possibly were enemies somehow now made us related. I scratched my head. What difference did it make if I descended from once-great landowners? My family's story was not like that of García Márquez's Buendía family—one generation tied to the next in a magical Latino country. Nor was I como el gringüito Harry Potter—with all kinds of tricks up my sleeve to impress people.

"I am not going to be one more invisible Mexican here picking up dirty dishes in restaurants," my papá told my aunt the last time she asked him to stay. "My people back home need me and I need them."

"OKAY, OKAY," el abuelo finally said, finding his chair and sitting back down. "THE TRUTH WAS MY FATHER NEVER EVEN MET PANCHO VILLA. . . ." Then he cheered himself up again. "BUT HE WAS A TRUE REVOLUTIONARY . . . YOU CAN BELIEVE THAT."

My father, too, I thought. The old man did not have to go so far back to make his point, whatever it was. La Revolución had not ended México's problems. And that was the purpose for a revolution, was it not, Santito? So I told him about my papá, not to boast but because I think he is the bravest man I will ever know. "My father fought in the highlands of Guerrero," I said. "That was before I was born."

El abuelo's ears perked up. "IS THAT RIGHT?" he said.

"I don't know much, Don Abuelo Milton," I said, "but the government had once granted the families there the rights to produce timber. Pero outside companies came in and took over. When the communities rose up in protest, the military came. My papá went to join the fight. In his youth, he said he was an idealist. Later, los narcos went and cultivated drugs. They brought wealth to the region but also engendered greed among the local officials. The families that had always lived there were forced to migrate in order to find work."

"ENGENDERED, EH?"

"*Engendrar* . . . It means . . ."

"I KNOW WHAT IT MEANS, SON," el viejito said, tapping la mesita with his long, skinny fingers. "BILINGUAL AND A SMART-ASS, HUH?"

"Disculpe, Don Abuelo Milton," I said. But I still wondered what his point was. "So, are you saying that it is okay to break the law if you think the government is wrong?"

El viejito was quiet for a few moments. He stroked his cottony beard as if realizing that maybe I was not as confused as I seemed by getting myself almost arrested. Then he said, "NEVER MIND ALL THAT FOR NOW, CARNALITO. WHEN YOU GET READY TO GO ON HOME, I'LL LEND YOU MY TROCA. BRING IT BACK WHEN YOU CAN. MEANWHILE, YOU KEEP YOURSELF OUT OF TROUBLE, YOU HEAR ME?"

Su Servidor sin Mérito

REGINA

Soon as it starts to warm up it's always something. Pero los insects are invincible.

Nobody knew about the Moth Destroyer. (Except Gabo, who didn't approve.) That's the name of my invention. With so many animal-rights people about, it wasn't like I thought I could go on the Home Shopping Network with my manual exterminating tool. It's a contraption I rigged one night when I was sure the moths were about to carry away my house and me with it. Although the Moth Destroyer is not patented, here is how it's made: It consists of three fly swatters arranged fanlike and wrapped tight with electrical tape to a paint roller stick.

I had tired myself out swinging fly swatters and rolled-up newspapers, using bug spray, and even going after them with a handheld vacuum. "It sucks 'em right up in midflight," I had said to my nephew one morning, all excited about my newest line of defense.

"That's cruel," el Gabito replied, who doesn't seem to be bothered by the moths or any of the other insects that mob the house.

"It's nothing bugs wouldn't do to us if they had the technology," I said, a little disappointed that he didn't have any interest in joining my crusade.

Above all, ants are my nemeses. Last summer they bit me up so bad in the garden I ended up driving myself to an emergency clinic in Canutillo, where half the time the doctor is out. This time the doctor was in. We don't have doctors in Cabuche. I don't like to think of the war the ants have declared on me, because they are winning. Eventually this will mean the end of my planting.

Next, I'll have the centipedes to worry about. These are not ordinary centipedes, neither, whatever that could mean. Flying ants, mice with bushy tails, low-flying bats, tarantulas, tiny lizards, and underground ranas that only come out after the rains. They quack. Don't even get me started on the arachnids. It's like Jurassic Park. A couple of weeks ago I woke up with a scorpion crawling around in my ear. I pulled it out without realizing what was stirring in there. I turned on the light. It was scrambling along my pillow, injured. I had broken off its tail. With all my screaming, Gabo came running. Before I was able to come down on the scorpion, my sobrino caught it in an empty coffee can. He slapped the lid on it and took it outside. I was pretty sure the scorpion would die anyway, with no tail to defend itself with, but I didn't say nothing to Gabo. My nephew is now calling his coffee can Salva Insectos. Or "Bug Catcher," in English, if he decides to patent it, he says. He keeps it next to his bed, ready for my next scream.

People have heard about the time of the butterflies—like in Manzanillo, México, when the monarchs fill the skies with their shimmering flutter. But around here what we have is the Season of the Moths. And they are not associated with rebirth, like the butterfly that comes out of its cocoon. Here moths mean death is around. That's when I go on moth patrol.

And during moth season this year was when I was caught in my boxers by none other than Miguel. At least he didn't find me pretending to sing karaoke like I was doing earlier that evening. But the humiliations were adding up. There'd been the dropped pie in the parking lot. Then there was the Fanta mustache that Sunday at el abuelo's that he never told me about. I discovered it when I got home and took a look in the mirror.

Now he saw my legs.

That evening, with my Gabo still away, I was standing on the back of the couch, in bare feet, toes gripping on for dear life. With my weapon in both hands, I was just about to aim for a moth—I'd never seen one so big. It was plastered on the ceiling fan like a wet maple leaf. Just then I heard a deep voice out of nowhere say, "She's armed and considered dangerous." Because it was pitch dark I couldn't see it was Miguel peering in through the window. But he could plainly see me. With Gabo being away, Miguel had come to check on things. I lost my balance and went flying forward with the giant moth swatter. Meanwhile, Miguel was outside being attacked. "Hey! Will you let me in already?" he called, running toward the door. "It's terrible out here!"

As soon as I got myself together (which wasn't too easy with the bruised shin I got against the coffee table), I went over and pulled him in quickly, slamming the door behind him. "I think you got a wasps' nest under the vigas," he said. "Something real big was buzzing around me out there. And it wasn't alone." It seemed hard to believe, but Miguel was more afraid of bugs than me. Sitting down on the arm of the couch, he put his hand to his heart to catch his breath. "I could use a Valium," he said. Where was I going to get Valium?

"I've got some aspirin," I offered. "I heard that's good for men to prevent heart attacks, after a certain age."

"Yeah, well, I'm not quite that age yet," he cracked. That was one wisecrack too many I had let slide. I was about to put that man in his place when I noticed he was staring at me. Not just at my face, neither. In all the commotion over our shared insect terror, I forgot that I was hardly dressed for company. Hardly dressed at all. As usual when alone, I was in boxers and a skimpy T-shirt. I ran to the bedroom to change.

It was too late to try to impress him with the new dress I had just bought at Sears. The only things I'd ever gotten there before were appliances. Not the big ones, neither. Just the handheld size. The big ones, like everything else, came from las segundas. I ended up putting on the jeans and blouse I'd been wearing earlier, when I cleaned the oven. My mother had always said that the older a woman got, the more she had to cover up. These covered me up pretty good. When I finally got the nerve to come back out, Miguel was still there. He was still looking, too. I almost made an about-face and went back in my bedroom. But then I said to myself, Steady, girl, you have company. Don't freak out.

MIGUEL

Finally the rains came. It was a relief, too. The days had gotten so bad I had to change my shirt two, even three times a day. I was teaching summer school and we don't have any air-conditioning in the classrooms. Then the rains came down like nobody's business, like it would soon be time to build an ark (as my ex put it). Then the sewage system on my street backed up for miles. There were no fishing boots tall enough to spare anyone. Not to mention it reeked to high heaven. Fire departments came out to help, volunteers, whoever could lend a hand to start the cleanup afterward. Some of the people in Anapra had to vacate and were taken to stay at the high school in Santa Teresa, where the Red Cross brought cots, dry clothes, and food.

Wastewater had backed up into all the houses. Sewage surfaced everywhere on the front walks, lawns . . . streets. Drinking water had to be brought in from El Paso. All the water was contaminated. Nobody could bathe, wash clothes, or anything else. (I went all the way to my abuelo Milton's just to shower.) The mayor brought in Porta Potties. For days and nights we had to go outside to the bathroom. Electricity was out. La Migra stopped and flashed infrared lights on people all the time. I swear, it looked like we were living under martial law. I sent my ex and kids to Califas to stay with her brother Fernie in Oxnard. Schools were closed, anyway. I stayed behind to deal with the sludge.

In our small desert city, flanked by the Texas border and the Mexican one, we're always having water problems. Water is a precious resource around here. It's a blessing from Father Sky. That's how you gotta look at it. And that's why I wear my jacket with the fringes all the time during our periodic droughts. The fringes are symbolic of the rain. I keep my Lakota pouch on me, too. I'm no medicine man. I just believe in paying homage to the old gods. I believe in respecting the land, respecting all the gifts of Ometeotl—Mother Earth and Father Sky, which were meant to be used by everybody. It don't really matter what your religion or spirituality—without water there'd be no life on the planet. The president, as a born-again, more than anybody, should be aware of water's basic association with salvation. Baptism takes place in the immersion of pure waters. Who'd want to take Christ into their lives by being dunked in an oil-slick river contaminated by chemicals?

First it was so dry, fires were sparking everywhere. Then the rains hit and got us all real bad. Up there in Cabuche, where esta Regina lives with her nephew, they were flooded. The road up to their place was washed out. Regina works during summer school, too, and she couldn't get down the mesa for three days. Our school stayed open because the rains hadn't affected it. The lousy thing about the school board is that it won't approve paying teachers' aides for days off. I keep telling Regina she should go to night school and start working toward a degree. Who knows? Maybe she's not cut out for it.

Then again, she's got a lot more going on than she gives herself credit for. One day she found me trying to start up my Mustang in the school parking lot. "Pop the hood," she said, like she worked at Pep Boys. She figured out so fast what was wrong I was barely out of the car, getting ready to tell her not to mess with it, when she said, "Start it up." And sure enough, it started right up. Impressive. More so, because she's like this "lady," you know?

Before my ex and the kids left for Califas, we decided to have dinner together at the "Big House." That's what I call the home, where I no longer live but still get to pay the bills. I ain't exactly a guest there, either. The only times I'm invited over is to cook, babysit, or do handyman work. During last football season, I suggested I'd go and watch the games on my wide-screen TV in the den with a few of the guys, like I always did, but needless to say, that didn't go over with Crucita. The TV was too big for my trailer, so that was that.

The electricity was back on, I had thrown out all the ruined carpeting, and except for the Porta Potti situation, the family was more or less comfortable. Now we'd have to deal with the mold. We were heating bottled water on the brick barbecue I had built with my father-in-law next door way back when. My ex-in-laws were still hanging in there. ("Don't worry, don't worry," they always say when I check up on them. Just like old electronics that outlast new models, the elders seem to have more durability than the young.)

Our street was lucky. Not just our street, but my own side of the street, especially. The trailer went unscathed by the storm. Some neighborhoods were inundated. One grocery store lost its foundation. That neighborhood got slammed with currents of mud, and produce and canned goods were floating down the street. The governor was asking Washington for emergency relief money. But when wasn't he?

While "family dinners" had been Crucita's idea since the separation, as usual it was left to me to put something together. My ex was in J-Town, either working on her new storefront church with the preacher or volunteering at the women's shelter there. We all knew she'd be late. "Make whatever you want, Mike," she told me when she called from her cell. "The kids aren't picky." Not the kids I knew.

I stopped by the Little Diner on the way home and picked up some chile colorado gorditas for everybody. Right away my son said the food was too spicy for him. He wouldn't even taste it. Xochitl announced she was on a diet. "Xochi, you're already a toothpick," I said to my teen.

"No, I'm not. I'm fat. Fat. Leave me alone." Híjole. We ended up making grilled-cheese sandwiches.

We were just about to sit down to our fabulous supper when the kids' mother walked in. "We need more sandbags around the house, in case it starts raining again," was the first thing Crucita said as she threw her keys on the counter and flung off her shoes, which hit the wall on the other side of the kitchen. We settled down around the island, where we usually ate, and my ex joined me in having the gorditas.

"Did you guys know that the border has had something like twenty times more water pumped out of it every year than can be replaced naturally?" I asked my children. Xochi's cell rang. She answered it but didn't answer me. Little Michael picked at the sandwich his mother had just cut off all the crust from. "Some of those people out there in J-Town don't have any access to clean water at all," I told them.

"Neither do we," Crucita said.

I'm not sure why, but half of what my ex-wife complains about makes me feel like it's my fault.

"I know," I said, ignoring the sarcasm. "Right here in the First World, if you can call New Mexico that, our own tap water is full of moyote," I said. Our pipeline flows underneath the dump. The storage tanks are situated inside the landfill and the water system is not exactly hermetically sealed. Inspectors "assure" us that horsehair worms aren't harmful if digested. "We're living in dire conditions, guys," I said. "Dire conditions require extreme measures."

"Here we go," Crucita said, jumping the gun as usual with me. "How many times do I have to tell you I am not leaving Sunland Park? I am not going to leave my parents. And I am not leaving my home." A big drop of water fell from the ceiling and splashed on her plate, followed by a slow drip. Everyone's roofs had sprung leaks. I stared at her.

"What?" she said.

"You what," I said.

Little Michael and Xochitl got up and left the room. Crucita folded her arms. Her tight body language implied that once again I'd managed to screw up by alienating our children. "What?" I said. "Our kids had to be tested at school for TB because it's on the rise again. The truck driver who just had lunch in a restaurant here is having breakfast in Utah mañana. Our crisis today in no-man's-land is tomorrow's national epidemic."

"Mike, do you ever stop lecturing?" Crucita said. Then without further ado she pushed back her chair and got up. "I promised this women's shelter in Juárez that I would try to raise some money for them. Their government funding was just cut off. I'm going to make some calls."

She left, and after a minute or so I got up and went to the living room. All our family pictures were still on the mantel. Crucita was sitting on the couch with the cordless phone on her lap and her phone book out. We stared at each other. She was wearing her hair differently, blond streaks going through her natural black hair. It came off incongruously becoming, like a lot about her. Crucita had always looked to me like a cross between a Tarahumara and Sally Fields. Lately she looked more like a sunburned Norma Rae than the perky Flying Nun.

We were all wiped out.

I sat down next to her. "Your daughter thinks she's fat," I said. "She weighs ninety-eight pounds soaking wet."

"She weighs one hundred and ten, like me," Crucita said.

"That's not fat."

Crucita shrugged her shoulders. Women and their weight—you could never win that argument, I thought, observing my own growing gut. She changed the subject. "Lots of horrible stuff goes on across the border and not just related to water shortage," she said.

"That preacher treating you all right?" I asked.

"I'd kick his hiney if he didn't. You know that," she said, almost smiling. "What about your friend up there at the school?"

I had told her about Regina's brother gone missing. I had tactfully left out my interest in the redhead, but women always sense these things. Before I could answer she asked, "Did you hear anything about her brother?"

I shook my head.

"Well, maybe I can ask around over there," she said, gesturing her head south, toward J-Town.

"You'd do that?" I asked, frankly surprised by the offer. We were not husband and wife anymore or even friends to go out of our way for each other.

Nodding, she let out a heavy sigh. That was my ex's way of reminding me how weary my presence made her. It was how she felt. She didn't have to justify it, she would have said, if asked. And had, plenty of times.

chapter

SIX

REGINA

LA BÚSQUEDA DE UN SUEÑO AMERICANO PUEDE SER TU PEOR PESADILLA.
Every time I go to the Grupo Beta office in Juárez and wait for la Señorita
Edwina to talk to me, I stare at that sign on the wall, like it is a snake getting ready to bite. "The search for the American Dream could be your
worst nightmare."

The purpose of Grupo Beta, a Mexican government agency, is to dis-
courage illegal immigration. They drive all around and hand leaflets that
warn of the dangers to immigrants trying to cross. La Señorita Edwina is
on the phone. She is combination office manager and agent. Short-
handed, she always says, "Maybe you want to volunteer?" This is my
third visit. After school, I waited in the long line to cross into México.
On the way back I'll wait in another long bumper-to-bumper line.

How I found out about Grupo Beta was from un trabajador near my
place. He was out picking cotton. I stopped while I was driving by. First
I honked. Honked, honked. Then I called to the men and women
hunched and sweating. Only one looked up at me. He finally walked
over to my truck. "Sí, señora?" he asked. Maybe he thought I was a pa-
trona myself and looking for gente to work for me. He took the opportunity of my interruption to remove the large straw hat he was wearing.
He wiped his brow, which was wrapped with a dirty kerchief. I wasn't
sure what I wanted to ask. It had something to do with finding out about
Rafa's whereabouts. The man seemed a little surprised that a woman who
looked like me, practically a gringa, would have un hermano in such a
situation. Then el trabajador recommended I go to Juárez and ask about
Rafa at the Grupo Beta office. "Maybe they found him," he said.

I reached into my truck and pulled out a bottle of water to give to him. He shook his head. "It's not my break time." Break time consisted of two ten-minute "breathers" out of a ten-hour day. As el trabajador went back to the field, I spotted a parked truck in the distance. Probably the supervisor, watching. I stared at the man as he returned to the endless rows of cotton. That had been me as a girl, I thought. Not a girl, but a robot, expected to have no feelings, no brain. That's why me and mi mamá got out of it. Getting legal status was easier said than done, naturally. We had to get our papers in order. That's all every immigrant in the world wants, to get her papers in order. To officially become a person. One day a machine will be invented to replace all the farm workers. Then what?

That bent-over, backbreaking, repetitive reaching down or reaching up was the reason I could not move my wrists some days. My wrists and most everything else. Being out in the glaring sol like that gave me melanoma. ("That's what happens when you go suntanning so much," the doctor told me.) Rafa couldn't have lasted much longer doing that work, neither. He was already starting to look like an old man. But my little brother had a goal. He was building a casita back home. "Almost done," he said every time I saw him.

"What has happened is that migrants are having to try more often to get across without being apprehended, and are using different routes to do so, which are more dangerous," la Señorita Edwina told me the first time I went by the office. Everyone had a theory about what could have happened to mi hermano. None ever sounded like it would have a good outcome. Her first hunch about Rafa's disappearance was that he might have changed his mind about the coyotes and gone in another direction.

"It is hard to come up with true figures," she said, "but we estimate maybe three thousand immigrants try to cross in a single day. It is impossible to track down so many. They show up all along la frontera packed in cattle trucks, water trucks, and the backs of pickups. The trucks drive up dirt roads and stop, and everyone jumps out and makes for the nearby border."

"No, señorita, you don't understand," I said, hoping to make clear who my brother was. He was no stranger to the routes. Rafa knew his way. He was of the Rarámuri, he liked to say, the people with the light feet. The only reason he needed a coyote was that was the law of the land now. If you wanted to cross, you had to pay *somebody*. Plain and simple. "My hermano was not naïve," I said. "He even spoke English. I am certain he fell victim to the coyotes he got mixed up with."

La Señorita Edwina was wearing a jacket that had PROTECCIÓN A MI-GRANTES stamped across the back. It came down to mid-thigh she was so short. "Well, then, señora," she said, looking up at me with that pitying face people make about such matters, "there really is nothing we can do but keep an eye out for him. Leave his datos and a photograph and if we hear anything we'll let you know." I'd come prepared with a stack of photocopies with Rafa's picure. In black marker I wrote a description: six-one, black hair, green eyes, a tattoo over his heart of a corazón with his and Ximena's initials. That proof of love had been his wedding gift to her. "Tattoos are for sailors and vulgar people," Mamá told them. It was after the fact. They didn't care. They were young and in love.

Grupo Beta was now also helping pass out fliers warning migrants about the Minuteman volunteers. They described them as "armed vigilantes" waiting across the border to hurt them. "They have guns," Edwina told me. "Why would they be carrying guns if they were not planning to use them?"

They didn't have these agents driving around the desert in their orange trucks when I was working the harvests. They supply water and bring people to aid stations. The Mexican government now even puts out a survival handbook. It advises migrants how to cross, with tips on avoiding apprehension by U.S. authorities. Those Grupo Beta agents are not supposed to send you onward but to coax you to go back home. When you try to come over with no papers and vanish, there won't be any dogs or search parties called out. You travel at your own risk. You are at the mercy of everything known to mankind and nature. There is the harsh weather and land, the river and desert. The night is and is not your friend. It provides coolness and darkness to allow you to move. But you can get lost, you can freeze, you can get robbed or kidnapped, you can drown in el río. You can fall into a ravine, get bitten by a snake, a tarantula, a bat, or something else. The brutal sun comes with day and anything can happen to you that happens at night but you can also dehydrate, burn, be more easily detected by patrols and thieves. Bandits could kill you as easily as rob you of not just your life's savings but that of your whole familia. Even of your village, in cases where communities have decided that getting one person out will help them all. If you are a pollo smuggled with others in an enclosed truck you could die of suffocation. Whatever happens to men, in my opinion, is worse for women.

The first time we crossed over I was on my period. I was thirteen. We made it to this side fine. Fine meaning alive. We had the help of Junior's grandfather. Despite my abuelo Metatron's firing him, Junior's family still had affection for us. When they drove out to the desert, to the designated meeting point and picked us up, my slacks were caked with dried blood. I wanted to die of embarrassment. I cried so much, Mamá kept saying, "Shut up already—don't be such an escandalosa." We were safe. That was all that mattered. Embarrassment is nothing when you're at the mercy of not just "your" coyote but all coyotes, all traffickers prowling out there for the victims of poverty and laws against nature. That's how I feel about it. From the beginning of time, the human being, just like all nature, has migrated to where it could survive. Trying to stop it means one thing only for the species: death.

Grupo Beta agents were sent out to help what could not be stopped. But like with everywhere else, there were corruption and abuses even within that agency, or so I heard. In Baja California and some other places Grupo Beta had been investigated for drug and human trafficking. La Señorita Edwina told me this when I started looking into what it could and could not do for me in terms of finding Rafa. Overall, she tries to convince me that their intentions are well-meaning.

PARA EL INSTITUTO NACIONAL DE MIGRACIÓN LO MAS IMPORTANTE ES BRINDAR AYUDA Y PROTECCIÓN, reads another slogan on a poster near the door that has caught my eye each time I leave with no news about Rafa. While Grupo Beto claims to be all about looking out for the welfare of would-be crossers, where would anyone begin protecting people they didn't even know existed?

6   6   6

Maybe it's the stress of Gabo's recent troubles, the steady three-digit temperatures before we got the chubascos, floods everywhere, or maybe my hot flashes, pero I'm dizzy all the time. "I'm just having a power surge," I say if anyone notices I'm sudando like I was in a steam bath. But in reality, it don't feel like it's a power surge but more like an outage.

Maybe it's my blood pressure. Mamá had high blood pressure. She also had diabetes, a weak heart, varicose veins, bursitis . . . what didn't she have? All her life Mamá had physical debilities. I remember when she was young my mother was anemic. She used to suffer from fainting spells. When we worked in los files, she fainted every day out in the middle of the field, picking pecans, chiles, tomatoes, apples, whatever. Berries. They were the worst. Imagine what all the thorns do to your fingers.

As I get older I keep thinking I'm going to be sick with everything, just like mi mamá. Instead, except for the discomforts, throwing the blankets off and putting them back on all night, and the fits I have over nothing that come with the Change, the doctor has told me, "Regina, don't worry. You're going to outlive us all."

I don't know if I want to outlive everyone I know. I was just telling that to la Tuerta Winnie while she lay at my feet underneath el portal. The heat of the day has begun to go down with the sun. Now the mosquitoes will be out in full force. The dog is not only half blind, but now she's got cancer. And every day our old heeler gets worse. I've been thinking about when she was just a little pup and Gabito was first learning to talk. I got her for the boy when he was only two years old, when Rafa and Ximena left him with me. That was my Christmas present to him. Gabo named her after his favorite bedtime story, *Winnie-the-Pooh*. They say don't give puppies to little kids; they don't know how to take care of them. The first thing Gabito did for the little dog was get her some water in a plastic bowl. It was one of my good Tupperware. He got it from the kitchen. He was trying to do something good so I didn't scold him. You should never scold a child or an animal when it don't know no better. Afterward, now that's different. You don't want them getting mañosos.

I could have the cancer cut out of la Winnie's thigh but the vet said it would cost nearly a thousand dollars. One day I drove the dog to a vet in Juárez. Doctors are cheaper on the other side. He wanted eight hundred dollars. That was still a lot.

I got la Winnie from one of my neighbors, an onion farmer. His dog had just had a litter of sixteen. Sixteen was too many for the mother and she ended up crushing some by accident. The farmer gave away the rest when they were ready. There's no more to tell about la Winnie. She's not Lassie. She don't rescue people out of fires. She has been a good watchdog. Even almost blind, she has gotten me up more than once when there were shots coming from the other side of my barbed-wire fence— where the true desert begins without end.

6 6 6

Gabo's in his room sleeping.

Last night, he was up sleepwalking again. Maybe it's not sleepwalking. I called Uriel. I keep inviting her down. Maybe one day she'll surprise me and show up. My old friend, with her Tarot cards and pendulums, over the phone said, "It's something else." She couldn't say exactly what, but something.

That's how me and her met, when she read my palms. Up near Cloud-croft, in Mescalero, to be exact, she had set up a table at the market. She read palms, the Tarot, whatever you wanted. She also sold smoked venison. It was good, too. The lines on my hands told her what I already knew. I'd never known money and never would. I'd had a true love but had my heart broken. I'd have three children. She never explained that one. "All I can tell you is what I see," she always says. I call Uriel when there's something I can't figure out no matter how I look at it. She keeps telling me that she "sees" Rafa alive. Who, what, where, why? "I'm a psychic, not a private eye," she says.

Ever since Gabo came back home he's been far away. Last night, I found my sobrino out under one of the big pine trees that surround the house. He was sitting on the ground, cross-legged, nearly naked, with a sábana wrapped around him. He looked like he was in a trance, like one of those yogis who meditate all the time. I don't know what got me out of bed, besides the fact that I had to go pee. On my way back to my room, I happened to notice something strange outside the window. By the tree, there was the whiteness of a bedsheet.

I opened the door. "Gabo?" I called out. It looked like it was him but I couldn't make sense of it. It was a full moon so it was easy to make him out. The whole ground was illuminated like there was a huge overhead lamp up in the sky. There was light on the creosote, on the ocote and yucca. A strange light. Light like dew on the leaves, like manna—the food of the angels. I tiptoed in my chanclas toward my even-stranger nephew, who was sitting so still with la Tuerta Winnie lying down next to him. When I got close enough, I thought he wasn't even breathing. It scared me.

He was breathing, as I discovered, but I had to put my ear to his smooth chest to hear his heart. It was beating so slow, I was afraid that any second it would stop. His whole cuerpito, tan delgadito, like no one ever bothered to feed him, as if I didn't make the best frijoles, the tastiest chile colorado, the finest gorditas, the most golden crust pies in all of Doña Ana County—just for him.

"Gabo?" I said, after a minute of staring into those blank eyes looking upward. Then I looked up, too. The sky was full of stars, all the galaxy, the Big Dipper, Little Dipper—what do I know about the stars? "Please, Diosito," I said out loud, "what should I do?"

La Tuerta, who has a hard time getting around now, managed to get up and lick my hand. I looked down again and Gabo was back. "Tía," he said softly, looking all surprised, "what are you doing out here?"

"Me?" I said. He had given me un susto, my heart beating fast enough for the both of us. "What are *you* doing out here, Gabo?" I asked him. And instead of hugging him and telling him how happy I was that he was all right, before he could say a word, I started yelling at him about everything that he had done to upset me lately.

"And can you explain to me why you still have that?" I said, pointing to that monstrosity of a truck that he'd been driving around. It belongs to el Abuelo Milton. Miguel told me at the school. "I can't believe my grandfather wouldn't even let me *look* at his troca and he let Gabo drive it home from El Paso. It's a classic, you know."

It may be a classic but it's still a monstrosity. "Make sure you take it back to him soon," I told Gabo.

"Don't worry, Tía," was all Gabo said, like always, as he pulled the sábana over his shoulders. I helped him stand up and we walked back to the house. Tuerta, too. She sleeps in Gabo's room now. Then they went to bed.

My sobrino hasn't been up since. It's already dusk.

It's *something,* all right.

While I cannot say why or how the thought has even occurred to me, I have the feeling that Gabo's spells have to do with his love for Christ. He calls it passion. I say obsession. But who can I ask? Padre Juan Bosco left us without so much as saying good-bye. He didn't bother to give one last farewell Mass or even put it in the Sunday bulletin. He just got up and left. We don't have a priest now at our church. Every Sunday a different one comes down from Las Cruces to take confessions and give Mass. Then he jumps in his vehicle and leaves.

I asked Herlinda Mora about Juan Bosco when I ran into her at el Shur Sav. I went one evening pretending I needed some baking powder for the tortillas in the morning. The real reason was that I had started checking up on Gabo, and I went to see if he was at work. I know he said the Arellano brothers are in jail, but they do belong to a gang. That means there are more of those hoodlums. The job of a mother (even a substitute one like me) never ends. Lately I keep reminding myself it's only until Rafa comes back for his son.

Herlinda's eyes were all red from so much llanto. They looked like she had busted the veins inside them from crying so much. Now she was starting to feel the shame she should have had from the start, I thought. Her parents barely in their graves, and she was already shacking up with the cura who had given their funeral misa. "He's gone," she cried out, hoping for consolation. When she didn't get it, she wiped her eyes. "He went to Rome," she said proudly, like he was some kind of emissary from the New World. Herlinda Mora never was a smart woman.

I guess Father Juan Bosco had to report to the big guys before they kicked him out—the equivalent of upper management. The new pope in training, I'm sure, don't have time to deal with one more malportado.

Management know-how is essential to running any kind of business. I am still considering signing up for night classes. The math teacher told me I have a knack for working numbers out quickly in my head. "Open up a pie shop, Miss Regina," she advised. Gabo gave me a better idea. "Start your own tiendita online, Tía. You know how to make quince-añera dresses, bake delicious pastries. You could cater . . . design every-thing, basically plan the whole event, if you wanted." That sounded like a lot of work for one person alone. That's why I need to learn about man-agement.

The doctor has another opinion about Gabo's sleepwalking. Of course, el médico didn't examine him. I can't afford to take my nephew in for something like that. Over the phone, the doctor in Juárez said Gabo was walking in his sleep because of all the stress he's under, possibly los-ing a second parent and all. If you ask me, that's not just stress, that's trauma. Even I know the difference.

MIGUEL

Before we recovered from the flooding, another serious problem came up. To my mind this one was motivated by unmitigated vigilantism at its racist best.

That's right. RA-CIST.

I don't have any problem calling things how I see them.

So when the Minutemen announced they were coming from Arizona to Sunland Park to set up a new chapter in our town, my neighbors and I had to have another urgent meeting. The Minutemen believe that the Border Patrol isn't doing its job. The organization claims to be just "concerned citizens." They wouldn't try to apprehend anybody they spotted crossing over illegally, just report them. But when you start taking the law into your hands, you best believe you are going to get lunatics in the bunch who'll do whatever they get into their heads.

"They're no better than the KKK!" Matilde shouted at the meeting. Matilde Benavides was the woman who said she would lead the protest. Matilde worked in maintenance over at the casino.

"No, what they are are borderland terrorists," another neighbor said.

"Renegades," someone in the back called out.

"Does that mean *renegados*?" Don Carlitos, the man who owns the land where my trailer sits, leaned over and asked me.

Vigilantes, I say. Unmitigated vigilantism.

But then again, that would be just this veteran radical's opinion. Something I do believe I have every right as an American citizen to express.

The Migra not doing its job? Bull crap. Those that live around here more than anyone else in the country, I think, are aware of the 24/7 vigilance we live under. Hey, it is our tax dollars, too, that go to maintaining "borderland security." And then, we are also the ones who get stopped just for being out and about.

The other morning my abuelo Milton was walking home from the panadería when some Migra asked him for his papers. What was an old man going to take from this country, even if he was illegal? Not Social Security. Not Medicare. Prescriptions are a lot cheaper in México. Gringos cross over all the time to get their medication at pharmacies there.

La frontera is a Berlin Wall great divide. The Border Patrol not only has million-dollar barriers with stadium lighting; they have motion sensors, helicopter sweeps and night-vision goggles. They are better equipped for combat than the boys at war.

Hell yes, I've given it a lot of thought.

One time, years back, my ex and I took the kids up to Vancouver. Crossing back from Canada was like being at a national park. Mi'ja needed to use the restroom and, lo and behold! There were not only nice, clean public restrooms right there; you could get out of your car—while in line waiting to cross over—and stroll over to use them. People were getting out to take pictures on the lawn by public sculptures.

What passes for public art at the Santa Fe bridge here is the pink installation—eight feet tall, with ninety nails hammered in halfway. They represent all the women who'd been killed by the time the memorial went up. Most were unsolved murders. Get out of your car crossing from J-Town and you not only get accosted by a slew of merchants selling everything from cartons of cigarettes to Chiclets to getting your windshield wiped with dirty rags, but the customs officers will bring out the dogs and detain your ass.

I went out with my neighbors to march the day the Minutemen held their first meeting in our fair hamlet. Some thought we should have given ourselves a slick propaganda name like the Minutemen had, just to make a point of how we felt our hermanos and hermanas on the other side had every right to be here. Someone came up with the Pilgrims of Aztlán. I suggested the People of Corn because it was our people who cultivated maize on these lands. I should have seen the jokes coming. Immediately I got shot down by everybody, saying we'd just be considered "corny."

Sometimes I think we *are* corny—still thinking we could get some redress for all the bullshit we've been subjected to on our ancestors' lands.

Fast-forward five hundred years and we now believe we can get unions back.

The TV news people came out. But there were only about three dozen of us protesters. The same people I've been working with for fifteen years. Where were all those who complained all the time when it counted? I've gotten tired of asking.

The Minutemen held their own press conference. They talked about how they were just "helping out the Department of Homeland Security—to be its eyes and ears in spotting and reporting crossings." They were also of the conviction that south-of-the-border immigrants are taking away jobs from "true Americans."

"Do *they* wanna be chicken pluckers or peel chiles all day long and work for below minimum wage and with no benefits? Go for it," I called to my fellow protesters over a bullhorn with a chorus of, "Minutemen, go home," behind me.

The truth is, a lot of employers don't want immigration laws to change. Like one grower put it, "Illegals kick butt out on the fields." But I have another way of looking at it. If the country made it easier for professional immigrants to come in, the competition would possibly drive professional salaries *down*. Thereby equalizing the distribution of wealth. Anyway, it's not about people sneaking in but jobs being snuck out. NAFTA, CAFTA, the new treaty with the Pacific rim, all the maquilas along the U.S.-Mexican border and Southeast Asia—companies went there and keep going there to take advantage of the cheap labor to be found abroad. Hell, just take the all-American great auto production, as a case in point; it was one of the first hard-hit.

"DON'T YOU GOT NOTHIN' BETTER TO DO THAN BE OUT THERE LIKE A MITOTERO?" el Abuelo Milton told me on the phone that night after he caught the weak turnout on the ten o'clock news. "WHY DON'T YOU SPEND YOUR FREE TIME DOIN' SOMETHIN' USEFUL, LIKE SHOWIN' YOUR SON HOW TO PLAY BASEBALL INSTEAD OF WASTIN' MONEY ON ESOS VIOLIN LESSONS?"

"Abuelo," I replied, finding I had to remind my ever-so-mucho-macho grandpa once again, "Little Michael's asthma won't let him play any kind of sports. I know it's related to the environment here."

"AWW," Abuelo said, "YOU'RE PARANOID. YOU THINK EVERYTHIN' IS POISONED. THE WATER, THE LAND, EVEN THE AIR. WHY DON'T YOU GET YOURSELF ONE OF THOSE OXYGEN MASKS, IF YOU'RE SO DARN WORRIED?"

"Everything *is* contaminated," I said. "Now, is that all?"

"NO, MUCHACHO, I'M CALLIN' ABOUT WHAT ELSE I SAW ON THE NEWS TONIGHT—THOSE TEN MUERTOS THEY FOUND OUT ON EL DESIERTO. . . . DID YOU SEE THAT STORY?"

Of course I had seen the news. I was the one who called my abuelo Milton to put on the TV that night.

"BUENO," he said. "I TELEPHONED THE STATION. THEY SAID THEY'RE HÓLDIN' THE BODIES IN THE CITY MORGUE IN JUÁREZ. THE BODIES ARE MORE OR LESS DECOMPOSED FROM BEIN' OUT THERE FOR A WHILE. BUT ANYONE INTERESTED CAN GO AND IDENTIFY 'EM."

"Abuelo, I hope you are not thinking what I think you're thinking."

"WHY NOT? AIN'T IT POSSIBLE THAT ONE OF THOSE PEOPLE COULD BE LA REGINA'S HERMANO? MAYBE THOSE COYOTES NEVER HAD 'IM TO BEGIN WITH . . . OR MAYBE HE RAN AWAY FROM 'EM WHEN THEY STARTED ASKIN' FOR MORE MONEY? OR—"

"Maybe he went back to México and was trying to cross again. . . ." I started contemplating the possibilities myself. After all, *something* happened to Regina's brother. He didn't just fall off the planet. What really got me from what she said was that this guy had been a guerrillero, un luchador, an ass-kicker, man. You can't bring a guy like that down easy. What the chingados happened to him?

"I THINK IT'S WORTH GOIN' TO JUÁREZ TO CHECK OUT."

"I don't know, Abuelo," I said, trying not to imagine the condition of the bodies, flesh and eyes picked off by buzzards. "I'd hate to put Regina through that . . ."

"WELL, SON." He paused and then asked, "WHAT WOULD BE WORSE? KNOWIN' OR NOT KNOWIN'?"

EL ABUELO MILTON

El Chuco is where I've spent my life, El Paso del Norte. Like they say, there's no place like home. As for my barrio, el Chihuahuita, it's older than me. It came together with the building of the Santa Fe Railroad back in 1881. Back in them days things were bustling around here, the railway, mines, copper mill smelters—where my jefito worked until he died with a pair of charcoal lungs.

Bueno. Nowdays what you can see from downtown besides los Franklins and la Puente is Fort Bliss, the country's largest army training base. Yes, sir. It's right here. That's why we were all so worried after 9/11. We figured we could be next. In el centro itself, besides the run-down businesses, are the old railroads. There ain't much else. You might say this town grew out of the Santa Fe Puente, where you cross back and forth to el Other Side. Not like a corn on your toe. N'hombre. It's a big city. It ain't nothing like the town it was when I was growing up. Now you got your convention center, the Camino Real hotel all renovated, even an art muscum. There are los mansions in Coronado Estates (I hear los narcos own some). But what you got mostly, near my barrio and the Puente, is a whole lot of gente.

Early in the morning, the day laborers crossing over here look like lines of ants moving steadily over the bridge. At the end of the day, same thing, only going in reverse. I can't tell you how many come over every day. Maybe a hundred thousand. Sounds like a lot. Looks like a lot. But crossing has never been easy.

Let me clarify—crossing over *from* México has never been easy.

The unruly Río Grande, where tanta gente used to wade through when the river was low, back when I was growing up, always caused problems between the two countries because it changed courses. So, you could see how it could get tricky. Sometimes it was on the U.S. side, sometimes in México. Then it was decided by the powers that be on both sides to run it through a concrete channel. They built a nice park, the Chamizal, that sits on both countries to commemorate the settling of that dispute. That was back in los sixties, I believe around when Kennedy was still alive—el best presidente the Mexican people ever had.

Los Franklins stand guard over history—man's and nature's. That's what they do. But there ain't nothing inviting about them. You wonder how people went over them back in the pioneer days. On the other hand, looking down from up there—the view of three states and two nations all lit up—is dazzling at night. I remember it from the times I used to take Lola up there, back when we were going out.

Bueno. You can cross by underground, too.

Tunnel smuggling has always been big business, not just around here but everywhere. I saw my share of tunnels when I fought in la guerra. When I was coming up as a boy—un chamaquillo no más, during Prohibition, running around working for the ladies of the night, bootleggers built underground tunnels to get back and forth. Along la frontera, people are still digging tunnels. Over in Nogales, a man was busted for having built one going into Arizona. It was nearly a foolproof plan, too. He had a cement factory on one side and his home on the other. He used the materials from the cement factory to line his tunnel. Bien trucho, hombre. He'd bring workers back and forth all the time. Eventually the authorities caught on.

Legend has it that in the Wild West days, Wyatt Earp come by here before he went to Tombstone and found it too wild for him. All kinds of desperadoes passed through El Chuco looking for refuge. The gunslinger John Wesley Hardin is buried over in the Chinese graveyard. Los chinos were here building railroads back in them days.

It's still pretty wild around here. Maybe no more than other places in the world. Just yesterday, a man got shot in broad daylight. He worked for a car dealership. He was shot by a woman. Her brother was driving the getaway car. And they got away, too. You gonna tell me drugs weren't behind that? Either that or the guy sold a lemon to the wrong people.

I seen a lot during all my years of owning a cantina. Las viejas can be just as vicious as any man. N'hombre. You gotta watch las güisas, también. Once a woman slit her man's throat, just like that, with a kitchen knife. Right there in front of me. Chingaos, hombre. That took a lot of nerve. And a lot of forearm strength, too, let me tell you, 'cause accomplishing that as neatly as she did wasn't easy. The vato was sitting at the bar with una ruca he picked up, having themselves a good ol' time, when in comes his jaina. Three strides from the door, count them, to where the man was sitting on a stool, cooin' with la ruca. The wife spins him around y que zúmbale su madre! Not even a word. Blood spilling out all over the place. The ruca went pale like she expected to be next. She couldn't even move. We all froze. I'd even forgotten about my gun behind the bar. We only stood there, wondering what next from that jaina loca who'd walked in just like that.

Then, without so much as uttering a word, the wife made an about-face and walked right back out. She took the knife with her so there was no evidence. And there weren't no witnesses, so there wasn't no crime, neither. Then a couple of los muchachos carried the vato out to the alley. We didn't want no trouble. The police could close down my establishment. I couldn't have that.

Things like that happened in my line of business.

Running a cantina for so many years, I could recognize a backstabber on sight. Yes, sir. I've known backstabbers and I've known front-stabbers. In my business you had to know how to protect yourself. One particular year during the fifties, back when Eisenhower was president, my establishment was held up so many times I got this close to shutting it down myself.

Then the word got around that I had a gun behind the bar—a very big gun—and that I was prepared to use it. And los buenos pa' nada that were coming around stopped bothering me. I'd take out my Colt .45 without hesitation. I'd won it in a card game from un hombre de Galveston. Hijo. What a good night that was. I sent that vato walking back home barefoot.

I put the muzzle right between the eyes of the last mensote that tried to rob me while I tended bar. I didn't always tend bar after the first few years. I had found a real good bartender, Ernest Chávez. El Ernie worked for me for years, until he died, in fact. Bueno. The last pachuco who tried to rob me found me behind the bar that night. I put that gun right up between his eyes and said, "I'm gonna let you live for one reason and one reason only, cabrón. That's so's you can go and tell the rest of the ratas out there that I mean to blow out the brains of the next one that comes in trying to rob my till. And if I ever see you on the street, you better run, güey," I said. "Now get." Then el Ernie and a couple of the muchachos escorted him out through the back.

No one bothered me after that. Besides, a lil while later, Lola's nephew el Alonsito became a chota. When he was a lil vato he used to come into my place with his shoeshine box. He made a lot of tips there. El Al—all grown up—made sure people didn't mess with my establishment.

Ernie died way back when Nixon was president. He got a bone caught in his throat eating a bowl of cocido. All my compadres are dead. Lola's gone. My kids are gone—not dead, gracias a Dios, just gone from El Chuco.

So all this is to say, being around as long as I have, I figured que esa Tiny Tears, acting like una mosquita muerta, could be big trouble. She had her eye on el Gabo, too. You could tell that right away at the barbecue. He's a handsome kid. Girls that age, all they got on their minds are boys. La Diputada Sofia ran a check on la ruquita for me. Sure enough. She already had a record. Theft. Sofia said the girl had once been picked up in relation to a homicide, too. A homicide. Imagínate, hombre. But they let her go since no one could prove nothing. Bad-ass little girl.

⚬   ⚬   ⚬

These days you can just call me un walking fool.

Me and Oso, both. He's just about walked off the pads of his patas and me, the soles of my old botas.

Oso's my new dog. I got him from the pound. Mikey took me there one day. I said, "I need a new pair of eyes." Something like twenty-six thousand dogs are put down here every year. Sounds ridiculous. We figured we'd save one. That's how we got Oso. When we first brought him home you could count his ribs. You could tell he'd been mistreated. Now he looks like a fat sheep. Oso's a mixed long-hair shepherd and Lab and he sees real good. He leads me everywhere. I don't know how old he is, but he's a real good dog. At night he lays across the front door, every five minutes jumping up barking. He sounds ferocious. woof, woof. He don't let people sleep. I say, "Oso, if there ain't nobody there, shut the hell up, will you?" Then Oso comes over for a pat on the head since he thinks I've just thanked him for being trucho.

Regina gave me a picture of her brother. With the picture in hand, I go over to Paisano to ask if any of the laborers recognize him. Pero nel. No luck. Young and old men alike shake their tired heads. It's six in the morning and they already looked tired out.

What's a viejo supposed to do with the time he's got left, anyway? Besides going down to the bus station near the Santa Fe Puente and sitting around talking to whoever was waiting to go somewhere, I hardly had nothing to fill up my time. Maybe I'd go get a pan dulce in the morning to have with my café. That was about it for my whole day.

So we go walking around downtown, over by the Stanton bridge, up and down Paisano and down and up Oregon. We go by the Tiradero as the merchants are setting up their puestos and all los hombres are out there already. That flea market's open all year long. Across the street you got the Kentucky Fried Chicken–Taco Bell combo in one lil building—men are waiting there. They're waiting in the McDonald's and Church's Chicken parking lots, too. Across from my old parish, El Sagrado Corazón, where Lola used to make me go to Mass, you got them waiting. "Maestro," they call out, "take me. I'll work hard for you. See?" They flex a muscle or try to. They flash a smile at us.

Me and Oso make our way down to all the bus stations with Rafa's picture that's falling apart from so much passing around. The one closest to my house is on Santa Fe and Overland. Then over to Los Angeles Limousines. I understand that some women take that one all the way to L.A. to get clothes deals at the garment district there. Then they come right back on that bus line and take the clothes to Juárez to sell. I go to the Plaza de los Lagartijos where all the women housekeepers wait to be picked up by patrones. The city used to keep live alligators in the fountain but the animals kept getting killed.

Once I even asked a couple of Migra parked on the street. "Let me see your I.D., sir," one tonto said instead of answering me about the photograph I was trying to show him. N'hombre. La perrera anda brava. They'll take anybody in.

Another time, me and Oso asked some pachucos standing around waiting—not for work but to make dope deals. I knew who they were—los Mexíka Tres Mil. Pretty bad pachucos, but they still ain't the worse. The Mexíka Tres Mil or the MTM, like they call themselves, come straight out of federal prisons. They operate inside the prisons, too. Maybe they're tied to the big narcos. I ain't claiming to know nothing. Just like my neighbors never hear nothing, I walk around but I don't see nothing.

Well, that's actually the truth.

The MTM ain't no lil ganga, neither. They're spread all the way down to Centroamérica. Matones mostly.

I ain't afraid of them, though.

One day I went right up to a couple of MTMs, me and Oso, and showed them the picture. "No, viejito," one of the vatos said, "we ain't seen your son. But we'll keep an eye out for him, how's that?" No one said he was my son. But hearing that, even all friendly, almost sounded like a threat. "How about your dog? You wanna sell him?" one MTM called out as me and Oso walked away. I didn't even turn around. Like I'm gonna put Oso to his death in the dogfight racket. Who knows. Maybe he'd win. But not eventually.

All up and down now there are los day laborers who cross over every morning, the skilled and unskilled, good workers and not-so-good ones. The borracho types hiding cuartos in paper bags underneath the muebles they're leaning against. You gotta look behind the tires to check for a hidden half-pint to make sure you don't pick up un tipo who'll be pie-eyed by noon.

It almost looks like something outta the Depression era, so many men needing work. But back then, they could've waited all darn day and no one would've come for them. Then again, back then they weren't allowed to cross over precisely 'cause there was no work. Now, during the chile harvest season, La Migra turns a blind eye at all the men that come to be picked up.

Sometimes, en los evenings, we go out walking again. We got a purpose now. Me and Oso make our rounds to the cantinas and todos los diners with our picture. Whenever I go up to people, at first they think I'm looking for a handout, 'cause of Oso and my cane. Then I say, "¿Qué creen? I'm looking for a friend, un amigo who's disappeared on his familia." Everybody seems to get that right away. The borderlands have become like the Bermuda Triangle. Sooner or later everyone knows someone who's dropped outta sight.

One time I took the picture to la Diputada Sofia. I won't say we've become old pals, exactly. I'm not about to ask her to tea. I can't say I haven't thought about it. But I think she took a liking to Gabo that one time she processed him. More precisely, I think she saw what I saw. I asked her if she noticed anything unusual about the boy. I was afraid that maybe I was seeing things like that 'cause my time was coming. I came right out and asked her, "Do you see a gold ring over the muchacho's head?" At worse, la Diputada Sofia might think I was developing a case of Alzheimer's.

"Do I believe that Gabriel is special, in other words?" she asked. "Of course. Don't you?" Then she laughed.

She does have a pretty laugh.

Sofia was happy to meet Oso, who is not angelic by any means but is still turning out to be a good dog. Everybody at the holding tank was happy to meet him since Oso's pretty friendly when he wants to be. "If you ever decide you don't want him anymore," one chota said, "we can always use a dog like this around here."

Like I was ever gonna let Oso work for la chota.

Sofia scanned the photo. "I'll pass copies out to my deputies to ask around." She knew the man I was looking for was a mojado. Not like we don't have them all around us. All I wanted was some news.

"Maybe he found himself a wife," one laborer said once. I imagined him with a big old grin. In the day people are all blurry. Sometimes I can see the color of the shirt, more or less, or sometimes the hair or los ojos stand out to me, but mostly they're casi mirages.

"Yeah, by getting married he could get his papers fixed and stay here," another chimed right in.

I don't know why that set me off. Maybe because getting to know la Regina and her sobrino, who's all but grown wings on him, I figured the missing man had to be un hombre noble. He wouldn't have abandoned his family like that. I said, "This was a man with a family. He ain't like you so-and-sos."

"WHO ARE YOU CALLING A SONSO?" the first man yelled. He thought I'd called him a dummy. He also thought I was yelling at him, so he yelled right back.

Oso can sense things right away, things that are there and that are not there, so he started baring his teeth and the men backed off.

I wasn't afraid of them, though. Even if I couldn't see them.

chapter

SEVEN

REGINA

Except for Uriel, I never had any friends. Mamá always said we didn't have time for them. Good times were for los lazyflojos who ended up on welfare and collecting government food stamps. No one we ever knew did that. Mejicanos needed to work, Mamá always said. At home, we had to keep the house clean. She didn't even believe in sitting down just to watch TV. We crocheted or mended while we kept up with a telenovela.

Despite all the work and running all over the place, my mother got fat. Well, not really fat, but fat enough that we believed it was the cause of her diabetes. All she could fit in for a while were huge housedresses, like campanas. They used to call them tent dresses. The diabetes got worse even after Mamá went on a diet. She lost all the weight. Mi mamá started dressing in culottes and matching tops, toda color-coordinated— chanclas, plastic earrings, and vinyl tote bags, even sunglasses if she could find them. Everything bright pink, orange, or lime green and with rhinestones, even better. She was real happy for a while.

Then the doctor told us they were going to have to amputate one of her legs. I've been thinking about that lately. About losing a part of yourself. But even after they cut off your leg you can still talk to people. You can tell them how you feel about them. You can live without half a leg. You can go on to live a pretty decent life, too. At least as decent as it ever was.

My feet and ankles swell up something fierce nowadays. Maybe I'll end up in a wheelchair like my mother. "Probably from so much work and never any dancing," Uriel said when I told her how Gabo had soaked and rubbed my feet. That gesture made me cry. I cried so much after he left for work, if you had sat me on the roof, my tears would have made another hole in it.

With Gabo's help, Miguel fixed the one causing seepage over my bedroom. My nephew was right. I kept myself too isolated. It was kind of awkward the first time Miguel showed up just to keep me company. One evening he was at my door with no reason or excuse. As usual, the mosquitoes were sucking on the very air. Right away I insisted he come in the house. "You want some tea?" I asked. "I just made up a jarra and put it in the fridge." He shook his head. "How 'bout some pie?" He shook his head and even shuffled his feet a bit.

"You wanna just talk?" I asked.

"Okay," he said. So that's what we did. We sat on my plaid patched couch and talked our heads off. Not just him but me, too, for a change. I didn't even care that he caught me with the cloth I dry the dishes with over my shoulder. He already knows I'm not elegant. Not being elegant don't mean you don't have class.

We were talking and even laughing. Then Miguel noticed the guitar I had leaning against the wall. I got it as a trade some years back from my vecinos. I gave the neighbor's two kids free haircuts. (I learned the haircut business from Mamá.) One day the father gave me the guitar. I can play a couple of chords. That's about it.

Miguel gestured as if to ask if it was okay for him to try it out. It turned out he plays like he could teach it. He played some old revolutionary songs like "La Adelita," "La Valentina," and even "Allá en el Rancho Grande." Then he started a tune I sort of remembered from my parents' time. It was pretty. When I hummed along, Miguel asked, "Do you know what this song is called?" No, I said. " 'Quizás, Quizás, Quizás,' " he said, looking at the guitar as he strummed, instead of at me. Maybe, Maybe, Maybe.

Then there was the most recent occasion. He brought up that pingo of a grandfather to talk about how the old man had taken my nephew sin papeles across the border. They went to look for his dad at the city morgue.

Gabo, with his new mustache, looks more like Rafa each day. He's stubborn like him, too. When we saw the news about the bodies found in the desert, there was no doubt in my mind that if Gabo could find a way, he'd go to Juárez to see if one of those muertos was his father. Then the phone rang. "I THINK WE SHOULD GO SEE FOR OURSELVES," el Abuelo Milton said. A couple of days later it was all set.

El Viejo has lived by the Santa Fe Puente all his life, so naturally he knows a few customs officers, sons and grandkids of people who drank in his cantina. When you're driving across, officers don't ask every single person for an I.D. It's the luck of the draw. You never know if you'll be the one who gets pulled over. People owe el Abuelo Milton. He did favors and made loans back when he had a business and money to lend. So el Abuelo Milton must've got someone to let Gabo cross back into the U.S. with no I.D. That's how I figure it, anyway. No one asked my permission and no one asked my opinion.

That evening I fixed us sopes while el abuelo and my nephew told me and Miguel about their adventure to the city morgue. Gabo and el abuelo both looked wrung dry from heat exhaustion and emotion. Somehow it had been determined by the authorities that the group of muertos had started out in Zacatecas. It didn't seem likely that Rafa would have been among them. Gabo and the grandfather had to see for themselves. They were sent all over the place. When they finally did find the morgue, they said only two of the cuerpos were identifiable. If you could call that what they described.

We ate in my little living room that's still bigger than my kitchen. My sobrino, standing up, pecked on a sope. Afterward, he let himself flop down on the couch. "There was a muchacho crying over his mother's body. He was about my age," Gabo said, staring down at his dirty feet. He was wearing huaraches, the kind made from old tires. Terrific. He crosses over knowing that he might not be able to get back in and he goes shopping . . . ? (He bought me three crepe-paper flowers on thick wire stems.) Then Gabo gave away his good shoes to someone on the street there. I'm not buying him no more shoes. That's all I gotta say.

"EL MUCHACHO SAID HE AND HIS MAMÁ LOST THEIR GUIDE." El abuelo picked up the story. "THEN THEY GOT SEPARATED FROM EACH OTHER. DAYS LATER, HE WENT BACK WITH HIS RELATIVES TRYIN' TO FIND HER BUT COULDN'T."

"He had his arm all wrapped up," Gabo said. "He got it messed up while he was out there, lost, alone."

"CAT'S CLAW BUSH," the old man explained. "HE GOT A BAD GASH THAT ENDED UP GETTIN' INFECTED."

"He could lose his arm," Gabo said.

"YEAH, THAT'S WHAT THEY SAID," el abuelo said. "ANYWAY, WHEN THE BODIES WERE FOUND, THERE WAS NOTHIN' LEFT OF HIS MOTHER . . . JUST PUROS HUESOS."

I tried to imagine what it was like for a boy to find the skeleton of his mother and the fact was that I couldn't. There were tears rolling down Gabo's cheeks, big globules. I was thinking about that word, *globules,* big, round bubbles, when Miguel asked, "Then how did he identify his mother? How did the boy know it was her?" He pulled out a wrinkled hankie from his back pocket. He patted his forehead. Then he dabbed his eyes.

"Sí . . ." I said, rubbing the top of my ear. I do that when I get anxious. I was having an outage.

"Was it by her teeth work or . . . ?" Miguel said.

"No," Gabo said, jaw clenched, holding everything back. "She had three fingers with flesh left. Each finger had one of her rings. One of them with the image of the Virgin of Guadalupe engraved on it."

"AY, JUST THINKIN' ABOUT IT ALL"—the old man gave a loud sigh, pretending not to notice all the carrying on around him—"IT SURE IS ENOUGH TO MAKE ANY MAN WEEP."

EL ABUELO MILTON

Last week el governor de Nuevo México declared a state of emergency. We didn't know nothing about it 'til me and el Mikey got stopped by a roadblock.

It was the entire police department of Cabuche—all twelve of them.

The state of emergency was supposedly related to the crossing of mojados and drug dealings being both out of control. But I think the governor figured it would be a good way to get some real federal funding. He asked for something like a million dollars to increase border security. El sheriff y los deputies were stopping every vehicle going down Main Street quesque checking for sobriety. It was a Friday night and no doubt about it, Regina's town on weekends had a line at the package liquors drive-through como you wouldn't believe. N'hombre. Just the sight of all them cars lined up for beer made me miss my cantina. Like I always say, people like to drink and it ain't my fault if they do.

They also like to gamble. That's why when Miguel told me that Cabuche may end up with a casino in the not-too-far-off future, I figured the town was ripe for it. It may sound weird, but gambling and people with no money go together, just like drinking and having all kinds of problems do.

Me and my grandson had just come down the mesa from Regina's ranchería. That was the day when I had somehow pulled off slipping Gabo back into the U.S. I don't mind admitting it was proving to be one of the longest days of my life. And it was not over yet.

Well, at least in more recent memory it was the longest. Back when I fought in el army I had some pretty long days, too. None as long as the time when my jefita left me. She was gone for a month. She took the children and went to her sister's over in Amarillo. "I had enough," was all she said every time I called over there on the telephone. She was referring to the "viejas." Rumors, no más, I'd tell her. But she left me anyway. I bought her a new Buick and told her I would teach her how to drive it if she promised to come back. She kept her promise and I kept mine. I didn't count on her "surprise visits" at my establishment once she could get around on her own.

After a while a man gets tired of going from flower to flower like some greedy bee. Lola was my true love. Once my children were big enough to come to the bar to drop off my supper or give me a message from home, I started behaving myself. No use giving your children the wrong idea about what you know is not correct. It'll only come back to bite you in the trasero.

That day, when I decided to take my adopted grandson, like I call him now, to the other side to check out the bodies at the city morgue, we had a heck of a time. It started out with my compadre's daughter, my goddaughter, who is an officer at the Puente. At the last minute she called to say she was sick and wasn't going to work. We had arranged for her to be on the lookout for us at the crossing to help get Gabo back in with no problems.

Then, mi ahijada called me again. She said for a hundred dollars one of her compañeros would look out for me. Bueno, a hundred dollars is a good chunk out of a man's monthly pension, but I had already promised Gabo. He was even taking off from school, which to that boy was almost a sin.

Everything that has to do with the realities of life is a sin to that boy. "Having too much of a conscience is gonna make your head explode someday," I've told him.

Me and el muchacho made it to Juárez that morning. Then, hijo. How many times did we get lost trying to find that bendito city morgue? People sent us all over the darn place. Pa' 'qui y pa' ya. We just went in circles and kept ending up at the mercado.

I couldn't see nothing anyway—mi carnalito was leading me around.

Then, at el mercado, Gabo decided to get himself some huaraches. He put them on and left his good zapatos with the first pobre vato he ran across. They say everything fits a beggar. Anyway, right after that we had a stroke of luck. We met up with a traffic chota who finally gave us the right directions.

That day at the morgue, híjole, los muertos were out in the open like gruesome wares at a mercado—all waiting for someone to come and give them names. In some cases even faces. You can't put that scene in your head without asking for nightmares. I only hope to God I don't end like that. And it could happen to anybody. Cañones. Not just to los mojados perdidos. There were not only the skeletons we went to check out but all kinds of muertos, shot-up men, lil children, and the bodies of unidenti- fied females. Gabo was describing everything to me. "They're not really blue or wax-looking, Abuelo Milton, but like something that was never even human." I was smelling and touching por donde quiera since I couldn't really see nothing. It was like we were in a house of horrors. I'd seen plenty of dead during the war so I knew what Gabo was talking about. I reached out. Tiesos, all right, so stiff if you raised an arm it would probably have broken off at the joint. The coroner or whoever was in charge there kept saying, "Don't touch. Por favor."

"How else am I supposed to identify anyone?" I asked.

Up at Regina's, we had all gotten tearful thinking about the skeleton of the mother with three fingers left. I was still shaken up from being at the morgue. I took out my flask with Jack Daniel's to cool me off on that hot night (since Lola passed I do have a traguito now and then), when sud- denly me and el Mikey both spotted the darn mess up ahead. A check- point had been set up right on Main Street. My nieto, driving that conspicuous souped-up Mustang like he was Mario Andretti, down- shifted quick. We automatically fell into the stalled line of muebles y tro- cas. Seeing all the chotas ahead, I took a fast swig and tucked the flask in the inside pocket of my chamarra. The deputies—six on one side of the road and six on the other—descended upon each vehicle as it pulled up. They had set themselves up right on the corner by the package liquors store.

"Oh, man, they're doing a license check," el Mikey said. Los deputa- dos were waving mag lights, radioing in I.D.'s, and looking into people's trunks and backseats. They even had a bus—testing for sobriety or for detaining suspects, no sé.

Before I realized it, my grandson had put his ranfla in neutral and was climbing over the stick shift with those long legs of his to the passenger side, where I was sitting. "Ándale, Abuelo," el Mikey said. "I don't got my license. Get in the driver's seat before they see us." Even though that news came almost as a shock, my nieto being a teacher and all, what choice did I have but to hop over? He was about to squash me. Everything happened so fast that I was in the driver's seat before I knew it. Just as I got behind the wheel, like an eighty-one-year-old geezer like me driving a red sports car was not about to attract any suspicion, a deputy was sticking his ugly bigotes in the rolled-down window. "How much have you gentlemen had to drink tonight?" He shined a flashlight in the car. I was afraid to open my mouth, which surely smelled of whiskey. I just stared at the deputy. His face was about an inch from mine. "None, sir." Mikey smiled and, putting on the charm, got out his registration and insurance papers from the glove box. El deputy had asked for them and for my license. No sooner did we hand them over but the other deputies went scurrying off to run a check.

We were found clean, or at least I was, so the line of officers, men and women, waved us forward with their mag lights. Then, without meaning to, since the Mustang was a lot more revved up than my old troca ever was, when I stepped on the gas, we shot off like Batman and Robin.

"HEY! SLOW DOWN!" one of the female officers shouted.

"STOP!" another one warned.

Before we knew it, we had the chotas on our tail. "OKAY, BOYS," they called on their speaker when we pulled over, "STEP OUT OF THE CAR, PLEASE."

Mikey looked at me as if it had all been my fault.

I shot a look right back at him.

Then we both got out, me a lot slower than my grandson, obviously. The two chotas came over, walking like they do, like they're ready for a shoot-out. One, un chaparro with a big hat on that made him look like a thumbtack, started patting my khakis, moving his hand up toward my chest, where my flask was in my jacket. I was just starting to wonder how I was going to handle a night in jail at my age, when out of nowhere a humongous explosion rang out. It was so loud all four of us stepped back. *Ching . . . !* It pretty damn near blew all our hats off.

"Holy . . . !" the Thumbtack cried out. "Holy . . . !" the other one said, too. Holy what I don't know. My near-deaf eardrums were vibrating. It sounded like an atomic bomb resounding all over kingdom come. You got to keep in mind they tested out the atomic bomb up in Nuevo México. Even ahora they test missiles up in White Sands. So thinking we were being bombed was not that far-fetched.

The police car radio went off, calling all its manpower. Down the street everyone started running around, getting in their muebles, taking off in every direction. Squad cars turned on sirens and sped toward the direction of the explosion. All kinds of gente were suddenly out on the street—running out of the bar, the drunk and the not-yet-so-drunk. Others got out of their carros y trocas at the package liquors line to check out the flames in the distance. People screaming bloody murder, "Ahhh! Ahhh!" N'hombre. It was complete pandemonium.

Me and el Mikey were just left standing there with our hands still up.

Turned out it was the warehouse outside of town that blew up. It contained all kinds of petroleum products. The news said later they figured it was vandalism. Vandalism? Breaking the windows would have been vandalism. This was a pyromaniac's orgasmic dream. Or at least that's what my grandson called it.

Speeding back toward El Paso, el Mikey behind the wheel, I took a look pa' 'trás. All I knew was that—híjole, hombre—once again smoke, gases, and blazes had overtaken the holy skies of Nuevo México.

REGINA

Gabo's sleepwalking was a challenge for my yierba know-how. I'd never had that problem presented to me before. A neighbor might come to me about a cold that wouldn't go away or maybe about suffering from gas all the time. But no one had ever complained about sleepwalking. I tried to treat it by giving him a cup of valeriana at night before he went to bed. Valeriana isn't tasty like manzanilla, which is soothing. It's a lot more fuerte. I thought if he was really knocked out he wouldn't get up sleepwalking. But I was wrong. I needed expert advice. A yerbero in Juárez recommended anís de estrellita. That tea didn't help much, neither.

My poor muchacho. He's been putting up with my teas all his life. When Gabo was a little baby and got colicky I gave him té de alhucema. Alhucema is a lavender tea. That was when he was only three months old. Mamá had just passed away and I didn't know who to ask about babies. But I knew something about the herbs I grew. When my sobrinito got a little older and he became chipil at night, I'd give him warm manzanilla tea in his bottle. Because of manzanilla I knew how to handle Gabito's earaches. You steep olive oil in the manzanilla flowers and apply it as eardrops. Chamomile works for big people, too, to calm our nerves. I don't like to drink it much myself. But it does make a good hair rinse.

While all the tesitos I tried on him would put Gabo to sleep right away, I'd still find him wandering around at night. One time he was in my truck. Good thing I'd started keeping the keys in my room. El médico offered to prescribe some sleeping pills or even some kind of antidepressant, but I said no. I was sure my nephew was not about to take any pills. Besides that, he was not crazy. Everybody knows that medication is for locos. Locos and people with money who have too much time on their hands so they complain about being unhappy.

When Miguel found out I was giving Gabo teas for his sleepwalking he brought over some osha root in a small pouch. He got it up in Taos when he went and did a sweat, he said. "Gracias," was all Gabo told him. Later, I found the amulet on the bureau in his room. "My faith in Cristo is enough," my nephew told me.

"The concept of a savior takes hold of some people and that's what they live and breathe," Miguel said later. We were sitting out on the portal that night. The bugs were behaving themselves. We were talking about Gabo and Miguel's ex, who had left him after she was saved by Jesus. "Well, looking back on it," Miguel said, "I don't think Crucita wasn't regenerated so much by Jesus as she was by the preacher."

"Lucky us," I said, meaning me and him. "We're doomed to doubt everything."

When I turned to look at Miguel his face was coming toward mine. Maybe my doom talk turned him on. I closed my eyes to let happen whatever was meant to happen. And sure enough, it happened. I got kissed. "You're not mad at me, are you?" Miguel asked afterward. My eyes were still closed. I wasn't mad. I was waiting for another kiss. I opened my eyes. I guess the spell broke because soon after that, he left.

That night I made myself a cup of inmortal. Inmortal is taken for a variety of ailments. One of them is for the enlarged heart of the aging. Sometimes I feel my heart is getting so big it'll burst through the chest cavity one day. And I cannot say if that would be a good thing or a bad one.

MIGUEL

As soon as they spot a red sports car, they're after you. Who has time to go to court to fight bogus speeding violations? All right, so I refuse to pay. That's why I haven't been able to get my license back. Between my teaching job, commitments to the community, the kids, my research project, and now, all the investigations, I can't even think straight sometimes. I barely paid my electric bill on time last month. Okay. Bottom line. Who wants to turn over to the government any more money than we're already forced to? If it ain't coming out of your paycheck, they gouge you at tax time—they get you coming and going.

I call our search for Redhead's brother my investigations. What I've come up with is zilch. Rafa is only one among hundreds every year disappearing or finally turning up dead because of heat and dehydration in the desert or foul play at the hands of coyotes. These days all I can see in my mind's eye lately is that skeleton mother with three fingers that Gabe and my grandpa saw at the city morgue in J-Town.

"YOU A REGULAR SHERLOCK HOLMES, AIN'T YOU, MIKEY?" My abuelo Milton sniped. He's got his own investigations going. One day my grandfather took me to meet the deputy woman who arrested the kid. "I got a hunch that they're selling drugs at the coyotes' house," I told her about the people who once called Regina.

"Why do you think that?" she asked me, eyeing me up and down like maybe *I* knew something I wasn't telling her instead of the other way around. That's the way it is with most cops. "It's a hunch, that's all," I said.

"Well, we can't go in without a warrant," the deputy woman said.

Nothing to do but walk softly and carry a big stick around here, I guess.

I tell Crucita all the time to be careful when she goes to el otro lado. I warn her to be wary of anyone who approaches her, whether it's a supposed traffic cop or even a girl saying she needs help and wants Crucita to go with her somewhere. "Don't trust no one," I say, knowing all the while she talks to strangers all the time.

"I am there doing the work of the Lord," she tells me. "I'll be all right."

"Then, whatever you do, do not take the kids with you." By law, one parent can't take a child out of the country without written permission from the other parent. I hate enforcing my joint custody parental rights, but I got to look out for the kids first and foremost, man.

While my ex is doing the Lord's work, I've gone back to researching my book on the "dirty wars." The term *dirty war* goes back to the seventies, when the Mexican government started using brute force to stamp out both armed and peaceful opposition. It's pretty widely known now how much training and influence actually came from the U.S government to quash any and all kinds of so-called communist threats. From the student protests in Mexico City in the seventies to the Mayan people's uprisings with wooden guns in the nineties, the military has shown no tolerance regarding dissension.

The problem is that shit happens on an ongoing basis. The wars ain't over. I hardly have a chance to keep up. The other day a lawyer was shot in J-Town on his way to court. No one saw anything, of course. He represented one of the bus drivers accused of some of the murders of women who worked in the maquilas. The word is the bus driver was a scapegoat. Apparently, the lawyer knew things that would have come out in court. Police officials, military, Interpol, state officials—who knows who's who, much less what anyone is up to. Oh, what a tangled frontera we live in.

When I was a teenager, we used to cross over to Juárez every weekend. J-Town always had a reputation as a good place to party. It still does. Hey, it's the birthplace of the famous margarita cocktail. Back then, Spanish rock was just starting up and they had some good live bands there on weekends. A carload of us would go drinking and carousing. The worst that would happen was the cops would stop us because we were kids and all hammered. They'd threaten to throw us in jail and then we'd pay a mordida and that was it. I had a girlfriend over there for a while. Carmelita. Maybe that wasn't her real name. Maybe she wasn't just my girlfriend, either. But she was there whenever I wanted to spend time with her.

Years later, something happened that changed J-Town for me. You can't pay me to cross over now. And you best not suggest taking my Mustang allá.

It was 1997 and Crucita and I were already married. Our daughter had made her First Holy Communion that day. So Crucita and I and the kids, my mom, who was in town for the occasion, my grandfather, Xochi's new sponsors, well, let's just say everybody, decided to go over to J-Town to have dinner. We made reservations at a nice place near Avenida Juárez called Mares Mazatlán. It was supposed to have good seafood. Aside from my upset stomach that I was sure had to do with my pasta-and-scampi dish, we had a good time. The kids were well behaved, even Crucita's beer-guzzling cousin el Pinky.

Everyone was getting up from the table, full, contentos, and my little girl beaming in her white lace dress. Crucita's parents, our new compadres, el Abuelo Milton, my mom, and I were all arguing as to who would get to pay the bill, when all of a sudden, like from a gust of wind, the doors were flung wide open. Man. I'll never forget it. Just like that, two gunmen were in the room, opening fire. Sparks from blaring rat-a-tat and people screaming and ducking with all the tiroteo. I got hold of myself and flung my body over Little Michael, who was closest to me. He was only about five then. Everyone was down on the floor, most people seeking cover under the tables and chairs. The gunmen took off as fast as they'd come in after they got the former police chief and his entire family. They had been seated just a few yards away from us in the middle of dinner. My kids had nightmares after that for a long time. Crucita had us all in family counseling. Truth be told, I think that was the turning point for any hope for happiness in our marriage.

That wasn't the first police chief to get hit, and most definitely he would not be the last. The dirty drug wars take no prisoners. A police chief could be targeted because he knew too much, because he had refused to cooperate with the local drug lords, or because he did and might talk, or maybe just as a warning to the next police chief.

That was the year the Juárez Cartel had left all the other cartels, all the way down to Colombia, in the dust. Amado Fuentes Carrillo, the head narcotraficante, was grossing something like—get this—*200 million bolas* a week. Who makes 200 million dollars a week, unless they've got an oil well in their backyard? And Fuentes Carrillo had even bigger plans for himself. That kingpin was planning on expanding into the methamphetamine and money-laundering markets. Then, be it tough shit or what, Fuentes Carrillo died undergoing plastic surgery. He was trying to disguise his looks. Everybody on all sides suspected foul play. It stood to reason. But it seemed that his ultimate demise was the result of complications under the knife.

"Poor México, so far from God, so close to the United States." Most of the cocaine, marijuana, heroin, and the raw methamphetamine ingredients consumed in the United States enters by land from south of the border. México is next to the world's biggest drug market and the world's biggest weapon supplier. The worse the dirty wars south of the border get, the higher the demand for stronger artillery. The narcos can even buy weapons off the Internet.

This is all going into my book.

Now, the sixty-four-thousand-dollar question, or in this case, billion-dollar question, is: How long can the United States contain what its vices and counterproductive prohibitions have wrought?

REGINA

Mamá was right. I always was a little bit loca. Crazy, I'd say now, is not knowing a happy moment even if it bopped me on the head. What was wrong with feeling felíz, even if just now and then? I don't know. When you grow up being told smiling is too much, just like you are told not to cry, you don't know what to do. So you stay still, like a statue with a pigeon on its head. That is why I didn't know how to react on the most beautiful día de mi santo that I've ever had.

Maybe I was overwhelmed. Overwhelmed I know. But I'd never been overwhelmed with happiness before. Not even on my wedding day. But then that had only consisted of me and Junior going to the courthouse and then over to his mother's house to eat afterward. To celebrate she bought us Kentucky Fried Chicken. Mamá would have nothing to do with that day and stayed home. She was overwhelmed with my decision to marry Junior, who was going off to die in the war. She wasn't wishing it on him. She just figured what were the odds that one of our muchachos going to the front lines would come back?

Since we left my grandfather Metatron's property, I'd never paid attention to my birthdays. Only my saint's day was observed. By observed, I mean I had to go to Mass. That was about it. No parties, no cake, no piñatas, and most definitely no break from whatever else I was supposed to be doing that day. We didn't observe my first name, Regina, who is the Queen of Heaven. Just my second name, Ana. Saint Anne—patroness of late-in-life mothers. Santa Ana's Day is in the middle of summer, when there isn't a drop of rain in the sky and los zopilotes are making circles over your head.

But this día de mi Santo was delivered up on the wings of the gods. The gods in my case being three men now in my life, an old one, a very young one, and one in between. Like the Three Bears. They got together on this one and decided to take me to a charreada. Charreadas are Mexican-style rodeos. We used to have them on my grandfather's land. But those were nothing like the extravaganza that el Abuelo Milton, Miguel, and my sobrino took me to in Sunland Park. They were just the way the men entertained themselves on their day off—lassoing and roping horses and calves. The one I was taken to for my santo was a big espectáculo. It had mariachis and food and I even drank a beer.

"Don't ask any questions, please, Tía," el Gabo said, as he drove me in the direction of Miguel's comunidad. It was Sunday. I figured he was taking me to brunch somewhere. I was a little upset with him because he had gotten off from work. He could use the day off—that wasn't it— but not to take me out or to spend money on his old tía. But they had it all planned, los Three Bears, the old one, the very young one, and the one who showed up that day in a charro outfit, the one who was just right.

"That's Miguel," I said to my nephew and el abuelo, who had me sandwiched between them in the bleachers of the arena. Of course they already knew that. That was part of the big surprise. I kept looking. I had to rub my eyes to make sure. It was Miguel, all right. He was dressed to the gills—spurs, sombrero with a rope headband, pointed boots, a wide leather belt with a pistol, long-sleeved guayabera, silver buttons on the outside seams of his tight pants, and a sarape strapped to the saddle of his horse. The works. "Miguel has a horse?" I said. It wasn't his, el Abuelo Milton explained. It belonged to one of his neighbors, who was with the charreada and had invited him to participate. Miguel sure knew how to ride. "Wow," I said.

"IT WAS ANOTHER OF THOSE SPORTS HE ACCOMPLISHED TO PLEASE HIS FATHER," el abuelo said. It was bright out. I knew he couldn't see Miguel or much of anything. You could still tell he was enjoying the rodeo, jumping up and clapping with everyone else. "DON'T WORRY. HE AIN'T GONNA DO THE PASO DE LA MUERTE OR NOTHIN' FANCY LIKE THAT." The Death Leap was the grand finale. It required the charro to leap onto and ride a wild mare on the run, el Abuelo Milton said. Miguel wasn't going to participate in the most popular event, neither. El coleadero is when a charro rides by a steer and gets hold of it by the tail. Then he wraps it around his boot. Once his horse picks up speed, he can run the bull off balance. The charros who did do it were exciting to watch. Even the bull riding, although I can't say it was my favorite part. Miguel also didn't do no lassoing of any kind. But he did make a fine picture on a very fine horse when he came out in the first event in la cala de caballo.

This opening act shows the judges how well your horse is trained. Miguel entered the ring at full gallop. Suddenly, he brought his horse to a complete stop, leaving a mark in the sand from its two hind legs. Then he turned the horse in both directions and then backed out of the ring. For a moment I forgot myself and I whistled with fingers under my curled tongue as loud as I could.

"AY!" el abuelo said, covering his ears.

"I thought you were deaf," I said to him, sitting back down.

As thrilling as it was seeing Miguel in the charreada, the men still had more surprises in store for me. It was the best day of my life. I swear. During the break, when the mariachis came out, Gabo disappeared. I looked around. I thought he was going to find Miguel. But shortly, there was an announcement over the scratchy, mega-loud speakers. I thought I heard, "EL JOVEN GABRIEL . . ."

"What?" I said. "WHAT?" I asked el abuelo, who had heard my whistle but now could not hear me shouting in his ear.

And then I saw my boy. I saw his crisp white church shirt and his pressed black pants, which I always creased just so, and there was my sobrino holding a microphone with los mariachis, dedicating a song to me. To me, his tía, and saying something about my santo. Gabo, in his young tenor's voice, sang a song I had heard only once in church, a long time ago. I think it was at a misa one summer in Chihuahua at the catedral. Gabo's voice changed last year. It's a man's now. "Salve, Regina," he sang, "to you we send up our sighs . . ." slowly and so nervously, I held my breath throughout. I held my breath for him and for me. I think I couldn't breathe. I looked around, and everyone in the crowd was holding their breath, too. They had all shut up at once, beer bottles in hand, and even las criaturas were suddenly quiet. Gabo sang like I heard only one person sing before. That was my older brother, Gabriel, his namesake.

I knew my nephew had a voice. But I had heard him only in the shower. I always lean close to the door to hear better. He's been practicing to a Plácido Domingo cassette.

Now, in the center of the lienzo, my Gabo sang with his eyes closed, his voice going out all over, bouncing off the nearby mountains and the faraway trees. And like I said, he had the crowd mesmerized. Nearly impossible for Mexicans at a rodeo. But he did it, mi'jo, with such resonance—a good word. A perfect word for a perfect voice. It wasn't just my opinion. Everyone was starstruck. Gabo is not a celebrity, but he looked like one con los mariachis. Only one violinist accompanied him, while the other musicians stood by with heads slightly bowed, like they were listening to a prayer. When my Gabo was done, there was still silence. Then all of a sudden an announcement full of static blared out the next competition.

When Gabo returned, his cheeks all lit up, I put my arms around his bony frame and squeezed him against my soft one that is giving in to gravity a little more each day. "HÍJOLE, CARNALITO," el abuelo said. "YOU'RE GOOD!"

I couldn't talk. When had they planned this, these men, the old one, the very young one, and the one I didn't know what to make of no more? One day he is a political activist Chicano, todo bravo and defiant. Next, he comes out like a nineteenth-century vaquero. The original southwestern cowboy.

And then, Miguel found us. I was in my inability-to-talk mode, which he was getting familiar with, so that's why I guess he spoke up first. "Nice, huh?" It wasn't nice. It was spectacular. Him, too. He smelled of cologne. Woodsy, pines, algo manly. Maybe it was the horse. Miguel sat down next to Gabo. I wanted to lean over and ask Miguel something. My mouth opened but nothing came out. I wanted to ask him why. But why what? And why should I ask why?

And then there came even one more surprise, from the three men— the ones who on that day I barely recognized. Who were like the little Russian dolls I got at la segunda, one inside the next. So many in one.

My next santo surprise was Uriel. Uriel, with her long, black hair and a little more of her than the last time I saw her, which was who knows when. She was making her way up the bleachers, waving, waving. Behind her was Uriel's newest husband, carrying a cake box. Like me, Uriel had always been good in the kitchen. "Regina!" she called. "Hey, woman!" and waving silver rings on all her fingers, including her thumb, which the new husband made. I started waving, too.

"Didn't I tell you we were gonna see each other soon?" she called out from three bleachers down, squeezing her sneakers between people. She came up as fast as she could. Yeah, she had said that the last time we spoke on the phone. I thought it was a prophecy. Maybe it was.

I looked at the three men, el Abuelo Milton, Miguel, and then Gabo. They were so proud of themselves. My sobrino was all smiles. I hadn't seen those dimples for a while. I smiled, too, all that day. I'll admit it. I don't care who knows. Smiled myself silly for once.

chapter

EIGHT

REGINA

When it's raining, you pour it. That's what Mamá used to say. And you can do that until you're all the way down to when China comes home. Every day for every dollar. That was another one of her favorite sayings, too, although there were days when we were lucky if we made a dollar. My mother learned to speak English pretty good. Faster than me. Maybe it wasn't perfect but she could sure defend herself. Her first language was Rarámuri. Pero Metatron knocked that out of her.

As soon as we settled down in Cabuche, mi mamá got involved in everything. She belonged to the women's group at the church. She went to bingo there every Friday night with as much devotion as she went to Mass on Sundays. She had her hair-permanent business. When it didn't work for me selling products for the home, she took over my "district," and really scored. She knew everybody. Half of Cabuche attended her funeral Mass. People couldn't even fit in the church. Up at the pulpit, Father Juan Bosco gave a teary-eyed eulogy.

She always went out. I always stayed home. Sometimes I wonder what my life would have been like if my mamá had not been so strict with me. For instance, I would have learned to swim, for sure. She thought if I went in the water, I'd drown. Come to think of it, maybe that fear came from when we crossed over through el río one time at night and I almost did. But who knows? Maybe I would have even made it to the Olympics. Or been an ice skater, getting to wear those skimpy outfits with fake fur around the collar and cuffs. Or, after I got my general equivalency diploma and started taking classes at the community college, I would have gone for the degree. Mamá said so much school was a waste of time. We needed to work.

Even though she always told me that it was unattractive for a lady to be chismeando, she herself had a lot of "comadres." Dropping off someone's rug-cleaner order from Amway, for instance, could take her all afternoon. Mamá and her customer would just blab the day away. One time I told my mother that. She was mad at me because the frijoles had burned. She was out dropping off an order of pet-stain remover. Beans take a while to cook. She put them on and left. I was out in the garden. When beans burn you practically have to vacate, the smell is so bad. She was angry, all right.

"And what were *you* doing, anyway?" I said. I said it under my breath, figuring she wouldn't hear me. "But puro huirihuiri all day." Next thing I knew my mamá was in front of me, her hand raised. I stared at her. I was twenty years old. I was too old to be slapped no more. She saw all that in my look. She put her hand down and walked away. After that, she was the one who always watched the beans. Mi mamá still made me do the rest of the housework. But at least I can say one battle with her was won.

I don't want to stymie my sobrino that way. *Stymie* is one of those words that sounds just like what it means. Not let him dream because I want him around to do my bidding, because I'm afraid to be left alone, because I resent so much how my own life turned out. I'm talking about my mother, not me. I don't blame anyone about my life being stymied.

⚬ ⚬ ⚬

After los aguaceros or monsoon, like the news called it, the garden buried in mud, the road washed out, us stuck in the house, roof leaking, pots and Tupperware everywhere, all I could ask myself was, "Where are the locusts?" Then I got my answer. The locusts came in the form of a rumor. No sooner had the new school year got under way, Mrs. Martínez told me what she was hearing through the grapevine in the office. Our jobs, and those of most of the staff, might be cut at the end of the school year.

School had started off like always, with a lot of work for everybody. I stayed more than my share of hours the first weeks, helping the teachers get their tasks done. I not only set up classrooms and straightened them out afterward, a lot of times teachers asked me to grade homework for them. I didn't think I was supposed to do that but I did. I didn't get paid for staying after school, neither, but if I didn't, I'd surely be replaced in the flash of an eye.

In the *blink* of an eye.

That's why I can be replaced so easily. It don't take a genius to do my job. There are some aides at the school who, because they work so hard, think they are irreplaceable. I am not one of them. "The school board is always at it about how they can improve the education of our kids," Miguel said when I told him what Mrs. Martínez was saying, "and the first thing they come up with is cutting budgets."

Gabo had started his senior year. He was still working at el Shur Sav. But he didn't let me see his schoolwork no more. He didn't even like me to ask about it. The year before he'd always come home and show me his grades. He was an honor student. Now he didn't even mention his classes. So it wasn't exactly una sorpresa when I got a call from his principal to come down for a meeting.

Dr. Patel was young for being the head of the high school, I thought. She must've been studying her whole life without stopping. "Chandra," she told me. "Please call me Chandra." Dr. Chandra was dressed in a suit that made her look like a dark Jackie Kennedy. She was wearing pearls. "You're not from around here, are you?" I asked.

I had worn my Sears dress for the occasion. It was the first time I'd had the chance. Since I purchased it, it had gotten too big on me. Cutting back on my meals had paid off over the summer, I thought that morning when I put it on and started looking for a belt that might help pull it in. Paid off for what? that nagging little voice I carry around in my cabeza-head for no good reason asked.

Dr. Chandra smiled and shook her head. "Let's talk about your nephew, shall we?" I smiled, too, and crossed my legs at the ankles just like she was doing. (This is how you learn things, by watching, I reminded myself.) She folded her hands on her lap and I did, too. Then she reached over to her desk and picked up a pen, which she started poking against a notepad. My hands went up for a moment and then I settled them down on my lap again.

"Señora . . ." she said.

"Regina, please," I interrupted.

"Yes, okay," the principal said, groping for a way to begin our discussion about my nephew. She swallowed and adjusted her glasses. It looked like she was putting on her principal's face. Her jaw became firm. "Gabriel is a very bright young man," she said.

Yes, he is, I thought.

"He scored among the highest in his class last year. He had, in fact, every chance to be valedictorian . . ."

"But . . . ?" I said.

"I am aware of Gabriel's personal situation—about his parents, I mean," she said. "Last year I made him see our counselor here. Did you know that?"

I didn't. Gabo used to be a better listener than a talker and now he wasn't neither. Even when he came in at night from work and I sat down with him to eat a quesadilla or sandwich, he'd eat in silence.

"I don't know," Dr. Chandra said. "He's lost a lot of interest in his studies. I'm worried as to how he is going to do this year."

I didn't know what to say. My heart was sinking down to my stomach. My hands were not politely folded on my lap no more but holding my panza. It felt like it'd been hit.

"He proselytizes all the time . . . did you know that? Is your family very religious? I mean this is a public school . . ." The principal waved both hands in the air, and the pen in her hand made her look like she was trying to conduct some faraway music. "I mean . . ."

"You mean what, Dr. Chandra?" I asked. My voice came out so small I hardly heard it myself. Was she going to kick Gabo out of school?

"Well, while there isn't exactly an official code prohibiting it, we are getting pressured to keep religion out of school business—any religion," she said, "and that peculiar tunic he's wearing every day is simply disruptive for our other students."

"I don't understand," I said.

"We're not going to suspend him or anything like that. But as one parent to another," she said, "I am very concerned about Gabriel. I mean, why is your nephew going around in a robe? He looks like a Capuchin monk," the principal said, all niceness suddenly vanishing from her original quinceañera manner. Now her eyes were searching mine with reproach. All mine could do in return was keep wincing like they were being attacked.

She went on. "Half the time he refuses to wear anything on his feet . . . and when he does it's those sandals. . . . He can't participate in gym class in those. He used to be athletic. We don't want to suspend him. Gabriel was one of our best students, over all, in fact. But I mean, my goodness. What . . . in . . . the . . . world . . . is going on?"

"I don't know, Dr. Chandra," I said, mostly because I didn't. "Gabo just came into this life that way."

GABO

Padre Santo Pío, Amigo de Jesús, the Holy Spirit, all the Angeles, and above all, Our Lord,

I am failing and yet my Lord does not forget me.

I fail to express my most ardent love to my Father in Heaven. I fail to show my infinite gratitude. I am at the bottom of the sea. What sea, Santo querido? The sea of eternal sorrows. And yet, my Lord has bestowed the grace which I have yearned for for so long. I know now what you were trying to teach me for so long about sharing the suffering of Our Lord on the Cross. I beseech you to kindly let Him know. I pray for nothing more than to accomplish that mystery.

Yet, I know how I am unworthy, Padre Pío, more than ever. I steal and I lie. People think I am un loco. If only that were the truth.

It started after el cura, my mentor, left without saying a word. I know that it is no excuse for my behavior but the only way I could fit his desertion into my head, Santo, was by telling myself that Padre Juan Bosco was not the Church. Like my tía Regina tried to tell me ever since I had run away to stay at his house, priests were men, capable of making mistakes. "Maybe even more than most," she said, "because they got so many rules imposed on them." As you know, Padre Pío, I do not want to be a priest. My greatest desire is to be un descalzado devoted to silence. (But Su Reverencia, if you permit me, I will always write to you. Although I worry I bother you too much writing to you as much as I do.)

The first time I went into la iglesia it was just to pray.

The priest had always said it was okay for me to do that, Padre Pío. He had given me a set of keys. I could tell that Herlinda Mora was also going there, keeping things up, dusting, cleaning . . . and waiting, too. One day, I went into the sacristy. I used to prepare everything for el cura as we got ready for Mass. I was filled with such longing. I found some communion wafers in a box. The communion host is only to be for those ready to take Cristo into their hearts. You must be free of all sin, but I had no one to hear my confession. I had stopped going to la santa misa. The only one given on Sunday was by the priest that came from out of town. A lot of people did not attend church anymore. He was not our priest. He did not know us. We did not know him. And who was going to tell his pecados to a stranger?

Then something happened, Santito, the kind of miracle bestowed upon sinners like me. God is so great, He is bountiful even to us. As Saint John the Divine had in the Book of Revelation, I heard a voice from deep inside: "*I know thy works . . . and thy patience, and how thou canst not bear them which are evil.*"

It was true I could not and yet evil was all around me.

"*And thou hast tried them which say they are apostles, and are not, and hast found them liars.*"

Padre Juan Bosco.

Then, as if the cura's weaknesses were contagious or I was excusing my own, I took a communion host out and placed it on my tongue. I yearned to taste the blessedness of the Lord again. After that, in el ropero, I found the humble robes of a Franciscan brother. They smelled musty and were filled with moth holes. I tried them on. They felt as if they belonged to me, Su Reverencia.

(Did you send them?)

All the signs were there. I am sure of it. Especially now, after the floods have destroyed so many of the casitas around here. Many of my classmates were left homeless. The great voice of Saint John told of the seven angels who were sent to pour out the vials of the wrath of God upon the earth.

It was suddenly clear.

The next day I wore my robes at school. At lunchtime in the cafeteria I stood on a chair and set upon revealing God's message. Tiny Tears was sitting at the usual table with her girls, as she called them. My heart reached out to her, most of all, Su Reverencia, with the Word.

"The first angel poured his vial on the earth," I said, at first speaking softly, "the second on the sea, the third upon the rivers, and the fourth was poured upon the sun."

(Contamination is everywhere in the environment, Padre Pío. El Chongo Man is always saying toxins are steadily killing everyone. The science teacher has told us that global warming will be the demise of the planet.)

"The fifth angel poured out his vial and the kingdom was left full of darkness." My voice grew a little louder this time. "Wars are going on all over the world. Disease and famine are spread throughout."

"No darker hour could we be living in than this one, when a great nation sets upon declaring wars in the name of peace," I told my classmates. The students were mostly ignoring me, talking loudly and playing their music. Some made fun and even threw food at me. I did not care. Why should I? My voice grew louder still, *"And I saw three unclean spirits like frogs come out of the mouth of the beast."* (It was the day after the president gave a speech on TV. All my tía had done the night before when I came home from work was talk about how it had been nothing but lies to placate the public. *Placate.* I looked it up. Yes, everywhere people were sleeping.)

The teacher who supervises the cafeteria in fourth period left to call the security guard. A group of chavas were upset, unas güeras, who said they were not Catholic and whatever they were was nobody's business. They said they were going to call their parents and complain that they were being preached to at school. One called me Satan's helper. "With that rotten costume and red hair," she said.

Some of the chavos, instead of throwing pieces of fruit and empty milk cartons, like others were doing, started threatening me. "Hey, shut the ef up, man," and, "I'm gonna go up there and kick your funky ass if you don't shut up," they called. But they did not. No one approached me. Tiny's "girls" were laughing—at me for sure, but when they saw me looking right at her, they laughed at her, too. Tiny just stared back at me.

The Spirit of God kept speaking through me. *"And I saw the dead, small and great, stand before God . . . and the dead were judged, every person according to their works."* Tiny Tears was like the living dead, Padre Pío. She had no recognition of the greatness of our Lord's love. She kept eyeing me with those heavily painted eyes and penciled-in eyebrows that make her look gastada, like la Mrs. Casas, the lunchroom cook, and not just a girl. Why could she not cry real tears over those tattooed ones that boast her mortal sins? With each second that went by, her gaze seemed more unrelenting.

The teacher came back with Mr. Ledesma, the school security guard. Both tried to coax me down. "Come on, son," he said. "If you don't stop, we're going to have to call the sheriff," the teacher said. But every time they put their hands on me, the hand of the Lord would shake them off.

Finally Tiny Tears got up.

My arms were still outstretched, waiting for her to be embraced by the light of El Espíritu Santo. But instead of coming toward me, she left, Su Reverencia. Her chavas followed behind, all with their shaved eyebrows, penciled, outlined purple bocas, tattoos on their necks and ankles, and pierced noses, eyebrows, chins, and even tongues. They looked like dancing girls from Babylon. I kept reaching out but they only laughed. ". . . *they hid themselves in the dens and in the rocks of the mountains; and said to the mountains and rocks, Fall on us, and hide us from the face of him that sitteth on the throne and from the wrath of the Lamb . . .*" I called out behind them.

Then, I crumbled, Padre Pío, falling, yo creo, into el Mr. Ledesma's arms.

"What happened to him?" I heard the teacher's voice come from far away. "His hands are bleeding," someone cried. *"His hands are bleeding."* I heard a choir all around me. *"His hands are bleeding."* I could not open my eyes. I could not stand up on my own. When I woke in the nurse's office, my hands were bandaged.

The Lord heard me at last.

Praise be, Adorado Santo. Gracias.

In the name of All that is the Lord's, your eternally grateful servidor

MIGUEL

"When a finger points to the moon, the imbecile looks at the finger." That was an old saying of the anarchists. When my grandfather told me about the Flores Magón brothers, self-proclaimed anarchists and their first attempt to overthrow the Mexican government a hundred years ago, it just about changed my life. Especially the fact that my abuelo's own father had been a Magonista. My grandpa hangs on to that like a gachupín hangs on to the family coat of arms. The anarchists of that era—from Russia to the U.S.—were set on taking over capitalism. They were against monarchies and despots like Porfirio Díaz, who kept reelecting himself in México. Magonistas believed in rights for all the workers—all the underdogs.

"Land and Liberty" was Zapata's cry. Zapata was one of the heroes of the Mexican Revolution, but before him came the Flores Magón brothers. It was Ricardo Flores Magón, in fact, who penned that slogan, Tierra y Libertad.

Industrial workers of the world unite! ¡Órale!

Sometimes I think I was born a century too late.

The Magonistas considered J-Town the optimum headquarters for an uprising. They had a customs house and a railroad there—in others words, money and good transportation. But Porfirio Díaz was not about to suffer enemies. No dictator does. The Magonistas managed to get some allies here in El Paso, but Díaz had planted infiltrators in the group and all the Magonistas were arrested. Ricardo Flores Magón died up in Leavenworth. The official report was heart failure. The bruises noted on the corpse's neck said differently.

"History," I tell my students, "depends on who you want to believe."

My abuelo told Gabe all about the Flores Magón brothers just the way he once told me. Regina's nephew has been through more than most people twice his age. He can handle all kinds of information. He reads like breathing air. So, hearing about Ricardo Flores Magón, an intellectual, former law student, writer, starting a movement with his brother to overthrow their authoritarian government—that must've been like a Russian novel for the kid.

But history does not mean much to the youth. It ain't real for them. Video games are more real than the past, the past being yesterday. I know. I teach the subject and I've slammed a book down on a desk more than once to wake a knucklehead who's fallen asleep in class.

But after Regina told me the kid was walking around in some kind of monk's robes and preaching scriptures at his school, I thought maybe I should talk to him myself. Guy-to-guy. One day I picked him up after school, and we drove over to the Sonic to get a couple of burgers. We pulled up to the speaker and put in our order. Right away, it started off bad. Gabe said he didn't want anything. But except for all the gauze wrapped around his hands, he seemed normal enough, dressed in a pair of jeans and a T-shirt. "You boxing now, dude?" I said, referring to the bandages. No reply.

I ordered some onion rings and a shake for him. A few minutes later an attendant came out with our order. "Girls used to bring orders out on roller skates," I said, groping for a way to start a conversation.

"Why did they wear roller skates?" Gabe asked me, accepting the rings and shake when I handed them to him but I saw he wasn't about to touch them. He rested the food on his bony knees, waiting, like he was being held captive.

"I don't know," I said, already feeling like an asshole. That's how it is with teens. They make you feel out of it. Trying to talk to my daughter these days, for instance, always ends up seeming like I'm interrogating her. No matter what I ask, "Dad!" is all she'll reply, rolling her eyes.

"My abuelo said he was talking to you one day about our local revolutionary heroes," I said. Gabe didn't even show facial reactions to my comments. He just stared out the windshield. "You know, I think that in his day Christ might have been considered an anarchist." Why the hell I said that, I'll never know.

But this got the kid to finally speak up. "I understand what you y el

Abuelo Milton are trying to tell me. But I must find out what God wants from me."

I ran a hand through my hair. Armchair revolutionaries, that's what we were, my grandfather and me both. Crucita was right. My worst enemies in the community were right. Too much talk and not enough action on my part. "Never mind," I said to Gabo, deciding to just eat my burger and shut up. I couldn't help him.

Meanwhile, things all along the border just kept getting more heated as the months passed. The latest thing was the weird shoot-outs between Border Patrol over in Crockett County and Mexican military protecting vans packed with marijuana trying to cross over. The Mexican government denied involvement, but the Texas officials said, "Well, if it looks like a duck . . ." Those Mexican military ducks shooting it out on U.S. territory were probably more afraid of the narcos they worked for than the Border Patrol.

Then the kid reached into his backpack. I tried not to be nosy, but I peeked over anyway. It was bulging but not with schoolbooks. Yeah, brown burlap. Where had he gotten a monk's robes anyway? I wondered. He pulled out a sheet of notebook paper folded in a square about the size of a silver dollar. "Here, read this, please," he said, handing it to me.

I hesitated but he pushed it against my hand. "Please, Mr. Betancourt." I put down my burger and wiped my hands on a paper napkin. I don't know why. The letter looked like it had been through hell and back already.

It was written in large, loopy letters. I glanced down quickly to see who'd penned it. Tiny Tears. That girl was all attitude.

"I found it in my locker this morning," Gabo said. "She doesn't come to school anymore."

It was addressed to Gabe. *We need to brake out El Toro,* the note said. *You have to help.* Apparently they had El Toro's breakout all planned. *He got you down as his brother,* the note said. *He got information about your dad.* They wanted him to hide bedsheets under his "robes." By being listed as a relative, as a minor Gabe could visit El Toro. "Are they kidding?" I said to Gabe. Did they actually believe he was going to escape from La Tuna through a window using a bunch of knotted-up sheets or how?

"No, they are not kidding, Mr. Betancourt," the kid said. "It has been done before. Un hombre escaped last year from there like that."

"Did he get caught," I asked, " 'cause I bet he did."

Now that anguished look on his face since I'd picked him up from school made sense. Gabe nodded. "But, the Palominos have worked it out better."

"Well, you ain't doin' it!" I said.

"What if El Toro does know something about my father?"

"That guy don't know nothing, man. Don't let them con you, Gabe. And even if he's stupid enough to try to break out, you are not getting involved with those people anymore. You hear me? Don't make me tell your principal about this . . . or your aunt."

He took the note back, folded it up again, and put it away.

"Gabe, man," I said, "promise me—on your mother's grave, you are not going to get involved in this." Gabe tried to open the car door and I reached over to stop him. "Promise me, man," I said.

"I promise, Mr. Betancourt," he said finally.

But I was left uneasy. Even though I had no intentions of snitching on Gabe to Regina, I decided to go see my abuelo that night for advice. With no news about Gabe's father our expectations had all but faded out. Not without some guilt, I avoided bringing the subject up about her brother to Redhead. When I arrived at my grandfather's, he was out. Going around with his new dog, I figured. At least one of us wasn't ready to give up.

REGINA

Mamá used to pray to Saint Anthony of Padua to help her recover items she'd misplaced around the house. Her knitting needles—in the basket next to her favorite chair with her yarns. Her prayerbook, just as she was running out the door to say a rosary at someone's house—already inside her purse. The crossword puzzle she was working on—stashed between the sofa cushions. She was always losing things: her reading glasses—on her head, the collected rent money—down her bosom without her realizing it. Things like that. No sooner was something missing, she'd cross herself and say a prayer to el santito. San Antonio, saint of the poor, kept busy by people like my mother—who was even capable of asking him to help her find a parking space—was a great man in his life. He made milagros happen even while he was still alive, appearing in two places at the same time in order to heal a very sick person.

I believe in the saints as people. I can't speak for them once they've passed. But Gabo talks to the santos all the time. He always lights candles to San Antonio. "Please help us," he prays under his breath before a little card with the saint's image he placed on the altarcito in his room. The altar used to be a desk. I found it for him at la segunda, an oak table with a pencil drawer. He was supposed to use it for his homework. The altar-desk now always has a white vela burning. There is a small wooden crucifixion and three polished stones from the Río Grande. There is also a picture of his parents, Karla, and himself when he was a little boy. That was the only studio picture the family had ever taken.

Who San Antonio turned up was Padre Juan Bosco. And he was wearing his collar. "Next time make yourself clear when you talk to los santos, will you?" I said to Gabo and walked away, leaving the priest standing outside just as he had once done to me.

But when my sobrino went to the door, el cura was still there. "May I come in," he asked, and then, "por favor?"

Just as I expected, Gabo invited him in. While el padre was in Rome Pope John Paul II had died. Father Juan Bosco filled us in on what it had been like to be there. Our parish priest was just one of the little guys. He had witnessed everything from the Vatican plaza "among all the throngs that had flocked there waiting for the Holy See's final hour," he told us.

"You didn't come to report to us about your trip, did you?" I asked.

"No, Regina," Padre Juan Bosco said. "I came to tell you both that I've resumed my duties at the church. I hope I will see you both in Mass again."

"You hardly ever saw me there to begin with," I said. I knew I was upsetting my sobrino, but I couldn't help myself. He had disappointed Gabo. "But I'm sure you can still count on Herlinda Mora's attendance. She doesn't seem to be very discriminating."

El padre blushed.

"Tía," Gabo said. Then he went to his room and came out with a brown bundle. I knew what it was even though I'd never seen the robes the principal told me about. Gabo handed them to el padre. "Gracias, Gabriel," was all he said. No reproaches. Humility was new for the priest. Father Juan Bosco took one of my nephew's bandaged hands.

I am the one who wraps them.

There are things you question. Then there are things you don't. But the priest did. "You didn't do this to yourself, did you?" el cura asked.

"Here we go," I said.

Then Father Juan Bosco turned to me instead. "I know I've always been hard on you, Regina. But if I may say it now, I did a lot of reflecting while I was away. The Bible states, 'Honor thy widows who are widows indeed . . . who do good works.' All your life I have seen it in you. I had no cause to doubt you, but I did."

I was so angry I had to take a deep breath before I could speak. "Padre, don't worry about me. But as for my nephew, shame on you."

Juan Bosco nodded. To both of us he said, "If you cannot have me as your spiritual adviser, perhaps you will allow me to be a friend."

Gabo looked like he didn't know whether to go toward me or the priest. But I felt it was mi'jo that needed the compassion. "Gabo came to you with his heart split open like an apple that you can't put back together," I said to el padre. "Just think of all he's been through. He lost his madre, his hermana . . . his papá . . . *my* brother. We may as well say it. We're never going to find him. You never knew each other, Padre. And Rafa probably wouldn't have had much use for you but I'm sure you would have liked him." I counted to ten. Get hold of yourself, Regina, I told myself.

Father Juan Bosco just stood there with his eyes down. It didn't help.

"And then you got up and left when mi sobrino needed you most," I said. The padre did not react, but Gabo did. My sobrino came and put his rail-thin arms around me so tight I could hardly breathe. I knew he was trying to shut me up. "Tía," he whispered, "don't you know?"

I pulled away and looked at him. His eyes were so dark against his pale skin. I felt lost. My head started to pound. I'd been lost for so long in so many ways I wouldn't even know where to begin to pull myself together, I thought.

Mi sobrino gripped my hand. "The First Epistle of John told me, 'Little children, keep yourself from idols.' So don't worry, mi tía. You have been more mother to me than I could have ever asked for . . . more than I deserved. Our friend was wrong, Tía Regina"—Gabo put my hand against his cool cheek—"yet, you let him in your home, just as you made room here for me. Don't you know how many lessons you taught us both?"

GABO

Padre Santo. In the Name of the Crucified Jesus, Su Madre Santa, and the Holy Spirit.

Your most fervent disciple will not burden you with laments of his numerous weaknesses. Instead, permit me to remember a glorious experience with the Divine that happened when I was just a chavalito. Some kids at school remember TV programs they watched as children to console themselves when they are afraid about having to grow up. They think of Big Bird or Barney. They remember their favorite toys, their Legos and their plastic superheroes. The other day, I was afraid. Then I remembered what once delighted me. It cheered my heart, Santo apreciado, thinking of what we once witnessed, my tía Regina and I. She had said in my ear, like it was a secret, "Don't tell anyone, Gabito. Don't tell anyone what we saw."

But Father Juan Bosco explained it to me when I relayed the secret in confession. "Are you very certain that you didn't read about this somewhere?" el padre asked. No, I had not. He came out of the confessional and opened my door. "Are you sure?" he asked again, scratching his calbo cabezahead.

He gave it a name, the "Dancing of the Sun." It had happened before, he informed me. The Church had recorded it. When la Virgen María appeared to los niños in Fatima, thousands saw it, he said. That was in Portugal almost a hundred years ago. It happened in a place called Medjurgorje, too, more recently. "Where is that?" I asked the priest.

"Near Bosnia."

Yes, I had heard of Bosnia because of the wars there, but not Medjur-gorje, where la Virgen María also appeared about twenty-five years ago to tell people to pray and do penance for their sins.

And it happened on my tía's ranchería to us.

We never talked about it. But one day, not long ago, I told her what el cura told me, that it was an official milagro of the Church. "But who would believe us?" she asked.

"Padre Juan Bosco believed me," I told her.

"Yes, he believes *you*," she laughed.

It happened when my mamá and papá left me there to go to school. I was eight years old. My tía Regina was showing me how to plant tomatoes. We took all the small plants from the greenhouse my papá had helped her build. It was made of netting and chicken wire held with postes. All she wanted was something to protect the seedlings and small vegetable plants until spring, when it was safe to put them into the ground. She does this every year; that is why I am able to remember so clearly what we were doing that afternoon.

Just then came great gusts of wind. The winds knocked down las plantitas we were carrying. They pushed me down, too. My tía laughed and helped me up. Then she fell. We were covered with the fresh fertil-izer we had just spread out in the garden. It seemed as if suddenly it might rain. It happens that way in the desert. Suddenly there is a storm. Just as suddenly it stops. But there were no rain clouds in the sky; the sky had just darkened.

The sun was between two thirds up from the horizon and directly above one's head. It was about four or five in the afternoon. First, it was my tía who saw what was happening. (That is how I know she is so blessed.) My tía Regina gasped, not a gasp of fear but a gasp of joy. She was looking at the sun, shading her eyes with her hands. I looked, too. Although the winds had died down as quickly as they had started, the sky was still dark. Yet the sun was bright as ever. But it was different. It was flat like a disc and it was whirling. "¡Tía!" I said, pointing at it. We clasped hands. Then my tía took off her sunglasses and put them on me. "You must protect your eyes," she said. "It's an eclipse."

But it was not an eclipse, Su Reverencia. No eclipse was recorded that day. (I have looked it up on the Internet.)

Then suddenly the sun, whirling like a disc, unhinged itself from the sky and started soaring fast toward the earth. My tía and I stepped back, as if we could avoid its crash. Then abruptly it stopped. Just as abruptly, the sun withdrew, ever-whirling, back to its place in the sky.

I took off los lentes oscuros and everywhere that my eyes rested upon was golden. I looked at my tía and her face, arms, and hands—they were gold, too. "¡Mira, Tía!" I said, pointing at her. She was pointing everywhere, too, marveling at how everything had turned gold, including me. My tía Regina picked me up and jumped up and down with me in her arms, both of us laughing. The sky cleared up almost instantly. The gold dust that seemed to have sprinkled the world faded, too.

Then we went back to our planting.

Su servidor, whose boundless faith in the All-Glory of the Lord will soon end the darkness that has surrounded him, G.C. y R.

chapter

NINE

REGINA

When I was a young widow, me, Mamá, and Rafa used to pick chiles all up and down this area. It was where Junior's people were from. I didn't have much to do with them after he died but we still settled here. We were in the chile capital of the world. We followed the harvest from La Union to Chamberino, la Mesilla to Caballo, then back down, through Arrey, Hatch, and Las Cruces. By September it would be time to settle down and work at one of the chile processing plants.

Once I got my widow's papers in order and my army widow's pension, I didn't work in the fields no more. Years later, Mamá got amnesty. Rafa was the only one who never got his documents fixed. Then he married a Mexican national, who insisted they have their children at home near her family in Chihuahua. They remained foreigners forever.

Funny, about the chile. I could make you any kind of mole you want. I use mulattos, anchos, guajillos, and pasillas but I don't use the chiles we picked all those years. They're not for the kind of mole my mother taught me to make. But that's not the funny thing about my making mole. The funny thing is I don't like chile. Even my famous chile colorado is too spicy for me. (It's now famous because after Miguel tasted it he told everyone at the school how delicious it was.) It might be the side of me that came with the red hair that can't take hot stuff. But Rafa was different altogether. He could practically eat the hottest chile all by itself, even while it made him do a jig. His son is not like him when it comes to food.

And lately, Gabo don't hardly eat at all.

It started the morning we woke up and found la Tuerta Winnie dead. She was lying in the kitchen next to her bowls. Without saying a word, we wrapped her in a colchita. Gabo and I carried the dog outside. We buried her next to the staghorn cactus that had claimed her eye. Now it had all of Winnie.

We went back in and silently got ready for our day.

That was weeks ago, but it feels like a lot longer than that. More bad was to come. That very night the sheriff and a deputy came to our door. Gabo had just got home from el Shur Sav. I was getting ready for bed. It had been a sad day because of how it had started. So when Gabo came in, we were still not speaking. We hardly spoke no more, anyway.

The pounding on the door startled us both. No more Winnie to warn us. Anybody could come up here, and we wouldn't know until it was too late. Too late for what? Just too late. The men wanted to ask Gabo a few questions, they said. Of course I knew the sheriff. We went back a long way. We were even in a class at the community college when we were young. He got his associate's degree. I didn't. He wasn't married back then. Now he was. "Buenas noches, Regina," he said. He had come to tell us about Miguel's ex-wife. She was gone. Nobody knew nothing.

"What do you think happened to her?" I asked.

The sheriff shook his head. "We just need to ask your nephew some questions."

I had to sit down. They came to ask Gabo about a note he'd gotten from Tiny Tears. The sheriff had an idea that Tiny Tears, or at least the Palominos, might have something to do with the kidnapping of Crucita Betancourt.

Kidnapping?

"Do you know for sure that she's really missing?" I asked. For a moment, I thought maybe she'd run off to elope with the preacher.

"Yes, ma'am, she's missing," the deputy replied, but didn't say how exactly they were so sure.

First one person's loved one has gone missing and before you find him, someone else's goes missing. Things that terrible don't just keep happening to people, I thought. To what people? Just people. That's when I imagined the canyon. It was a canyon as treacherous as I could possibly visualize it. My mamá was born in La Barranca. She spent her life trying to get out. I wasn't born in the Copper Canyon like her. But I exist in a different kind of canyon. There's a lot of gente down here, too. Not just me. So it's not like I feel sorry for myself or even alone about it. I am sure not everyone in this canyon is condemned to stay down here with no way out his whole life. I was determined to see that my Gabo got out. Stand on my shoulders, I'd say to mi sobrino. On my cabezahead, if you have to. Now all I could hear in my head were echoes. Gabo! Gabo! Gabo! I kept calling. Don't let him be lost in here, I prayed.

"Are you sure you did not mention Miguel's name to your friend María at school?" the sheriff asked Gabo.

"Who's María?" I asked.

María was Tiny Tears's name, María Dolores. She was a pain, all right, muchos dolores.

The sheriff was not being mean to my nephew. He even said he'd prefer not to have to take Gabo into the station. He was just trying to establish if there was a connection between the message Tiny Tears had given him, that Miguel told the authorities about, and the anonymous ransom letter that was left in the teacher's car.

"A note was left in Miguel Betancourt's car?" I asked. The sheriff nodded but offered no details. Gabo went to his room. He brought out the letter and handed it over. "I told her on the telephone that I couldn't help them. I said that I had promised someone on the grave of my mother."

"You didn't ever say who that someone was?" the deputy asked Gabo.

"No, sir," Gabo said. We were clutching hands.

"The note here states they had information about your missing dad," the deputy said. I looked at Gabo. This was all news to me.

"Satan always lies to mock you," Gabo told the deputy. The deputy and the sheriff exchanged looks, quién sabe what they thought. The sheriff assured me that he did not consider Gabo a suspect but his questioning him about the woman's disappearance made me feel no better.

Miguel was being questioned, too. "Ex-husbands are always persons of interest," the sheriff told me when I stopped by the station and spoke to him about it. The El Paso police were questioning Miguel, not our sheriff from Cabuche, New Mexico. When it comes to legalities, living in a town divided into two states can make life somewhat confusing. Otherwise, as long as you're going about your own business, it really don't matter.

Crucita disappearing after Miguel tried to have a talk with my nephew was probably too much for el Chongo Man, because right away he stopped talking to me. Maybe he thought Gabo had something to do with it, even if only indirectly. Then again, he stopped talking to mostly everybody at the school. "Poor guy—it must be rough," Mrs. Martínez whispered to me when he seemed to not see us in the office one day.

"I know how he feels," I said to la secretary, who just looked at me. Me and Gabo had been in a private state of near-mourning over Rafa for more than nine months. No one at the middle school but Miguel knew. I followed him out to his car as he was leaving the building, "Wait, please!" I called. "Wait." Miguel could hear me, I was sure of it, but he kept walking, lanky strides carrying him fast toward his vehicle. "Espérate," I then called in Spanish, like it was a language problem between us and not the preponderance of tragedies in our lives building sound barriers.

Finally, he stopped, but did not turn around to look at me. I was right behind him, looking up at his ample back and at that ponytail of his that I had come to adore. Yes, adore. Adore as in found very endearing or adore as in I had in fact fallen in love with the man, which one it was, I wasn't sure. "Miguel," I pleaded, "you must believe Gabo. He don't know nothing. You never wanted to see him hurt and he never wanted to hurt you."

Miguel turned around slowly. He couldn't even look me in the eye. "Regina, I don't blame Gabo. And I am not angry with you." I pulled my sweater tight around me like I was cold all of a sudden. Then, getting in his car, he said, "Right now, I don't know who to blame. Most of all, my kids just need their mother back."

MIGUEL

I have repeated it a dozen times. I don't know how it got left on the dash-board of my Mustang. It was parked in the teachers' lot at the school. The top had been up. The car did not look tampered with to indicate any break-in, not the tiniest scratch by the lock. I checked it all out before I even read the note. I looked all around, too, as if I might catch whoever had messed with my ride. No one in sight.

Exactly two days after I saw Gabe, I got a little note of my own. My note wasn't in large, loopy writing. And it was very brief. The briefest of messages and direct. Composed of letters cut out from the newspaper, pasted on with school glue: BETANCORT—my surname was not the only misspelling—A THUOSAND DOLLARS FOR YOUR WIFE. DONT CALL THE POLIC.

Yeah, it could've been Tiny Tears. But with no trace or clue about any-thing, I got no choice but to suspect everyone.

For a while I was the main suspect for the cops.

They thought I might have made that anonymous ransom note my-self. After they asked me to take a polygraph, which I passed, I heard that Prescott Burke had volunteered to take a polygraph. Yeah, they checked Silver City, where her "fiancé," the preacher, lives. The only thing they found out was that the Reverend Prescott Burke and Crucita would not have been getting married anytime soon since the man already had a wife. So you can just imagine his old lady's surprise when the FBI came to their door. It seems he hadn't seen Crucita for a while before she dis-appeared. And he had plenty of alibis to prove it. After we each were cleared, the officials on both sides no longer seemed predisposed to finding her. Since she was involved with someone while we were still married and it was a married dude to boot, it seemed they thought she was capable of any kind of duplicitous behavior. So there was some speculation that maybe Crucita had just run off, maybe even with someone new.

Perfect, I thought. The victim herself was now a suspect.

The Feds took Crucita's computer so I never got a crack at going through her files myself. I just needed something to go on. One day I decided to go to the women's crisis center over in J-Town where she had been volunteering. I parked my car near the Puente and walked across. I found Casa de la Mujer by asking around. Yeah, the director told me, they knew my ex and had heard. "Women who come to the center sometimes disappear." She said it as plain as that, like there was no point in sparing my feelings. Maybe she was jaded. One more woman obliterated, like a foot soldier lost in an undeclared war. "Sometimes their tragic fates are not left to the imagination," she said. The director, an older, rubia, well-dressed woman, was a volunteer herself. The year before, their receptionist had been shot and killed in their own parking lot by her estranged husband. It was no surprise to anyone that abusive husbands would target a place that offered refuge for wives who, in their minds, had been so bold as to leave them. "Around here, Señor Betancourt," the director said in English, "men still think they own the women." Aside from being left with yet one more possibility as to what may have happened to Crucita, I had nothing else.

I stay up nights reading, all the while thinking how bad I've messed up.

Maybe she did decide to leave everybody, but I can't stop thinking the worst.

6 6 6

During the last month, I've gone through every single article I ever collected for my book on the dirty drug wars searching for a clue to something. I ran across all kinds of reports on the killings of hundreds of women all along the border in the last fifteen years. When I'd look over them before, just like with all the levantones—the kidnappings off the street of people who were suspected in some way of being a threat to a cartel—I could only ask myself, With so much money involved, how can anyone ever expect this savagery to stop? How much does a Mexican cop make? Forget that. How much did the former Mexican president make who took off to Switzerland after he left office?

It was hard to fathom how little girls and young women fit into the equation of omnipotent kingpins' power. But you start thinking about what drugs do to people's heads and how mutilated the bodies were and you can figure out the rest. There were snuff-film theories and theories about rich sadists. At least ten women have accused police of sexual assault and violence. So the cops are always suspect.

The governor of Chihuahua who was in office when the first murdered victims turned up actually blamed the girls, stating they had asked for it by being out at night. When he was reminded that girls worked the night shift in the maquilas, he still blamed the victims. No good girl would be out unescorted. And surely, he said, the girls were dressed provocatively, so they got what they deserved.

There was the case of an Egyptian who left the U.S. because of sexual-assault charges and in México was accused of at least one of the murders, but suspected to be behind others. He got arrested but the killings continued. Women kidnapped for organ harvesters was another conjecture since some women's bodies were found with vital organs missing—like Gabo's mom.

One guy was convicted of a couple of murders then he got away. He's still at large. There were the maquila bus drivers who were accused of some of the murders. Many others are suspected to be related to the drug cartels. Some Mexican gang members were picked up in the U.S. There have been all kinds of theories, all kinds of patsies, and even a few convictions. Usually when they bust someone it's a case of domestic violence. In México, a woman can't even press charges of domestic violence unless the wounds last longer than fifteen days. Some years back, if the judge did find a man guilty, the fine was a grand total of about twenty bucks.

That was four hundred victims ago. *Femicide* is the term that's been given to all of it. And the murders continue.

Tracing my ex's steps on that day myself has only made me go in circles. She crossed over about eleven in the morning. The customs officer remembered her because he knew her. It seems she went over to the other side almost every day at the same time. She was intent on getting that church started. She went to the storefront she was getting ready and met with several of her "brothers and sisters." They were all questioned. More than once. By everyone, including me.

After she left her new iglesia-in-progress, she disappears.

I say it in the present tense because it's like an hour—between 1 and 2 P.M.—that I have frozen in my head. She slipped through another dimension, and she's still there somewhere, like Alice in the looking-glass.

◊ ◊ ◊

Things fall apart; the centre cannot hold.

One of my all-time favorite books in college was *Things Fall Apart* by Achebe. It was about how one man of the Ibo tribe experiences the breakdown of his world. Things thereafter would never be the same. The title of his novel came from the Yeats poem "The Second Coming."

Like my abuelo might say, we need a second coming around here all right.

Things fall apart; the centre cannot hold; / Mere anarchy is loosed upon the world.

It wasn't the Magonistas who brought anarchy to the border. There is no cohesive center where a line divides. Anarchy is its natural result.

Crucita used to always tell me I needed to get in touch with my feelings. "You're like so many men," she'd say—she was a psych minor. "You guys don't let yourselves feel your emotions."

She was right, but I didn't know it then.

I was out of touch with my feelings.

I mean, I knew I loved her and the kids. I knew I wanted to look out for them as best I could. I just didn't know how to show how I felt.

Three weeks have gone by and Crucita is still lost in the looking-glass.

My ex-wife's vehicle was found in a garbage dump on the other side, in Lote Bravo.

The car had been stripped and torched.

There was no way to get any kind of evidence from it.

How did the police there even figure out that the vehicle they found was, in fact, Crucita's?

Like I say, I suspect everybody. Even if I don't suspect some officials for being the culprits, I suspect their incompetence.

I moved back into my old house, empty as it is, and left all my papers in the trailer.

I sent the kids to stay with their uncle Fernie. They call home every day, if I don't call them first. Xochi says, "Dad, do you think we'll ever find Mom?" She asks me the very same question every day the very same way. *Dad . . . do . . . you . . . think . . . we'll . . . ever . . . find . . . Mom?* What I can't stand is that implicit in the question is that my child is asking me to give her something I feel I don't have the ability to do—return her mother to her. *Will you ever find my mother?* is what I hear. And I, a man with the best intentions, who obviously could not love enough or the way my wife had wanted me to express myself, have failed my whole family miserably. I could not even keep Crucita from harm's way.

The worse part is the not knowing. Aside from the ransom note left in my Mustang we never heard anything about her again. Is she still alive? We don't even know that much. "That piece of crap Toro and his little Palominos have no souls. They're wicked to the core. They would just as soon kill someone for the fun of it than try to extort money," I told Gabe one day when he came over to see how I was doing. I took a leave of absence from school. At first I was all over the place, on the news, crossing over to the other side, driving all over the place trying to track those little pendejos down on my own . . . organizing posses. Then little by little, with no sign and no word, people started losing interest in finding Crucita. Some days I can't get up from bed. Or better put, the couch. I can't go to the bed my ex and I used to sleep in together.

"Don't blame yourself, Mr. Betancourt," Gabe said. He was with the priest that had come to his barbecue party. Juan Bosco, or J.B., as I like to call him, and Gabe offered their help. But the kid knows better than anyone there is nothing they can do.

Regina didn't come with him. We haven't spoken since that day she came running out of the school after me. I've picked up the phone ten times to call her. Ten times I've stopped myself. I want to apologize. I want to tell her how afraid I am to get together with someone and fail again. Fail is an understatement. I've been carrying so much anger inside me so long I don't know who I'm mad at anymore. Even if the note I got came from the Palominos gang, I knew Gabe didn't have anything to do with Crucita's disappearance. And if he didn't, Regina sure didn't.

So, for now, we're a pair of U.S. Mexicans living in parallel universes. People we care about go AWOL.

"Unless you can be inside a man's brain and replace memory, a sense of family duty, cultural norms, and everything else he grew up being told what it is to be a man, this ain't working for me," I told the therapist when I decided to quit.

Before I got divorced I joined a men's circle up in Taos. There were about eight or even as many as a dozen of us sorry asses at any given meeting. We weren't exactly "Iron Johns" searching for our feminine souls. But we were aware of our reliance on our macho selves. We built a sweat lodge in the back of one of the guys' houses. We stayed out all night praying, chanting, talking, and trying to be honest with ourselves, some for the first time in our lives. A couple of the guys there admitted having been physically abusive. Some had drinking or even drug problems. Eventually, I stopped going.

Not because I couldn't relate. In some ways I had related too much. I just felt, like Crucita always said, I was a man who couldn't let himself feel.

Now all my feelings are beating in my head like a water drum.

EL ABUELO MILTON

"Here's what we are going to do," I said to el Mikey when I went to check him out at his house one night. He wasn't answering the phone no more. He didn't return my messages. ¿Qué diablos pasa? I asked Oso. Maybe my grandson had gone and done something stupid to himself. So me and Oso drove up to Sunland Park to check it out.

I found el Mikey alive. He only grunted when he saw me at the door and went back to lay on the couch. "Chingaos, hombre," I said. My nieto looked like ese Rasputin con una long beard. Y más pa' ya que pa' 'ca. He was in some scruffy sweats, like he hadn't changed in a month. 'Cause he hadn't. That was obvious. It wasn't a month but he sure stank like it.

When Crucita first disappeared, Miguel had been on the TV news appealing to the kidnappers. He would drive all over the place with fliers—the airport, hospital, and bus terminals. His gente in Sunland Park, they'd been helping to look, too.

Then my grandson shut down. That's what happened. I wasn't having none of that, not from a Betancourt. "Ya ni la muelas, hombre. Where's all your fight gone, son?" I asked, showing as much disgust as I could muster. "Listen," I said, "I've been thinking about this whole situation. The chota in El Paso can't cross the state line to look for those lil pachucos. And the New Mexico police ain't had no success in finding them, neither. Looks to me like the job's been left to us."

The other night, I heard on the news that the bodies of two mujeres were found by the Santa Teresa border, naked, tied up, stabbed. No, I ain't saying that's what happened to la Crucita. I mean, all the missing and murdered mujeres in the last years. But they mentioned it once and that's it. You never get to even find out their names. It's like it don't matter. I do not think they could come up with a horror movie worse than the situation we got going en la frontera. In fact, we heard that the very consultant for that movie *The Silence of the Lambs* was brought in to give his opinion of what he thought was going on after the first three hundred missing girls and women turned up dead in Juárez—all having obviously met their end in the most vile ways. "Yup, it's a serial killer, all right," was his grand conclusion supposedly. "Maybe even two. He might not even be Mexican." Then he went back to Hollywood.

Esa Tiny Tears—my number one hunch as to who knew what happened to Crucita—had up and dropped out of sight, too. Maybe by her own doing. Maybe not. María Dolores, that's her real name. The diputada told me. Sofia said la ruquita left her sick baby with her mother up in Mesquite and took off. La baby was born an addict. Tiny Tears's mother didn't seem all that upset that her hija was gone. She told the authorities she didn't bother to report it because it wasn't the first time her hija had run away. "The last time she took off, she came back with this," the mother supposedly said to them, referring to the criatura in her arms.

"What d'you think, hombre?" I asked my grandson. At first el Mikey just stared at me, looking up from the couch. There were about twenty empty cups of take-out coffee all around, that yuppie expensive kind. "Ain't you got nothing better to do with your money?" I said, picking up the trash. "Learn to make yourself a pot of coffee, will you?" On the dining room table, all over the floor in the living room, everything was covered with papers and newspapers. By el teléfono, all kind of notes. "What's the matter with you, Mikey?" I asked him. "You on the phone all the time but you can't call your abuelo back? Who do you talk to, anyway?"

For the first time, Mikey spoke up, with a voice that sounded like someone was strangling him. "My kids," he said.

"Well, I've spoken to your kids, también," I said. "Frankly, they ain't doing too good, neither. So what me and you's gotta do, Mikey, is get out there and do our own tracking down of those Palomino pachuquito outlaws. That Toro-Vaca-Rata's back on the street hurting kids. Chamacos just likes yours."

"My kids," he said again, like his brain was on "repeat."

"Son," I said, reaching down and lifting up that big bulto of a grandson I had by the front of his sweatshirt, "get off your trasero and let's do something for those kids' sakes." Once I got him on his feet I said, "How 'bout we start with you taking a shower?"

chapter

TEN

REGINA

It was November, and a windstorm was howling all around outside one night when we were woken up by a *tun, tun, tun. Tun, tun, tun.* Válgame Dios, I thought, quickly putting on Mamá's chenille bata. (That's what I use, Mamá's old bathrobe.) I got my rifle out of the ropero. Then *tun, tun, tun* again.

"Who is it, Tía?" Gabo whispered. He peeked out of his room, more asleep than awake, like me. For once, he had been sleeping soundly in his bed. I shrugged my shoulders, tiptoeing with the rifle in my hand to the front window to take a look. It was the sheriff's vehicle, headlights glaring at the house.

When I opened the door the sheriff and a deputy stepped in. They removed their hats and apologized for disturbing us. "I just wanted to come up and make sure things were all right up here," el sheriff said. Why shouldn't they have been? Although my place is a ways from town, I never worried about break-ins or nothing. But the sheriff had never come around checking on me before, neither. "What happened?" I asked.

"Do you mind putting down your weapon, ma'am?" The deputy asked. I still had the rifle in my hand. I leaned it against the wall and crossed my arms. One minute you were in your warm camita dreaming about what you were going to cook on Thanksgiving. The next, you had law enforcement in your home acting like you were a potential criminal. The sheriff smiled at his deputy. "I think she's right to try to protect herself, living out here and all."

Now I really was worried. "What's happened?" I asked again. Gabo, who had put on some clothes, came over to hear.

"Asmo Rosado, whom I believe you know, got out on bail today."

"Who?" I asked.

"He also goes by the alias El Toro Arellano," the deputy said. "He pretends he's with the Arellano family cartel of Nuevo Laredo. But he's only a local petty thief."

"Do you think El Toro would come here?" Gabo asked. He put an arm around me. Then I put an arm around him. We looked like we were holding each other up.

"I don't know anything about Rosado or his intentions," el sheriff said. "When I heard and remembered that you folks knew him, I thought I'd take a little ride out here to check things out."

And that's what they did. They walked around the property with flashlights and got back in their vehicle and slowly drove off. Gabo and I watched from the windows. Then my nephew went to sleep on the couch with his new pistol. Me with my old rifle, I went to bed. El abuelo gave him the gun some time back. Where he got hold of it, we didn't ask. "GET YOUR TÍA TO TEACH YOU HOW TO USE IT," was all he said. Oddly enough, Gabo, not being capable of smashing a bug, was glad to have the weapon. It didn't take much shooting practice—hitting cans here on the property—before my nephew got the hang of it. Must be the old rancho blood he carries in his veins.

MIGUEL

"WHAT DID I TELL YOU?" my abuelo Milton growled, pounding his cane on the kitchen table. I was sitting on a chair half tilted back and lost my balance. "Ching . . ." I muttered after I banged my head against the wall behind me. Because it was daytime, the old man had to stretch his neck just like his dog did at every sound. "GET THE HELL OFF THE FLOOR."

I wasn't spacing out. I was saying a prayer to the Great Spirit. I joined a new sweat lodge up by Ruidoso. Both men and women this time. We'd done a sweat for my whole family the week before. Ever since Crucita's father, who was even older than my abuelo Milton, heard the news, he was in the hospital. His wife at his side wasn't looking too good, either. If anything would've broken that old man it would be for something to happen to his only daughter. And something had.

My grandfather, far from becoming debilitated by bad news, was more ornery than ever. "YOU ALWAYS GOT TO GO AFTER THE WEAKEST LINK. THAT'S HOW YOU'LL CRACK THOSE PACHUCOS," he said.

The so-called experts weren't getting us anywhere. So we decided to form an emergency strategy committee, my grandpa and I. These were dire times, all right. We called a meeting at his house. Gabe and the priest were invited, too. The kid had as much invested in finding any of those gangbangers as we did. There was no doubt in our minds that the Palominos and the Villanuevas had had something to do with the disappearances of our loved ones. But we knew no one could prove anything. More important, no one could find them.

But, jeez. When I saw Regina's nephew it nearly scared me. That boy was wasting away. And yet he didn't act sickly or fragile. On the contrary, leaning against the sink, hands in his pockets, thumbs out, listening, he looked damn near intimidating. A lean, mean retaliation machine. Ready for anything, was how I assessed the teenager's stance. And yet when he spoke, his voice was still gentle. "Mr. Betancourt, ¿Cómo ha estado?" he said when he came in, taking my hand in both of his bandaged ones.

The hands, that was something else altogether. "His palms bleed," Juan Bosco said, pulling me aside when I had asked Gabo again and still got no answer.

"Are you sure?" I asked. "Did you check them out yourself?" J.B. nodded.

Dag.

All Catholic kids go through a phase of desiring holiness. I had been a little like that myself, once upon a time, before adolescence. There was a time between the years my mother forced me to be an altarboy and when I actually went to Mass every day on my own. I think it was a month in seventh grade. You know, it's when you're afraid that what the priests are telling you about your thoughts and dreams is all true and you're going to hell for being a degenerate. Once I got in high school, hell didn't seem so bad a future prospect and I got over it.

But a stigmata?

"Are you sure?" I asked Juan Bosco again, who nodded but said no more.

J.B. had come around since the days when he only cared about the longtime residents who supported the parish in Cabuche. "My superiors advised me to keep out of political issues in the States. But I don't think like that anymore. Had I not gone into the seminary what would my life have been like scrambling around to feed a family of my own?" he said. Sometimes growers or foremen chased him off the premises when he went to see how the workers were doing. One grower pulled out a rifle. He even fired it hopefully in the air. But the priest had not turned around to see. A day or so later, J.B. went back. He and a member of his church or two who always went with him, not only to check that workers were not being abused and were actually getting their pay, but to offer whatever help they could. How little it might be. From the use of a telephone back at the parish office to call family back home to getting medical attention for a worker, if needed.

"HOW LONG HAS YOUR PAPÁ BEEN MISSING NOW, CARNALITO?" my abuelo Milton asked Gabe.

"Ten and a half months, Don Abuelo," the boy replied.

That long? I thought. I noticed the priest look at Gabe like he hadn't realized how much time had passed, either. Juan Bosco was wearing his collar but not a jacket since it was a hot day for fall. He shook his head. Then he asked me, "And your esposa?"

"My ex-wife," I corrected him. "Nearly a month now."

"And still no leads?" J.B. said. My abuelo and I both shook our heads.

I didn't know why, but looking at Gabe and thinking of my own broken family, suddenly I felt like crying. Men don't cry, my grandfather would have said. I had always been told that by him, the colonel, the priests in school, back when they gave you a good whack for looking at them cross-eyed. Everywhere and from everyone you had to take it like a man. The colonel busted me in the jaw so hard one time I thought they were gonna have to reset it. I surely did not cry at my father's funeral. But I had cried at the birth of my daughter, tears of joy. I wasn't at mi'jo's birth because Crucita had a Cesarean and fathers weren't allowed back then. I touched my throat; it was tight. Maybe I was just coming down with something.

"innocent gente disappearing into thin air," el Abuelo Milton said. "that's unacceptable." Then, reaching into his back pocket, he struggled to pull out something. He laid a huge-ass gun on the table.

"Hey, Abuelo," I said, pushing back my chair.

"Do you think that will be necessary?" the priest asked.

"we only need it for protection," el viejo said.

Protection was a double-edged sword, I thought. Ironically, everyone claimed to want protection or give protection, no matter whose side they were on and who they had to hurt to accomplish either aim. But as for my old grandfather, the question as to who he wanted to protect was a moot point. Blind in the day and nearly deaf all the time, he was more of a hazard than anything else. I most definitely did not want him driving around like Mr. Magoo. As for how tough he was, well, his bark was much louder than a denture bite. I stood up and sat him down. "Cálmate, Abuelo," I said, patting the old man's shoulder. "We get it. The weakest link."

The very next day, sans my grandpa, "the committee" started going to the basketball court in Santa Teresa after school. Regina's nephew had quit his job. She didn't know anything about it, he said, or about what we were up to. "This is the most important thing now," he told us.

We had put two and two together as to why Gabe had always found

Jesse at the school. He must have been making his rounds peddling his merchandise to kids. Juan Bosco, Gabe, and I went there three times before Jesse Arellano showed up on foot. But show up at last he did. The wiry gangbanger did not have his car anymore since the cops confiscated it. When he saw us, he was all grins, like a dumb fool. That's when I realized that the wild look in his bug-eyed ojotes was due to nothing short of him being high. It was a wonder he recognized us.

"What's up, eses?" Jesse laughed, then spit.

I spit, too.

Jesse put his hands out to have Gabe throw the ball to him. "Come on, let's see what you got," he said.

For a second, I half wished I'd brought along my grandfather's Colt .45. But where would that get us? We had decided to leave both el Abuelo Milton and his gun at home for everyone's safety. "Just stay by the phone," I told the old man by way of making sure he didn't feel left out.

"DON'T WORRY ABOUT ME," he said. "YOU JUST FIND THAT WEAK LINK AND OPEN YOURSELF UP A CAN OF WUP-ASS LIKE I TAUGHT YOU WHEN YOU WERE KNEE-HIGH," my abuelo said, stomping his foot. "BACK IN MY DAY, I WASN'T AFRAID OF NOBODY. AND I'M STILL NOT."

The main objective was to find Crucita and Gabe's dad or at least track down those who knew what happened to them. So I kept calm. At first, we pretended we were only there shooting hoops. The punk probably knew better but we were all biding our time at that point. "What's wrong with your hands, man?" the gangbanger asked Gabe.

"Nothing," Gabe replied, but it was pretty obvious that it pained him to grip the ball.

" 'The blood-dimmed tide is loosed, and everywhere / The ceremony of innocence is drowned.' " I quoted Yeats's poem "The Second Coming" out loud, snatching the ball right out of the little creep's grip and passing it to Juan Bosco. The priest couldn't play worth shit and dropped the ball. Gabe snatched it up and made a basket. After a few hoops had been shot, the priest stopped, out of breath, and called time-out. "Let me ask you," Juan Bosco said to Jesse, cutting the crap, "where can we find El Toro?"

"What do you want with him, you sick fuck?" the punk asked. He looked over at Gabe suspiciously. "I always knew you two were perverts."

J.B. and I scarcely knew what was happening when Gabe suddenly pounced on the Palomino like a cougar. I swear that kid leaped about five feet. "Stop! Let him go!" Juan Bosco begged the kid as we both tried to pull the boys apart. By the time we succeeded, bandaged hands and all, Gabe had done a job on Jesse's face. The kid walked away, arms crossed, each bandaged hand tucked under an armpit, as we picked Jesse up.

J.B. put the request another way, handing Jesse a handkerchief, which the punk didn't accept. "What will it take for you to tell us where we can find El Toro?"

"You know how much it takes, pendejos," Jesse replied, rubbing his fingers together. He wiped the blood off with his shirtsleeves. "How much you two perverts got on you, anyway?" Turning to me: "Or you? You think you all that 'cause you a teacher? I got a brother who's a teacher, man. He went to college and everything. Sheet. He don't make in my baby finger all month what I can earn in a week, a day even." The punk had gotten even more wound up with Gabe's attack. He strode right up to my face, which in his case, meant my chest. "You wanna piece of El Toro? You think he got your wife? Well, he ain't the only one!" He laughed like un loco, clapping his hands loud.

J.B. stretched his arm out in front of me to stop me from smacking the living daylights out of that punk. At that moment, I didn't care if I killed him then and there, but the priest was right.

"Vámonos," the gangbanger said, with a come-on wave. "I'll take all three of you to him right now." Then, swinging around, he looked over at Gabe, who only glared at him from a distance. "But it's gonna cost you, you wannabe-priest pervert."

It was Juan Bosco who reached in his back pocket and pulled out his wallet. He took out two crisp one-hundred-dollar bills and held them up. Jesse waved his hand and laughed like the offer was absurd. Undeterred, the priest pulled off his watch. "Mira," he said, waving it in front of him. "I got this in Italy. It's solid gold. Take it. Just take the money and the watch and tell us where your brother is right now. We'll all go together . . . in my car. It's right there." He pointed to his carcarcha.

The punk stared for a second, as if debating if that was as good an offer as he was about to get. Then he grabbed the watch and bills from the priest. "Sheet. You think I won't take you perverts to him? That fucker ain't my brother, anyway."

J.B. was a little sharper than I gave him credit for. That was the watch Gabe had bought him as a souvenir from the mercado in J-Town. He had told us it didn't even run anymore.

REGINA

Back when la Winnie was born on that onion farm, I remember all the puppies that had been crushed by the mother. By accident. But still. Six of them. I helped the farmer and his wife gather them up because the mother was so protective; she was baring her teeth at us. She tried to take a bite out of the farmer's hand, too. While the mother was busy wanting to attack her master, I slipped the dead newborn pups out from under her. They were so small. Their ojitos still shut. They never even got to see light or taste milk. She just crushed them, by accident, like I said. "Here, we'll just put them in this," the farmer's wife said, bringing over a sack, the kind they used for the onions. She brought her husband the first-aid kit, too.

But he kept saying, "I'm all right. Don't worry about me, now. Everything will be just fine."

Driving on the I-10 east toward Tornillo, where el Abuelo Milton told me on the phone that they were headed, I kept saying to myself, "I'll be all right. We'll all be just fine." I said it like a rosary, over and over. But I kept remembering that onion farmer, for some reason. Gabo's dog. I picked out la Winnie right away when I came back a few weeks later. She was the más metiche of the litter, getting in todo. She'll make a good watchdog, I said to myself. I was right, too.

I wasn't wrong that day, neither, driving above the speed limit, trying to catch up to Gabo, who was in el cura's car with Miguel and that hoodlum. What were they thinking? I asked myself. What were they thinking? I was driving as fast as I could. I won't say I was driving as fast as I could without getting a ticket because, before I knew it, the state police was on my tail. But it wasn't just any state police. It was la Diputada Sofia, the chief deputy who had arrested Gabo. The very same one who was involved in his case. And it wasn't a coincidence, neither, that she was right behind me. She made me pull the truck off the road and get in her car to ride with her and a deputy. I had to sit in back like I was a hoodlum myself. "It's the law, sorry," she said. She'd got a call from el abuelo herself. "This is too dangerous," she shouted over her shoulder, driving with the siren on y todo, "Your nephew and friends should have just called us."

La diputada was radioing in for help. We were on our way to make a premature bust. She already knew where we were headed. The house in Tornillo, close to the border, was used by the same coyotes who lived in the green house in El Paso. La diputada knew all this. She knew all kinds of things. Their names. Their expanding criminal enterprises. "Why didn't you tell us?" I asked her, pushing myself forward on the seat and shrinking back when she nearly sideswiped an eighteen-wheeler we went around. We now had another state police car right behind us. A few minutes later, there were three.

"I'm sorry, ma'am," she said. We had never met before. She looked like she might be a little older than me but la diputada moved like one of Charlie's Angels. "We couldn't tell you. We were planning a sting on these people—here and on their house in El Paso."

"My sobrino has a gun," I told her.

For a split second she turned and looked at me and then kept driving at full speed.

"Kids," her deputy said. "They're all alike at that age. . . ."

"My nephew's not just any kid," I said, sounding like everyone talking about their kids.

"No, not all kids are the same," la Diputada Sofia reprimanded the deputy, who said nothing after that the whole ride. Riding, riding. Sirens going. Day turning to dusk and suddenly to black night like a blanket thrown over our heads.

"We'll catch up," la diputada said. She didn't sound too sure. She just put her foot way down on the gas pedal until we couldn't go no faster.

You can't catch up from down in the canyon, I thought. She had lived there, too. You could see it in her eyes. In her "aura," like Uriel would have said. She was someone like me. We get to witness a whole lot of things before it's our time. Things people wouldn't believe. You just say barbaridades like, "Don't worry. We'll catch up," like she kept saying, speeding down the road.

We never caught up to el cura's car. We never even spotted it. I don't blame the priest for nothing. He probably wasn't even speeding, knowing him. They just had too much of a head start. They were flying. We were still on the ground. But my boy, he was flying.

MIGUEL

I gave away most of the colonel's money. Not all at once, but over the years. The only times I got involved in conventional politics was when I made donations to the Gore campaign and later to Kerry's—just to be let down twice. I always give to Amnesty International and to Human Rights Watch, all the usual old lefty favorites. But at some point you ask yourself, How much can you do to absolve yourself from the sins of the father? I've put aside for the kids' college funds. The house is in their names, just in case I get terminally ill and want to give up to my last dime to the Mother Teresa charity in hopes of saving my soul. I'll pay for Crucita's recovery. After that, Jesus will have to look out for her.

My abuelo asked me if I'd take him to the pretrial hearings. Regina's there, too, of course. I watch her across the courtroom, in her homemade blue suit, those ravishing legs of hers crossed so primly at the ankles. She stares straight ahead. Redhead still doesn't talk to me. I don't blame her. There are times when I can't stand myself, either. But I'm working on it, back in counseling with a new therapist. I think this one gets not just my hang-ups but the whole hard-ass cultural baggage crap I lug around. Who knows? Maybe it is all just me. All I know is that it will be one long, lonely life if I don't ever get that woman back.

I saw the coyote and his woman there. Tiny Tears identified them. She said she first saw him in front of his house the time she went with Gabe, Jesse, and El Toro. She stated he was so busy hollering at someone on a cell phone that she was able to get in his house without his noticing. Tiny Tears herself is looking at doing some serious time.

As a witness I'll make sure of that.

We found El Toro in that house in Tornillo. He was so messed up on drugs—heroin, meth, snot, who knows what, how much and, most of all, who cares—if the cops had not arrested him that night, he'd be dead now. Instead, they rehabbed his ass so he could rat on the Villanuevas. Because he is such a brownnose the D.A. says he'll probably get some time off for it. One day la rata will be back out on the streets.

When we first pulled up to the house in Tornillo, that stoned punk ass Jesse jumped out. "Come on, come on," he said. When we hesitated to get out of the priest's car, he said, "Don't worry, man. The boss ain't here."

"You mean El Toro?" J.B. asked, still in the car. The three of us didn't move, even when Jesse was halfway to the front door. "Naw, man," the gangbanger said. "El Toro ain't the boss around here. I'm talkin' about *the* boss. The one that looks kinda like you. . . ." He pointed at my ponytail and started laughing. I figured he had to be talking about the coyote back in El Paso, the same one Regina and I met up with the first time we went to el Segundo barrio.

While I didn't own a gun and my grandfather couldn't persuade me to take his, I did accept his switchblade. At least I could defend myself if need be, I thought. More out of desperation than bravery, we followed the crazy dude past the unlocked door. We were out in the middle of fucking nowhere.

As soon as you got inside you sensed something nasty was going on in that place. The unthinkable. It wasn't just a meth or crack house. It reeked like bad fish. After our eyes got adjusted to the dark, we realized there were two naked girls flopped on a run-down couch. The shades were drawn so what little light there still was for the moment didn't help much. "Put a lamp on," the priest ordered with the authority he was ac-customed to having, I guessed. Someone flipped a switch. It was Gabe. We saw right away that one of the girls was Crucita. At first I feared she wasn't alive.

"Oh my God," I said under my breath, rushing over to her, feeling for a pulse, a heartbeat, patting her face to revive her.

After that, everything happened so fast, no matter how many times I try to reconstruct it all, for the cops, for my own sake, for the sake of ever-elusive justice, there are still blanks. There will always be blanks in my recollection of Wonderland.

In that den of iniquity that evening, Gabe and the priest found El

Toro sprawled out on a bed in one of the two bedrooms. But the amoeba was unconscious. "He's in there," Gabe said breathlessly.

Crucita was mostly out of it, but she still feebly tried to fight me off as I gathered her up in my arms. She didn't know who I was. She didn't know who she was.

Then we recognized the other girl. It was Tiny Tears. She was slumped, her body all contorted, her eyes open. "What are you doing here?" she asked us. Maybe she didn't know who she was talking to, like she claims. Like the defense attorney insists.

The kid started to go to her.

"Gabo," the priest said to stop him, like maybe he thought she was possessed. She looked possessed. That twisted face of hers chilled me to the bone. The kid only wanted to save her, the girl with the tattooed tears. He tried to lift her, just as I had lifted Crucita. "Let go of me," Tiny Tears said. "Leave me the fuck alone, asshole." So he backed off. He left her the fuck alone. What else did she want?

Maybe she knew it was the kid or maybe, like she says now in court, she didn't know. She was too out of it, her lawyer insists.

All the while Jesse was laughing como un pendejo. But he didn't get in my way as I carried Crucita toward the door. By then it was pitch-dark out and we heard all the sirens outside. "Let's go," the priest said.

REGINA

My mamá always thought I wasn't really cut out for much. I know that. Her son Gabriel, yeah. And little Rafael. "He could have done so much with his life." My mother lamented his decisions all the time. "Rafa's got a mind for mathematics. He's got a good hand for drafting. He could have done anything he wanted . . . but you, hija," she always said, without finishing, and then she'd laugh a little laugh. Just enough to make me feel like she was sitting on my chest.

Rafa had been dead about a week, the coroner said, when the police found his body. He was in la coyota's house in el Segundo barrio all that time. They discovered my brother's corpse the same night we were out in Tornillo. The police went to the coyotes' in El Paso. They were planning a raid all along. But with us going out to the other place, they had to make their bust right then. The coyotes had my brother making methamphetamine. He didn't die by accident. From mixing up chemicals, I mean. He died because they wanted him to die. Rafa's body showed signs of being repeatedly zapped with a Taser gun. They kept him locked in un cuartito, no bigger than a walk-in closet. They had him naked, too. But besides that, la diputada said, "even with an autopsy we'll probably never really know what was the actual cause of his death or why they kept him captive. Sociopaths don't use logic. They only think they do."

We were on our way to the coroner's so that I could identify the body. I knew it was him. The man they found had a heart tattoo over his heart. When we got to the coroner's, walking down the hall that smelled of Pine-Sol, it seemed the hall kept getting longer and longer. Walking, walking. Then we got to the room where they had my brother.

"CALL ME," el Abuelo Milton had said on the phone. "I'LL GO WITH YOU." But I didn't. There are just some things you must do alone. Facing death is one of them. A young woman in a white lab coat went in with me and la diputada. She pulled the sábana back from my brother's face. He'll always be my brother. He'll always be Rafa, who could have been a great math teacher, a revolutionary leader, a farmer, whatever he wanted. Whatever he wanted? Was that fair to say? Maybe not about a dead man.

El Abuelo Milton thought seeing Rafa dead would be too difficult. But no, the worst part was over, the not knowing, fearing that something horrible was happening or may have happened to mi hermanito. Now, another kind of difficulty started. This would be the feeling of having been helpless to stop it. *Helpless* is not a word I like to use in relation to myself. But there it was, like my little brother's body in front of me. Maybe it wasn't even him. It could have been any undocumented man caught up in the evils of border crossings. I pushed the sheet down to check for the tattoo. I traced it with my finger, for a moment wanting to pinch the flesh. Wake up, Rafa, I wanted to say. Let's go home.

"Yes, that's him," I said and then I felt the diputada's arm go around my shoulder to lead me out of the room because my feet weren't moving on their own.

◊　◊　◊

Mrs. Martínez gave me a book about the Change that she'd ordered on-line. (Mrs. Martínez and I were kept on at the school. Some of the newer staff weren't so lucky.) It talks all about women's anxieties, the rational and the crazy stuff. The book says that while the Change takes away your short-term memory, you might start remembering events from a long time ago. That explained some things. The other day I bought some oil for my troca. The next day I bought another can of oil. I forgot all about the first can. Until I went to put it in. Who put oil in it? I asked myself. A ghost? Then I found the receipt. Things like that keep happening around here. Then one night I started remembering all of Junior's letters from the army that I'd lost way back. My mamá had taken them. Who else? It was just her way. She wanted to keep me from tormenting myself. The harshness was her way of saying, Don't expect too much from life.

Every night now, I sit down and write out each of mine and Junior's letters to each other word for word. Or at least I think it's word for word. I could be making it all up. "Preciosa Paloma," he'd begin each one. I called him "precious dove," too. As kids on my abuelo Metatron's rancho, we had started the Secret Order of the Holy Dove. "While I am off to battle," he wrote, "I leave you to care for all the innocent creatures." Walking home from the chile plant where I worked that year, I pretended all the pajaritos, dogs, cats, horses, roosters—any animals I passed—were in my charge. I'd throw migas around and leave scraps of food out for them. When he came home we were going to study to be veterinarians. That's what we told ourselves. We were just kids. No dream is too big when you're that young.

"No dream is too big when you're young," I said to Miguel. He called and called. He wants to pick up where we left off, he says, on my answering machine. How can you do that? You can pick up something but not what you left behind. One day I answered the phone. "Regina," he said. I think he was crying. Maybe not. "Regina," he said again.

"I know," I said. "I know."

There are a lot of things I can talk about. Like whether or not my garden is gonna come up this year. I can take orders for the Martha Stewart look-alike shawls I'm knitting and selling to people in town.

But I cannot say my boy's name. Not yet. That's the door I can't walk through. If I start talking, there's no turning back. But what am I afraid of now?

δ   ε   δ

Gabriel Campos y Rocas.

Aire y Mar.

"We are the people of the earth," Miguel says. Not all of us.

I look up at the stars. What do I know of stars? He is one of them, my Gabo.

There's nothing left to do now but to say it.

The little house off the road was dark when we all got there. Like nobody was around. Sirens and bullhorns and police jumping out. I saw el cura's car. I told la diputada, "That's el Padre Juan Bosco's car. Be careful, please. They must be inside." La policía were rushing about. I couldn't make things out. Someone was shouting something over a speaker.

"Gabo!" I called out. The diputada told me to hush with her mano going down.

"Gabo!" I called out again.

The screen door pushed open. Someone came out. "Put your hands up," the police speaker voice said. "Put your hands up."

"Gabo," I said, not shouting this time. It wasn't Gabo. It was the priest. He put his hands up. "No disparen," he called. I didn't see Miguel. Later, he emerged carrying a woman in his arms. It was Crucita more dead, or wanting to be dead, than alive. But right at that moment, I don't know what was happening. Then I saw the red spiky hair. "Mi'jo!" I called. "Mi'jo, put your hands up," I said, practically under my breath. I know he didn't hear me. I'm sure of it.

Before I knew it guns were going off. This way and that way. From all directions. Not from Gabo. I found Gabo's gun one day. It was buried in the garden.

But my Gabo went down anyway. Even in the dark I knew he'd gone down. The red hair wasn't there no more, behind el cura.

€   €   €

I believe María Dolores when she says she loved my sobrino. What was there not to love? "I know he didn't think much of me," she told me, chain-smoking, the first time I went to see her. "Man, you should have seen him that day in the cafeteria. His eyes were shooting fire at me, like I was the lowest of the low. Or at least that's how I felt. He made my girls laugh at me. But I loved him with my heart and soul." She started crying. She didn't stop, even when I got up to leave.

"I'll come back tomorrow," I said.

All the girl does is cry. Her makeup smears. Her teeth are going brown from all the nicotine. Her right hand don't open no more from how bad she cut it. She was clutching the shard of glass when they got her. Tiny says she still don't remember anything from that night. She was put in detox before she went to the regular jail.

Sometimes I bring her child. Sometimes she asks me not to. She don't want the baby to remember her mother that way. I don't know what the baby will remember.

The little girl didn't even have a name. Tiny gave birth to her in a bathroom at a gas station. She only called her "Mini Me."

María Dolores Jiménez, known to everyone as Tiny Tears. A seventeen-year-old mother who is going to trial as an adult. That wasn't my decision. That's the decision of the court system. My decision is to care for the child. Tiny Tears don't want it. Her own mother didn't want it, neither. The toddler was about to go to foster care. I wasn't raised like that. My mother may have been harsh but she wasn't like that. She always said, "There are always enough frijoles in the pot to feed everyone."

So I visit Tiny Tears and leave her a little commissary money for things she needs—tampons, cigarettes to trade, lo que sea.

One day at the main office at school, I said, "Buenos días," to Mrs. Martínez and the staff like I always do. Instead of a good-morning back, my longtime co-worker came around the counter and, standing right in front of me, she slapped me. She slapped me hard, too. I just stood there. My cheek was burning. My eyes were burning. We just stared at each other. "How can you go see that little monster?" she asked, gritting her teeth. She was talking about Tiny Tears.

The next day, when I went to sign in for work, I hesitated to say good morning. But again, as soon as Mrs. Martínez saw me, she came around the counter. This time I stepped back. Instead of striking me again, she put her hands on my shoulders. "My oldest was killed on the street twelve years ago," she said. "He was coming home from school and got shot by a drive-by. He wasn't even in no gang." What oldest? She had never talked about an oldest before. She pulled out a school picture. "That day. I remember it so clearly. He stopped by the office here first. 'Bye, Mom,' he said. That's all. Just 'Bye, Mom.' "

Gabo's favorite book of all was Matthew. I practically had it memorized myself he quoted so much from it. Father Juan Bosco tells me he has his doubts about Matthew. He thinks Matthew might have made up some things about Jesus. That's all of el cura's intelligence talking. I read Matthew to find Gabo. Sometimes I just like to feel the pages like I'm reading Braille. I feel my sobrino there. Maybe it don't make sense to no one else. But it does to me. Gabo talking to me through Matthew. "For if ye forgive men their trespasses, your heavenly Father will also forgive you."

Easier said than done.

Father Juan Bosco asked me to take Mini Me to church one day. I figured it couldn't hurt la baby to throw some holy water on her. We baptized her "Gabriela." My goddaughter, Gabriela, has three new teeth coming in all at once. Sometimes I freeze a piece of cloth soaked in manzanilla and give it to her to suck on but she likes frozen fruit best from el Shur Sav, especially strawberries. She surely didn't like the gingerroot I rubbed on her gums. She might have her mother's temper.

But Tiny Tears's rage, like everything else about the monster girl that no one loved, was out of control in that house in Tornillo. Being raped every day. No food, just poison in her veins. The public defender says the girl herself is a victim.

Victim is not a word in my vocabulary.

She pushed that shard of glass into my muchacho's flesh. That's how she did it. It punctured his kidney.

She was standing right behind him as he was coming out of the house. I never saw her. She was like the moon in the daytime.

It was enough, the first time. It should have been enough. But it wasn't.

After she punctured my boy's lung, catching him by so much surprise, I am sure, him collapsing into her arms, she pulled it out and pushed that same sharp and very pointed glass from a broken window straight into his corazón.

The thing about those bad videos they make about our lives out here is that you can rewind. Like, you can rewind to just before someone beautiful dies.

And press stop.

You can't do that in real life.

ACKNOWLEDGMENTS

My heartfelt gratitude goes out to the following: literary agent Susan Bergholz for her ongoing hard work and faith, editor Judy Sternlight, who made this book happen, as well as everyone at Random House for their enthusiasm and work. Also to Stuart Bernstein, agent and backup. Abrazos de agradecimiento a mis amigos y colegas for taking time from their busy lives and work to read early drafts and offer suggestions: H. G. Carrillo, Helena María Viramontes, and Anthony Nuño. On the home front, my love goes to my son, Marcel, who, now all grown up, continues to bring out the best in his mamá and keeps her going. Also, Robert A. Molina, whose love and work turned a place into a home: thank you.

Finally, the forgotten underclass throughout the world, whose lives, services, and labor are taken far too much for granted, are remembered. May one day the leaders who govern over humanity earnestly seek ways to even the playing field for everyone to live with dignity.

ABOUT THE AUTHOR

ANA CASTILLO is the author of *Peel My Love Like an Onion,*
So Far from God (a *New York Times* Notable Book), *Sapogo-*
nia, and *The Mixquiahuala Letters* (winner of the American
Book Award), as well as the short-story collection *Lover-*
boys. Her books of poetry include *My Father Was a Toltec,*
I Ask the Impossible, and *Watercolor Women Opaque Men*
(a novel in verse). She is the recipient of a Carl Sandburg
Prize and a Southwestern Booksellers Award. She lives in
New Mexico.

Visit www.anacastillo.com